"I don't wan[...] Jack grated.

"You don't know anything about me."

"I know you're a good man. And I know you've been hurt." Carrie knew he was wasting himself up here alone, and that his isolation brought him as much pain as peace. "I'm willing to listen to anything you'll tell me. I do want to know you, Jack. Very much."

Her quiet insistence nearly turned him inside out. She wanted to know him, and part of him wanted that so badly, he ached. There wasn't a man on earth who didn't want someone to accept him simply for the person he was, to care about him despite all his weaknesses, his mistakes, his flaws.

But once those flaws were exposed, she would see him as he saw himself, and she'd never again look at him the way she did now.

Dear Reader,

Happy New Year! We look forward to bringing you another year of captivating, deeply satisfying romances that will surely melt your heart!

January's THAT SPECIAL WOMAN! title revisits the Window Rock community for the next installment of Cheryl Reavis's FAMILY BLESSINGS miniseries. *Tenderly* is about a vulnerable young woman's quest to uncover her heritage—and the once-in-a-lifetime love she discovers with a brave Navajo police officer. Don't miss this warm, wonderful story!

It's a case of unrequited love—or is it?—in *The Nine-Month Marriage*, the first story in Christine Rimmer's delightful new series, CONVENIENTLY YOURS. This starry-eyed heroine can't believe her ears when the man she worships proposes a marriage—even if it's just for their baby's sake. And the red-hot passion continues when a life-threatening crisis brings a tempestuous couple together in *Little Boy Blue* by Suzannah Davis—book three in the SWITCHED AT BIRTH miniseries.

Also this month, fate reunites a family in *A Daddy for Devin* by Jennifer Mikels. And an unlikely duo find solace in each other's arms when they are snowbound together, but a secret threatens to drive them apart in *Her Child's Father* by Christine Flynn. We finish off the month with a poignant story about a heroine who falls in love with her ex-groom's brother, but her child's paternity could jeopardize their happiness in *Brother of the Groom* by Judith Yates.

I hope this New Year brings you much health and happiness! Enjoy this book and all our books to come!

Sincerely,

Tara Gavin
Senior Editor and Editorial Coordinator

Please address questions and book requests to:
Silhouette Reader Service
U.S.: 3010 Walden Ave., P.O. Box 1325, Buffalo, NY 14269
Canadian: P.O. Box 609, Fort Erie, Ont. L2A 5X3

CHRISTINE FLYNN

HER CHILD'S FATHER

Published by Silhouette Books
America's Publisher of Contemporary Romance

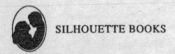

SILHOUETTE BOOKS

ISBN 0-373-24151-8

HER CHILD'S FATHER

Printed in U.S.A.

CHRISTINE FLYNN

admits to being interested in just about everything, which is why she considers herself fortunate to have turned her interest in writing into a career. She feels that a writer gets to explore it all and, to her, exploring relationships—especially the intense, bittersweet or even lighthearted relationships between men and women—is fascinating.

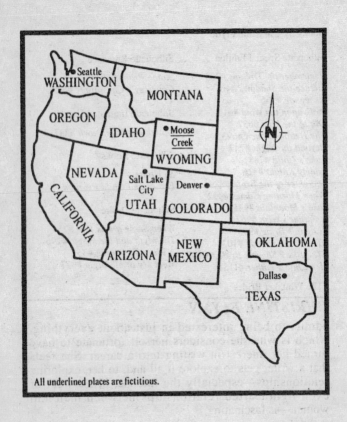

All underlined places are fictitious.

Chapter One

Jack Holt was the last person on earth Carolyn Carter wanted to see. The memory of their parting three months ago was still too fresh, the knowledge of how little she'd meant to him, still too painful to risk adding another bruise to her heart. But what she wanted didn't matter. A child was lost—and Jack could help.

With that thought, Carrie closed the passenger door on the four-wheel-drive Jeep and told the rangy, rawboned gentleman behind the wheel that she was ready whenever he was. Minutes ago, Sam Evans, the semiretired sheriff of rural Moose Creek, Wyoming, had come into the little storefront newspaper office asking for volunteers for a search party. She'd had no choice but to mention Jack. Not only was he intimately familiar with the area where the lost little boy and his father had been camping, but he also owned a wolf-dog that could outtrack any bloodhound.

The sheriff put the vehicle into gear, swerving slightly

on the icy pavement when he pulled out. "You really know this guy?"

"I met him a few months ago. When I first came here." Carrie added, trying desperately to ignore the apprehension knotted in her stomach. "He helped me when I got stuck out by his cabin."

Sam's mouth formed an inverted U when he pressed his lips together and gave an acknowledging nod. Beneath his brown cowboy hat, his bushy gray eyebrows formed a single slash. "Well, I'm glad for your help with this, Miss Carter. I never had call to meet the man myself. Don't know too many folks who have, 'cept the warden and the Chapmans," he went on, motioning the volunteers in the truck behind him to pass. "Bert and Lucille only know him 'cause he goes into their store to stock up and fill his tanks. But Phil, he's our game warden," he added, in case that fact had somehow escaped her note, "says that dog of his is nastier than an elk in rut."

"Felan's...protective," she conceded, speaking of the dog she'd told the sheriff about. "But I'm sure he can find that boy. All he needs is something with his scent."

"As dark as it'll be soon, I hope you're right. A seven-year-old alone in the wilderness doesn't stand much of a chance. Not this time of year." The grim note in the older man's voice was mirrored in his craggy features. "That kid's dad has to be beside himself. Don't know what the fool was thinking, leaving him sleeping to go fishing."

Carrie remained uncharacteristically silent. She'd offered to help in the search herself, but as a reporter, she was to ask questions and gather information. A child named Dustin Raynes had wandered from camp about six hours ago near the Teton Wilderness. Night would soon fall, it was already below freezing and the father couldn't find the boy's tracks in the snow. Moose Creek, population 1,206, had been the nearest place in the remote area to find help. Those were the facts so far.

One other little fact nagged at Carrie as she nursed the knot of apprehension growing beneath her breastbone. This was the first "big" story to hit Moose Creek since she'd begged the editor of the little weekly paper for a job last month——and she didn't care about the story at all. All she cared about was getting to the child before something happened to him. Had she still been working on a big city daily, she would be expected to intrude on the father's self-recrimination and interrupt the searchers by asking probing questions about the child's chances for survival. She felt sure that Ben, her boss at the friendly little newspaper, expected her to do that now. But she was coming to realize that she'd probably always lacked the edge it took for that sort of reporting. Just as she'd realized a few other truths about herself since Jack had jerked the rug out from under her.

"You want me to come with you?" the sheriff asked when, ten miles out of town and seemingly a hundred miles from nowhere, he pulled to a stop at the side of the recently plowed road.

"It might be better if you didn't. Felan won't hurt me," she added, speaking of the dog that had once terrified her. "We learned to be buddies. But Jack's probably the only one who can control him around strangers."

"Do you have the note?"

She held up a folded piece of paper containing a request for his help and indicating the search area. If Jack wasn't home, she'd leave it on his door.

"I won't be long." Pulling a stabilizing breath, she opened the door. She had to walk in from there. The cabin was back in the trees.

Hunching her shoulders against the cold, her breath trailing off in a pale fog, she followed the packed snowmobile

trail that paralleled the creek. Dread knotted with the need
to hurry as she picked up her pace. There was something
a tad ironic about rushing to see the man who'd left her
with no illusions about herself, a badly bruised heart—and
carrying a child she couldn't tell him about. She'd come to
regard that child as a gift, a gift she knew he'd never want
to share. But right now she was just grateful that the
changes in her shape weren't all that noticeable. Not with
her long jacket covering her from neck to knees. All she
wanted was to get through this without unearthing all the
memories she wanted so badly to forget.

The memories were there anyway. Each step she took
brought them closer, reminding her of the first time she'd
followed the burbling creek down this lane, the first time
she'd noticed the smoke threading from the chimney of the
weather-grayed cabin. She remembered pulling her car to
a stop very near where the sheriff parked his Jeep. She even
remembered what she told herself as she'd sat in her car,
glaring at the sleet that had poured from the sky.

The longer you put it off, the harder it will get.

Maybe that was why she wasn't letting herself slow
down now.

Five months earlier

The longer you put it off, the harder it will get.

Carrie blew a resigned breath, repeating the admonition
to herself as she reached into the back seat of her car for
her jacket. The past month had been the pits. Right up there
in the top three of worst months in all of her twenty-eight
years, not counting the time she'd been assigned to cover
society events for the newspaper she'd worked for in Phoenix, or the summer she'd had to live with her Aunt Liddy
and Uncle Pete when her mother had gone off to find herself. It therefore seemed only fitting that she should find

herself in the middle of an ice storm, in the middle of nowhere.

At least she wasn't lost. She knew exactly where she was, give or take a few miles. According to the map she had so carefully marked for her move from Dallas to Seattle, she was about ten miles south of Moose Creek, Wyoming. She would have been in Moose Creek by now, too, had the weather not turned so lousy.

Maneuvering as best she could behind the steering wheel, she struggled into her heavy white jacket and zipped it over her purple sweatshirt and the holey jeans that were too comfortable to part with. The rain had started coming down in buckets just outside of Cheyenne. About an hour ago, it had become mixed with ice. Now, all she could hear ticking on the roof of her boringly practical beige sedan was sleet, and the road was getting slicker by the minute. The wind didn't help traction, either. The gusts buffeting her car and the rental trailer containing all her earthly possessions kept threatening to blow the whole lot into the ditch.

At least there was a shoulder along this section of the highway. Crossing the pass a few miles back, the winding road had been edged by towering forest and mountain on one side, and a thousand-foot plunge into space on the other. She hated heights.

She wasn't too crazy about the cold, either. But, she figured the chances of a sudden heat wave were roughly on par with her winning a Pulitzer, so she flipped up her hood, pushed open her door—and felt her breath catch when the arctic air whipped shimmering crystals of ice at her face. She had forgotten how the Wyoming wind could suck the heat straight from a person's bones. But then, she'd been a child the last time she'd been in the state, and the memories she'd carried all these years were of a different sort. When she thought of Wyoming, she remembered only warmth, laughter and a feeling of security that had eluded her ever since. She definitely had not remembered the land being so wild, so rugged. Or so vast.

In the last two hundred miles, she had seen little beyond endless ranges of magnificent, jagged-peaked mountains, an eternity of autumn-tinged and windswept plains, and miles of log fence. The fences had run out a long time ago. Other than a ranger station and a few buildings at the junction miles behind her, the only evidence she'd seen of anything resembling civilization were a couple of signs for a Lazy J dude ranch, and the cabin set a quarter mile or so back from the two-lane highway.

It was the cabin she headed for now. She couldn't tell much about it, set as it was against the sleet-grayed forest, but there was no mistaking the golden light glowing from its windows, or the paler gray of smoke the wind swept from the chimney. The narrow, rutted road leading to it was edged by a forest of pine and aspen on one side and a creek and a few cottonwoods and pines on the other. Had the situation been ideal, she'd have been able to drive right up to the cabin, but the rain had made mud soup of the narrow little lane. Since she had no desire to get her car and trailer stuck in the mucky, crystalizing mess, walking was her only option.

She had to hurry. It was only four in the afternoon, but night came early in the mountains. With night, the temperature would drop even farther. Ice already glazed the edges of the mud puddles. Since the pass ahead was at yet a higher elevation and would be in worse shape than those she'd already crossed, she had no choice but to find the nearest accommodations and hole up for the night. She only hoped that the cabin was part of the dude ranch and that the ranch's owner wouldn't mind renting her a room cheap. Her budget was even tighter than her schedule.

A six-foot-wide creek, boulder strewn and barely running, paralleled the cow-path of a road. To avoid the puddles solidifying in the ruts, Carrie hurried along the wide strip of pebbles and ankle-high, yellowed grass separating water from roadway. Head ducked against the sting of wind-driven ice pellets, she hunched her shoulders and jammed her hands into her pockets. The loose hood of her long jacket muffled the burble of the creek and the whistle of the wind through the brush and trees, but it offered no insulation at all from the unmistakable howling that, to Carrie, was more chilling than the wet and the cold could ever be.

At the sounds, her heart gave a jerk and kicked into double time. Coyotes were out there. Or maybe, she thought, the long, mournful sound the wind whipped around her was made by wolves. She didn't know for sure. Nor did the distinction matter. Coyote. Wolf. Dog. All she cared about was that the bloodcurdling howls belonged to something carnivorous.

Shivering again, this time more from nerves than the cold, she picked up her pace. She had nothing against the animals as a species, but ever since a Rottweiler had left its teethmarks in her thigh when she was nine years old, she'd had a distinct fear of any canine weighing over a dozen pounds. Try as she might, she'd never been able to overcome that fear. It had taken twenty stitches to close her wounds. If an animal was capable of growling, she wanted nothing to do with it.

She thought about going back to the car. It was only fifteen yards behind her. The cabin was twice that distance. But if she did that, she'd wind up spending the night behind her steering wheel.

You can do this, she coached herself, her glance darting anxiously into the dark forest of thick-trunked firs rising on her right. She didn't like it, but she could do it. After all, she'd been surviving situations she wasn't crazy about all her life. As a reporter, having to cover some of the stories she'd been assigned over the years was certainly on the list. The week she'd sat through the Vasquez murder trial had given her nightmares. And while losing her job when the *Dallas Daily News* downsized last month ranked considerably lower on the trauma scale, it was something that had definitely rocked her sense of security. If she kept all that in mind, a little stroll in the miserable cold while surrounded by wild beasts should be a piece of cake.

She trudged on, determinedly telling herself with each foggy breath that being cold was no big deal and that the howling was *not* growing closer. It really wasn't. If anything it had become more distant—which was why the flash of movement to her right was so much more startling.

Her head jerked up, the lash of frozen rain stinging her skin. The needlelike sensation scarcely registered. Fear paralyzed her, rooting her to the rapidly freezing ground and slamming her heart against her chest. Through the dull gray of sheeting sleet, she caught the unholy glow of yellow eyes a frantic instant before a huge, gray-furred beast materialized from the stand of glistening firs. Suddenly she was nine years old. The snarling animal's upper lip was curled and quivering, exposing teeth as long as paring knives.

Jackson Holt turned from the wide strip of insulation he'd anchored between the wall's exposed two-by-fours and measured out another length. He'd finally finished closing in the porch yesterday. Just in time, too, he thought, considering the turn the weather had taken that afternoon. If he'd learned anything in the two years he'd lived in this particular corner of Wyoming, it was that once the temperature took a dive in the fall, that was the end of decent weather until summer. Since the mercury had fallen ten degrees in the last hour alone, it appeared that winter was getting a head start on itself this year.

Ice rattled against the paned windows, the cold wind

leaking through the new siding as he bent to slice through the thick pad of aluminum and antacid pink fiber. There were some people, he supposed, who dreaded the isolation that would come with the impending snows. But the loneliness that had nearly driven him out of his mind that first winter was simply the price he paid for the small measure of peace he'd finally found. At least he wasn't in prison. Being behind bars would have killed him for certain. Here, away from everything but the land, the animals and the buildings he was paid to tend, he was free to come and go as he pleased. More important, he was responsible for no human being other than himself. Having been betrayed by people he'd trusted and having betrayed people who'd trusted him, that was exactly how he planned to keep it.

The wind picked up, rattling the shutters. He should close them, he thought, then glanced toward the clearing beyond the window, watching for his dog. It wouldn't be long before Felan showed up. It was almost suppertime. The part-wolf, part-German shepherd he'd found in a mangled heap after getting up close and personal with a bear, never missed a meal.

The faint sound of a scream penetrated the howl of the wind.

Jack took a step closer to the window, listening. Hearing nothing but a shutter hinge in need of oil, he shrugged and turned back to his task. What he'd heard was probably a cougar. The big, beautiful cats could make a sound eerily like a woman's scream. Hair-raising to those who'd never heard it. Unnerving even to those who had. He knew they were out there, usually unseen, almost always unheard. Ghost-cats, they were called. Puma. Mountain lion. Panther. The stories woven around their stealth were as otherworldly and chilling as the sound that had just torn through the air. On the other hand, what he'd heard could simply have been a trick of the wind's high-pitched whistling. Nature created all manner of illusion in this untamed place.

It wasn't an illusion. He knew that the instant he heard Felan's ferocious barks. The dog was even more antisocial than Jack, which was why Jack was dead-certain from the racket that something had crossed the animal's path. The only time Felan sounded that vicious was when he had something cornered—usually the occasional poacher or an old grizzly. He obviously had no respect for painful lessons of the past. But quick and half-wild as he was, he was no match for a cougar.

The curse Jack muttered was low and succinct. Grabbing his rawhide coat from the peg inside the kitchen door, he shrugged it on, then snatched his battered old Stetson from another peg and his rifle from the rack by the refrigerator. Seconds later, broad shoulders hunched against a drizzle of frozen rain, he rounded the rustic old cabin to follow the dog's menacing barks. He had no desire to spend another winter nursing his only companion.

Dusk was gathering rapidly. The heavy overcast stole even more daylight. Leaves of crimson and yellow crunching beneath his boots, his glance skimmed the copse of golden aspen encroaching on the small compound, then sharpened as slim white trunks gave way to the heavier bark of fir and pine. A dozen ground-eating strides later, he noticed a beige sedan and orange rental trailer parked up on the highway—and Felan near the edge of the road.

The dog was ten yards ahead of him, gray hackles raised and teeth bared. The ashen light and icy drizzle erased definition, softening the edges of the landscape and making it nearly impossible to see into the trees. But a few steps later, Jack caught a glimpse of stark white on the opposite side of the rutted lane and stopped dead in his tracks.

From where he stood, the woman the dog had backed against a tree looked like an apparition. The frozen mist shimmering around her made her look as if she were covered in pearl from head to knee, the wide hood of her jacket obscuring most of her face. From what little he could see of her, her skin was as pale as ice.

"Felan. Back off," Jack commanded, his attention split between the animal getting in one last growl and the slender figure trying to disappear through the mottled trunk of an old pine. Huddled into herself, there didn't appear to be much to her. He moved closer, but he still couldn't make out much of her face—until her head jerked toward him.

It was then that he caught the impossibly delicate lines of her features, and the abject terror in her haunted brown eyes.

His intention was to step between her and the animal to block each from the other's view. But he'd no sooner ordered Felan to stay and started toward the woman, than she bolted from the tree.

Jack's arm shot out, his commanding, "Don't!" lost over the dog's warning bark. The worst thing she could do was run. Acting like frightened prey would have Felan on her in a heartbeat.

His own heart slammed against the wall of his chest, adrenaline surging to charge after her when he suddenly found her in his arms, clinging for dear life.

Jack's first thought was that he'd actually managed to get the rifle out of the way before the thing could get trapped between them and accidentally go off. His second, was that she hadn't been running away. She'd been running to him. Her arms were locked around his waist and she was as close to him as she could get without crawling inside his open coat. He wasn't so sure that wasn't what she had in mind. She was pressed so tightly to him that he felt her shaking from his chest to his thighs, the kind of shaking that came from deep inside, rattling everything from organs to teeth.

He closed his arms around her before he could think to do otherwise.

"Hey," he muttered, totally disarmed by her desperation. He angled his head, trying to see her face. The way she had her head tucked into his chest, all he could see was a swath of white fabric. "It's all right. Nothing's going to happen to you."

Except for the shaking, she didn't move.

"You're okay now," he assured her, increasingly aware of the feminine curves beneath that concealing jacket. "Honest."

A long moment passed. Then another. Though he didn't feel a single, slender muscle relax, he finally heard a muffled, "Is it gone?"

"No. But he's backed down. See?"

As if his presence gave her courage she might have otherwise lacked, she slowly lifted her head from his chest. That was the only separation she allowed herself.

"Make it go away. Please," she begged, the fear in her shaking voice as palpable as the vibrations of her body. "Make it go away."

Jack dropped one arm to his side, his fist clutching his rifle. Compensating, he tightened his other arm around her back. He was sure that part of her trembling had to be from the cold. Every breath they expelled vaporized in a puff of fog that the frigid wind promptly whipped away. Cold wasn't her concern, though. The way her eyes were fixed on the dog now placidly eyeing her, Jack doubted she even felt the pricks of ice pellets against her pale skin.

"He's just sitting there. Don't make any sudden moves and you'll be fine. Are you okay now?"

She didn't seem to be listening. Frightened as she was, she couldn't seem to make herself look away from the dog. Or make herself let go. And the longer she clung to him, the more aware he became of her feminine shape.

There was definitely more to her than he'd first thought. The fullness of her breasts pressed against his chest, and even through her jacket, he could feel the gentle, tantalizing flare of her hip where his hand rested at her waist. She was taller than she'd first appeared to be, too. Around five foot five or six, he'd guess, liking the way she fit him. Shelby had been five foot four and when he'd held her, the top of her head hadn't even reached his chin.

At the thought of his ex-wife, his jaw locked. The feel of the woman in his arms had him trying to pry her loose. It had been nearly three years since he'd held a woman. It had been longer than that since he'd had one in bed. He didn't particularly appreciate being reminded of that fact. Nor did he think it wise to consider that this ephemeral creature had his body hardening just by leaning against him.

He bent his head toward her, thinking to break her hold, and caught the faint scent of something soft and powdery. Need hit him like a fist. He missed the way a woman felt. The way a woman smelled. He missed softness.

Telling himself that all he missed was sex, trying to ignore the fact that this particular woman felt and smelled like pure temptation, he took a step back. She moved with him, gripping his shirt. It felt as if she also had a fistful of his coat in back. Because he hadn't buttoned the coat, sleet was sliding down his open collar and melting with his body heat. The effect wasn't nearly as cooling as it should have been.

It seemed she wasn't going to let go until the dog was out of sight.

"That's it, Felan. Go back to the house. Now."

The command was met with a deep, reverberating bark. The response was simply the canine equivalent of "Okay," but it caused the terrified woman in his arms to jump and cling tighter. Jack nearly groaned. The motion brushed her stomach against his groin and he could still feel her breasts through his shirt. Even when Felan wheeled around to dart through the trees, she didn't loosen her hold.

Jack was not a masochist. Since torturing himself with the feel of her while he turned into a pillar of ice was not his idea of a good time, he figured they'd better head for the cabin, too.

"He's gone. Okay? You can let go now."

His voice was gruffer than he intended. More impatient. Still, she didn't move. She simply stood there with her breath coming in ragged little puffs and his coat clenched in her fists.

"Look." He took her gloved hand by the wrist, breaking the hold for her. "We can't stand out here in this. My cabin's just the other side of those trees. If you'll let me go, we'll get inside and you won't run into anything else out here."

The threat of some other beast lurking in the rapidly encroaching night had her pulling back in an instant. Crossing her arms as if to provide herself with the hold he'd denied her, she stuck like a shadow to his side. The sleet pounded the gilded leaves from the aspens, stripping the branches down to skeletons, but the footing was surer beneath the sweeping, protective branches of pine where the ice had yet to reach. The path was scarcely wide enough for one person, much less wide enough for two. But she matched him step for step to the wide, railed porch with the deadwood chairs he'd made but never used.

Warmth reached out the moment he opened the door, light spilling onto the porch's weather-grayed planks. "Come on," he coaxed, brushing ice from his shoulders and sleeves before he ushered her inside. "You can warm up by the fire," he added, then closed the door, leaving her beside it while he headed through the kitchen to the back porch and let Felan in out of the weather with strict orders to "Behave."

Carrie didn't move from inside the front door. Sagging with relief, she closed her eyes and pulled the first unrestricted breath she'd managed in the last five minutes. The clean scent of pine mingled with wood smoke. They were the same scents that clung to the man she could hear moving toward her. Never again would she smell that combination without finding some measure of comfort in it. She was safe. The huge dog with the wild eyes and razor-sharp teeth hadn't ripped out her throat or otherwise mangled her body. She'd been so certain it had been about to lunge for her. If she could only stop shaking...

"Are you all right?"

The deep, smoky voice sliced through her lingering apprehension. There was richness in that voice, a sensual huskiness that would have played utter havoc with her nerves had her nerves not already been shot.

She opened her eyes, prepared to answer her rescuer, only to find herself faced once again with seventy pounds of mottled gray fur.

Adrenaline surged. Carrie's back flattened against the wood of the door behind her. The scarred animal reminded her of something out of a child's nightmare—her own, probably—and its yellow eyes were trained on her from a rug in front of a huge, stone fireplace. Fire crackled behind its massive head, the flames leaping behind panes of glass making the beast appear truly demonic.

"I said, are you all right?"

She opened her mouth, but nothing came out. With her glance glued on the dog, her only response was to swallow as she gave a pathetically unconvincing nod.

"Come here."

It didn't occur to Carrie that the resigned command was directed at her. Not until she felt her rescuer's hand close around her arm. The moment it did, her glance darted to his face.

When she'd first noticed him, her mind had been too focused to absorb anything that didn't have to do with immediate survival. She'd seen him only as big; as protection. A mountain of stone in split rawhide and denim.

That had been her initial impression when he'd materialized in front of the snarling animal, placing himself between her and what she'd felt was certain harm. Now, letting him lead her past a deeply cushioned tan sofa, she was aware of the piercing blue of his eyes and, since he'd taken off his hat, the fact that his nearly black hair was pulled back in a long, low ponytail. With his attention on the dog, her glance skimmed his sharp blade of a nose, the grim line of his firm mouth, the deep, masculine creases in his cheeks. Tall, broad-shouldered, commanding, he was the sort of man people noticed, the sort men envied for his powerful presence and women wanted for that same reason.

He also looked vaguely familiar to her, though she had no idea why. All she cared about at the moment was that he'd lead her to stand directly in front of the dog. Nerves jumping, she started to step behind him. The animal was obviously a pet, but how anyone could have tamed such a beast was beyond her.

"Don't," he insisted, his voice low and firm. "Shrinking back sends him the wrong message. Lower your hood."

"What?"

"Lower your hood," Jack repeated, watching her watch the dog. "Let him see you without your head covered."

Though she reached for the loose cowl, she was more intent on making sure the animal wasn't about to attack than on what she was doing. Grasping the fabric on either side of her head with her gloved fingers, she slowly pushed the hood back to her shoulders, then pulled her wary glance to the man beside her.

The moment she did, heat jolted through Jack like lightning. He had already been impressed by the delicacy of her features, the lushness of her lovely mouth, the haunting quality of her darkly lashed eyes. Now, he could see that her tousled hair was shoulder-length, and a glossy, golden brown that was shot with shades of fire. It fairly begged to be gathered in his hands.

Ignoring the tightening in his gut, he focused only on her uncertainty.

"Give me your hand."

"My hand? Why?"

There was more concern than challenge in her voice, and enough hesitation in her expression to make it apparent that she wasn't going to voluntarily expose any body parts to the animal sniffing at her sneakers. Knowing they weren't going to get anywhere until she forgot about the dog, he picked up her hand himself and began pulling off her glove.

"Do you have a dog?"

The concern was still there when she offered a quiet, "No."

"Do you know anything about them?"

She shook her head, her eyes on his face as he tugged off one royal blue knit finger after another.

"Felan's part wolf," he explained, increasing his grip ever so slightly when he felt her pull back. "He senses fear in people the same way he does in prey. If you show fear, he'll act aggressively. If you act aggressively, he'll act to defend himself and his turf. He has enough domesticated canine in him to be social, but even pets need to be introduced to strangers."

He gave her the glove, impatience vying with sympathy as he held her newly bared hand loosely in his free one. "He senses you're not a threat by the way you act toward him and how I treat you. Right now, he's just curious. Let him know your scent and he'll be fine."

Her hand felt cold in his. It also looked incredibly delicate in his bigger, rougher one. What touched him, though, was her almost childlike vulnerability when he curled her fingers in his palm and drew her hand forward. "Maybe you will be, too, once you realize he's not going to treat you like a meal."

Carrie had never before been so close to anything so wild. The animal's big head reached her waist, and the gray fur that had looked mottled from a distance was streaked with rich sable and tipped with white along his erect and pointed ears. The eyes that had glowed yellow before were actually shades of amber and pale green. There was an intelligence to those eyes, too, and cunning. As he dipped his long, black snout toward her hand, she could feel the fear rising in her throat.

"I'm right here." The richness of her rescuer's voice flowed over her nerves like warm honey, calming her, soothing her as he drew her hand even nearer. His tone grew hushed, as intimate as a lover's. "Nothing's going to happen."

She searched his eyes. She saw kindness there. Protectiveness. And a kind of deep-seated sadness that caught her totally unprepared. "You're sure?"

"Very sure," he replied, his certainty replacing everything else.

She took him at his word. The dog's nose was wet. And cold. But she didn't move as the animal sniffed at her fingers, her wrist, the sleeve of her jacket. The imposing man beside her supported her wrist loosely in his callused hand. The quality of his touch hadn't changed at all, but as she felt his heat warm her chilled flesh, she began to realize that his touch coaxed rather than insisted, encouraged rather than forced. He hadn't used any real pressure at all. It was simply his certainty, and the formidable power of his will that caused her to do his bidding.

Jarred by the realization, her gaze jerked to his. He was watching her, openly, waiting to see if the introduction would alleviate any of her fear. But there was something more lingering in the depths of his eyes. Something masked, but not so well that she couldn't see it. The strange sadness she'd glimpsed was gone, making her wonder if it had been there at all. He was watching her now the way a man watches a woman when he's trying to figure out how her skin would feel to his touch, how her lips would feel beneath his, how she would taste.

The thought sent a shiver through Carrie that had nothing to do with cold or fear, and everything to do with how hard his body had felt next to hers. She'd been too frightened before to feel anything more than gratitude for that solid strength. Now, with his eyes steady on hers, she was aware of a faint quickening deep inside.

Slowly she drew her hand away, shaken as much by his physical effect on her as by what she'd just allowed him to do. There wasn't a soul on God's green earth that she would have trusted to draw her so near such a beast. Yet, this man's command over her had been as certain as the mesmerizing control he held over the animal resettling itself on the hearth rug.

He seemed to sense the change in her. Stepping back before she could, seeming to need the distance himself, he lowered himself to his haunches beside his dog and absently began stroking its thick fur.

"What were you doing out there?" He looked up from the dog as it slowly rolled to its side, exposing his belly to the same treatment his back had been getting. "You having car trouble?"

"No. No," she repeated, suddenly reminded of what she'd been doing before the hound from hell had shown up and she'd thrown herself into this man's arms. "My car is fine. I saw the signs for a dude ranch," she started to explain, then cut herself off, too discomfited by what she'd done to ignore it. "Look," she murmured, feeling heat creep up her neck as she started again. "I'm sorry about what I did. The way I acted. Out there, I mean."

She pulled her glance from the denim stretched over his powerful thighs and motioned toward the road, mentally groaning when she thought about how he'd tried to pull away—and about how she'd clung like a barnacle, refusing to let him go. At the time, all she'd cared about was how protected she felt next to him; how safe. Now, having never behaved that way in her entire adult life, she just felt embarrassed.

"Forget it," he muttered, sounding as if he rather wanted to forget it himself. "It was nothing."

"Not to me, it wasn't. But I'm usually in much better control of myself. Honest. It's just that big dogs and I don't get along very well. I have sort of a thing about them."

"A thing?"

"A phobia," she conceded, thinking he probably knew darn well what she was talking about. He'd just seen it in action. "It goes back to my childhood, but I won't waste your time with that," she continued, wondering if someone who appeared to be in as much control as he did could relate to fear at all. "I saw signs for a dude ranch and thought...hoped," she amended, casting a quick glance around the sparsely furnished space, "this might be part of it."

"Sorry," he said, giving his head a slow shake. "The place you're looking for is another couple of miles up the road. But they've closed down for the season."

Carrie's bangs fluttered as she released a breath. "Is there a motel around? I'd planned to get to Moose Creek tonight, but as icy as it's getting, I'm afraid to go much farther." She edged back, adding a few more feet between the mound of fur on the floor and herself. Despite her surprising capitulation of moments ago, she still didn't trust dogs. If its master hadn't been there, she'd still be glued to the door. "Do you know of any place near here?"

A log in the fireplace snapped in half, sending a spray of sparks up the flue. Outside, the gray light of day flirted with twilight.

"The closest place without going over a pass is about twenty miles south of here. Even if there was something closer," he added, looking as if he wished there were, "that road will be sheet ice before much longer, if it isn't already."

That was not what Carrie wanted to hear. She wasn't going to waste time lamenting the fact, however. Already her mind was racing. She could spend the night in her car and keep the heater running, as long as she kept a couple of windows rolled down a bit so she wouldn't asphyxiate herself. But if she did that, she'd use up her gas. She had plenty now, but if she ran the engine just for heat, she wouldn't have enough to make it to Moose Creek once the sun came up and thawed things out.

"Great," she muttered.

"Yeah," he echoed, sounding as if he'd tossed around an alternative or two himself, and was no more thrilled with his own conclusion.

"Is there anyone else out there? Waiting in the car?"

She shook her head, water dripping from her jacket to the wood brown carpet. "I'm traveling alone."

She didn't understand the look he gave her. From the way his mouth thinned, it looked almost as if he wished she hadn't been by herself. Or maybe, Carrie thought, watching him treat the deceptively docile-looking animal to one last stroke before he rose, he was just a little put out by having to deal with her at all.

His jaw was working as he looked from the sofa behind her to the front door. "Seems you're stuck for the night."

He motioned to the end table by a comfortably overstuffed brown plaid chair. "The phone's over there if you need to call anyone. If they want to know where you are, tell them you're at the caretaker's cabin at Cougar Ridge."

Carrie hesitated, her glance swinging from the phone to the big man heading past the neatly stacked boxes in his knotty pine kitchen. There was no one to call. No one expected to hear from her until she reached Seattle. "You're the caretaker?"

"Yeah," he repeated, the grudging note still in his voice. "Name's Jack."

"Jack?"

"Holt," he added, pulling open the windowed kitchen door. Beyond was what appeared to be a closed-in porch. "Get what you need for the night out of your car," he said, running a glance from her shoulders to the drawstring hem above her knees. "You'd better get it now before the ice freezes your doors shut. That thing keeping you dry enough?"

He was referring to her jacket. Thrown by the question, or maybe the concern, she gave him a nod.

"Fine, then. I'll get you a flashlight."

"Wait! Look…Jack," she added, edging into the kitchen as he disappeared through the door. Even if she couldn't see any preferable alternative to staying where she was tonight, the offhand way he called the shots had her digging in her heels. Too much of her life had been dictated by circumstances beyond her control. That tended to make her a tad possessive about decisions. Specifically, her right to make her own.

"It's not that I don't appreciate your offer. It's very kind. Really. But I don't want to impose on you. Or your family," she added, when she noticed a roofless dollhouse through the open door. "I'll come up with something."

"I don't have a family." The flat pronouncement came

from the far end of the porch. "Short of staying in your car and using up your gas trying to keep warm, I can't see that you have much of a choice."

She barely caught his last words, muffled as they were by the wall between them. But the frown knitting her forehead had nothing to do with the way he'd pointed out the drawbacks to an idea she'd already discarded, or even his confirmation that she was alone with him and his beast. What had her puzzled was the incongruity of the miniature mansion under construction on the workbench, and the dearth of any other decorative or homey touch in the place.

There wasn't a single picture on a wall, a flower in a vase or curtain on a window. To the right of the front door was the living room with the tan sofa, the plaid chair, tables made of heavily lacquered slices of tree and an entire wall of books. To the left, was the kitchen, which was cursed with countertops in a shade of dark orange that had been popular around the time of her birth. It was separated from the living area by a large knotty-pine table and chairs that matched the cabinets. The door from the kitchen led to the porch. The one cut into the back wall opened to a short hallway that led, she assumed, to a bathroom and a bedroom or two. The place was very basic, very neat and, except for the fantasy of a dollhouse on his workbench, as masculine as it was austere.

Carrie stepped back from the kitchen doorway. A fishing pole stood by the almond colored stove, and boxes of canned and paper goods, what looked like a winter's worth, were stacked on the scarred, beige linoleum floor. Unpainted pine shelving was propped against the side of the relatively new almond refrigerator. From the looks of things, he was either just moving in or some sort of renovation was taking place.

The man who'd introduced himself as Jack Holt reap-

peared in the doorway, glancing at her as if he'd really
rather hoped she'd disappeared.

"Here." He held out a foot-long, yellow flashlight. "It's
getting dark in a hurry out there. You might need this to
see your way back. I'd help you, but I've got a couple of
things to do before I lose the daylight."

It was clear enough that he knew there was nowhere else
for her to go. It was equally clear that, while he was willing
to put her up for the night, he wasn't interested in playing
protector. Or host. Not that she expected him to. But as she
accepted the flashlight with a quiet and reluctant,
"Thanks," and he called his dog so it wouldn't follow her
out the front door, she couldn't help but think him a man
intent on keeping his distance.

He hadn't even bothered to ask her name.

Chapter Two

As far as Carrie was concerned, going back to her car held all the appeal of a toothache. It wasn't that far. A three-minute walk, max. Less than a tenth of her daily jog. But it was still sleeting, daylight was fading and coyotes were out there. Somewhere. Had she not dropped her purse by the tree, she wouldn't have bothered with the trip at all, but she needed to retrieve it before something wild ran off with her ID and credit cards. Then, there was the matter of the houseplant she'd left on the front seat. She couldn't let the pathos that had lived with her since college meet its demise by freezing to death. They'd been through too much together.

Nothing if not loyal, she hurried along the narrow, rutted lane, all too aware of the wildlife lurking in the woods and the cold wind that seeped through her jacket. The temperature was dropping like the proverbial stone, the ice thickening its glaze. The cold merely had her shivering. The feeling of keen, assessing eyes on her back had her edgy.

She glanced over her shoulder as she neared her car, nerves prickling. Her progress was definitely being followed, but not by a wolf, or coyote, or the beast called Felan. By Jack. He stood at the bend in the lane. He seemed to be watching her. Or maybe he was watching out for her. Whichever it was, something about his stance said he wasn't too happy to be doing it.

Carrie found her brown leather shoulder bag, already crusted with a thin layer of ice, in the stiff stalks of grass, then headed on to her car. All that mattered to her as she retrieved the gym bag she'd packed for her five nights on the road and the cardboard box containing her plant, was that he was there. Just knowing he wasn't far cut her apprehension in half. About her surroundings anyway. It didn't do a thing to alleviate her concern about her implausible responses to him.

He was gone by the time she started back to the cabin. Back working on his chores, she assumed. It was getting too dark to see very far, but she knew he was somewhere around the cabin or its outbuildings as she balanced bags and box and followed the beam of his flashlight. If the isolation and austerity of her reluctant host's surroundings were any indication, the man was very much a loner. In some way she couldn't quite define, she suspected he was also as scarred and distrusting as his fanged and furry friend. At least he didn't strike her as any sort of sociopath. She'd covered enough stories about the type working in Phoenix and Dallas to know there were plenty of crazies out there, and she'd yet to hear of an ax-murderer who offered the exact location of his lair to his victim to pass on to her next of kin. Jack seemed like a basically decent guy, so she didn't fear for her physical safety. Not as far as he was concerned, anyway. His hound was another matter entirely.

"Let me take that."

The voice came from ahead of her. Squinting against the bite of frozen rain, she looked up to see Jack near the corner of a large, weather-beaten garage tucked back in the trees. In the diluted glow of the yard light anchored under the eave of the roof, she could see that he'd turned up the shearling collar of his rawhide coat. The battered black Stetson rode low on his forehead and a coil of heavy, orange electrical cord hung from one hand. Had the cord been a rope, he could have passed for the hunk in the cigarette ad the girls from advertising had tacked up in the ladies' room at the *Daily News*.

He looped the coil over his shoulder and started toward her, his long, lazy stride seeming to mock the miserable weather. Beneath the shadowing brim of his hat, his carved mouth thinned just before he reached to take the two foot square box from her. He clearly couldn't imagine why she'd bothered with it.

Carrie's hold tightened. "I can manage," she assured him, tipping up her shoulder so the straps of her purse and the bright blue canvas bag wouldn't slip off. "I don't want to take you from your chores."

"And I don't want you trying to juggle all that and losing your balance on the stairs. They're getting slick." He slipped his big hands between her arms and the box. When she didn't immediately let go, he cocked his eyebrow at her. "If you fall and break something, I'll have to set it. I doubt you'd want your leg looking like Felan's." He gave the box a little tug. "Or for me to get that personal."

The threat made her let go. His proximity made stubbornness seem foolish just then, and the thought of his callused hands anywhere on her body had her blood heating. She preferred to think it was only with embarrassment.

She cleared her throat, stepping back. "What's wrong with the dog's leg?"

"It healed crooked."

His tone was flat, his expression no more inviting. He was hardly being chivalrous in his offer of assistance. He was simply being practical.

It seemed he wanted to be sure she understood that distinction, too. Tucking the box under his arm like a big football, he headed for the porch, leaving her standing in the sleet.

"Be careful with that! Please," she added, clutching bag and purse as she skirted an icy patch of leaves in favor of surer footing in the grass. "It's fragile."

"What is it?"

"My roommate."

Some of the length left his stride. "Your what?"

"My roommate. We've lived together for years."

She had the feeling he was frowning again as he crossed the weathered planks, shook the sleet from the brim of his hat and shouldered open the door. She knew for a fact that he was when she scooted in after him and watched him close the door with his booted foot.

Setting the box on the pine table, his glance raked her from hood to toe. "What is it?"

"A plant. I got it my freshman year of college. Except for certain members of my family, it's the longest relationship I've ever had.

"Hey," she murmured when his eyebrow arched. "You live with a wolf. You should know that some relationships defy logic."

She thought he might smile at that. Or maybe give her a glimpse of himself by claiming to know nothing about relationships, since he appeared to have relatively few.

All he did was step back, holding his hands up, palm out. "I didn't say a thing. All I care about is that I don't have to worry about Felan wanting to get at it. Don't worry about the dog," he added, since she'd already sent a couple of worried glances around the room in search of his buddy. "I'll keep him with me."

His reassurance should have put her more at ease. And it did. In a way. But as he headed out the kitchen door, Carrie realized she was still too disconcerted by her earlier behavior around him to relax a single freezing muscle. She still couldn't believe she'd actually allowed him to lead her right up to his dog. He'd obviously made her feel safe somehow, but she'd never felt that way with anyone in her entire adult life. Longer than that. She hadn't felt that way since she was eight years old and her mom had uprooted her from Moose Creek. It had almost felt as if, just by being with him, nothing could harm her.

It's because he rescued you, she told herself, needing desperately to understand the pull she felt toward a man she didn't even know. A man, she reminded herself, who was making it apparent he wasn't at all eager to know her. It only made sense that she'd have a certain trust for him, though. Considering how grateful she was to him for what he'd done, she decided what *she'd* done was perfectly logical. For anyone but her.

She shook off the thought with a shiver and dropped her purse and bulky bag by the sofa. Another shiver chasing that one, she toed-off her wet running shoes so she wouldn't track water and wet leaves over the carpet and headed for the braided hearth rug. The fire burning inside the metal and glass insert in the fireplace kept the room nicely warm, but her feet felt like ice and her hands weren't far behind. As chilled as she was, she would love to shed her jacket and curl up under the Indian-print blanket folded on the back of the sofa. But making herself that comfortable in a stranger's house seemed awfully presumptuous.

She had just opened her jacket to the heat when she heard the kitchen door open behind her. Turning at the sound, she saw Jack walk in, shouldering a huge, green sack.

She started to smile, the quiet greeting coming as naturally to her as breathing, only to find the expression stall halfway.

He stood solid and still as a small mountain, one arm looped over the weight he bore easily on his broad shoulder, and his cool blue eyes steady on hers. As if he were trying to decide whether or not he'd done the right thing allowing her stay, his glance narrowed on her face, then moved over her hair and down the front of her baggy sweatshirt. When his eyes returned to hers, she felt their intensity clear to her toes. But his expression never changed as he pulled his glance and shrugged the fifty-pound sack to the floor.

Without a word, he opened the stitching at the top of the bag, then filled the large aluminum bowl at the end of the counter with the brown nuggets. The bowl was barely back on the floor before the shaggy wolf-dog wandered through the open kitchen door. The instant the animal saw her, his tail dropped and his ears flattened.

Nerves already jangled, Carrie stiffened.

Jack sighed.

"Easy, fella," he murmured, preferring to calm the dog rather than the woman. He stroked his big hand over the dog's ruff, digging in harder where he knew his buddy liked best to be scratched. "It's okay. She's not hurting anything. She just has to stay here tonight."

The reassurance in his tone made Felan relax, which was more than Jack could say for the woman thawing out by his fireplace. She was definitely uneasy. What struck him was how hard she was trying not to be. Her hands were knotted together tightly enough to break her fingers. Yet, when he met her eyes, she actually managed a wary smile.

"I guess he isn't used to strangers."

"We don't get many visitors here. He's just protecting his turf."

Her chin inched up in acknowledgment. "He's good at it."

Jack didn't expect the sensation of warmth curling through him just then. It seemed to have something to do with her smile as she held his glance, with the tilt of her head, the faint huskiness of her voice. There was an openness about it, about her, that seemed to draw him in, along with a languid sensuality that defied her best efforts to deny it.

His glance slid down the long line of her throat. Above the edge of the bright purple sweatshirt she wore over faded and frayed jeans, he could see the fine line of her collarbone. Between the open sides of her long jacket, he caught the soft, feminine swells of her breasts. He'd yet to forget how they'd felt pressed to his chest. They would fit his palms perfectly, he was sure. *She* would fit him perfectly.

Before his glance could move lower, or his imagination ran wild, he turned away and picked up the dog's water dish.

"How old is he?" he heard her ask over the rush of running water.

"I don't know. He was grown when I found him."

"How long ago was that?"

Her question was either an attempt to get her mind off her fear of the dog nosing his kibble, or to ease the awkwardness of being stuck with a stranger. Aware of that awkwardness himself, he muttered, "A couple of years. Look, lady—"

"It's Carolyn. Carrie," she amended. "Carter."

His only acknowledgment was a tense nod. "I've got some things to do. Why don't you just…"

Just what? he wondered. He didn't have a clue what to do with her.

She wasn't his responsibility, he reminded himself.

"May I help?" she asked, cutting into his hesitation.

"Help?"

"With whatever it is you're doing. I know I must have caught you in the middle of something, and I'd be glad to help if I can."

"Thanks, but I don't think so. What I'm doing is pretty much a one-person job." He actually could have used an extra pair of hands. What he didn't want was her presence. "If you have anything you need to dry out, you'll have to hang it by the fireplace. The dryer's disconnected right now. If you're hungry, help yourself to whatever's here."

He motioned to the groceries he'd picked up in Moose Creek a few days ago. A winter's worth. Except for the perishables, he'd yet to put anything away. He couldn't. Not until the porch was finished and he could put the shelving up.

"Would you like me to fix something? Dinner I mean? It's the least I can do for staying here tonight."

"That's not necessary."

He hadn't spoken gruffly. At least, he didn't think he had, but he saw her smile slip as surely as if he'd said he wanted nothing from her but that she stay out of his way. That *was* all he wanted. He just hadn't intended to be so blunt about it.

"I'll get you some bedding," he concluded, thinking it best to get his dealings with her over with. He'd done what he'd had to do when he'd offered her shelter, and he'd offered that only because he had enough on his conscience without adding some stranger's death by exposure to the list.

He practically stalked past her, his left hand sliding down the front of his coat, releasing buttons. Boards creaked under the heavy thud of his boots on his way into the hall by the easy chair. To Carrie, he seemed to consume space as he moved through it, his raw energy sucking the oxygen out of the room. Or maybe it was his sudden impatience that made the air feel hard to breathe.

A minute later, she heard an unseen door close solidly and he reemerged from the hallway.

"The bathroom's through there. First door on your left around the corner." He dipped his dark head back the way he'd come, then dropped a couple of thick, navy blue blankets on the end of the sofa. A white-cased pillow landed atop the stack. "You'll have to sleep here. The spare room's full."

"This is fine. Perfect," she amended, because she was truly in no position to be picky. "Thank you," she added, the words sounding so inadequate for all he'd done.

He didn't allow her to say anything else, and if he said anything in response, it was lost to her as he headed back through the kitchen, his stride as brisk as the wind outside. Felan, his muzzle dripping water from his bowl, trotted out right behind him.

Carrie blew a breath of relief the moment the door closed. She was usually pretty good at talking to strangers. The knack had been honed when she was a child, a survival skill for coping with all the times her mother had moved them from wherever it was they'd just settled. If she hadn't been good at making friends fast, she'd never have had any at all. Now, she communicated with strangers for a living. Coaxing information and facts out of people, getting them to open up, was simply what a reporter did. She'd never been into digging for dirt like some of her colleagues, and she had a tendency to back off rather than badger—a lack that had cost her at least one promotion. She simply possessed a genuine interest in people, which was why she would have liked very much to know what a caretaker took care of in such a remote place. But she hadn't been able to get the man to talk about his dog, much less himself.

Enormously grateful for the absence of the canine in

question, she slipped off her jacket. Doing what Jack the Unsociable had suggested, she draped it and her wet gloves over the edge of the empty mantel above the fireplace and moved her shoes to the hearth to dry. Despite his invitation—instruction, actually—to make herself comfortable, she wasn't sure that was possible. Stuck in a strange man's house in the middle of nowhere, with no TV and nothing to work on, the best she could do was pace between the sofa and the wall of books, stopping every once in a while to skim the titles.

Carrie was on her third trip back to that wall, when she noticed the titles that didn't seem to fit with those she hadn't been all that surprised to find. Aside from an impressive selection of techno-thrillers and mysteries and a small library on forestry, land management, buffalo, bears, cougars and coyotes, were dozens of tomes on capital investment, stock and bond strategies and the commodities markets. Had there only been a volume or two of each, she might have dismissed the titles completely. The sheer number, coupled with their dog-eared condition, spoke of a subject that had been thoroughly studied. Recently, too. The copyright date on the volume lying facedown atop several others was last year.

The combination confused her. It had been her experience that those with a true affinity for the environment had little interest in the world of high finance, and those who truly understood Wall Street's buzzwords expressed an interest in the environment only when it was profitable. She didn't doubt Jack's kinship with his rugged surroundings. Not only did he look as if he'd been born there, but the man had a half-wild animal for a pet. From the austerity of the neat little cabin, it appeared that his physical needs were minimal. Far too minimal to require the kinds of money a graph penciled inside that one book indicated. But no one knew better than Carrie how deceptive appearances could be. She'd glimpsed the pain he masked with indifference. However briefly, it had been there. Surprising her. Touching her. Now, given the interests revealed by his choice of reading material, she would bet the new job she'd finally landed in Seattle that Jack was far more complicated than he appeared.

An hour dragged by before he surfaced. Looking totally preoccupied, he entered the kitchen, but he was there only long enough to open a large can of stew and dump it into a pan to heat. He reappeared ten minutes later to dish up half for himself, then told her the rest was hers before taking his, along with half a package of wheat rolls, back to the porch, presumably to eat while he hammered. Two hours after that, he returned to rinse his dish and turn out most of the lights. She wasn't sure he was even going to speak to her until he stopped at the foot of the sofa where she'd finally curled up under the blankets with a book on bears that she'd pilfered from his wall.

"I hope you don't mind." She held up the book. Except for the wary glance she darted toward the dog sitting obediently behind Jack, her expression matched the apology in her voice. "I needed something to do. I'd have asked first, but I didn't think you wanted me to disturb you." When he didn't disagree, she returned the slender volume to her lap. "You have a very interesting collection."

"Help yourself to whatever's there," he muttered, motioning the dog toward the hall. "I'm turning in, so I won't be putting any more logs in the fire. I usually let it burn down at night, but the heater will kick on in a while. You shouldn't get too cold out here."

He'd been avoiding conversation with her all evening. From the way he ignored her comment about his books, he seemed to have every intention of continuing to do so now. He was giving her a roof and blankets. That was it. "I'm sure I'll be fine. Thank you."

His only response was the lift of his chin, the tacit "You're welcome," all he would allow before he disappeared behind his dog.

The room was as black as pitch when a muffled thump had Carrie surfacing from under the blankets. She could have sworn she hadn't slept at all, but the illuminated digits on her watch glowed 6:34 in neon pea green. The last time she'd looked, it had been 2:57.

For a moment, all she heard was the tick of frozen rain still blowing against the window behind her. Then, the soft thump came again, followed by the creak of the floor. She heard another creak moments later, hardwood protesting as two hundred pounds of carved granite moved over it. The man on the other side of the wall was either an early riser or a restless sleeper. Carrie could easily identify with the latter, which tended to make the former next to impossible.

She lay listening to the sounds of movement and stared at the weak ray of light that filtered from the hall, presumably from beneath his door. The light suddenly disappeared, robbing the room of shadows. Thinking he was about to come out, she held her breath. A full minute passed, yet the door didn't open. After another minute went by and he still didn't emerge, she readjusted her pillow and snuggled back down. The room was cool, but it was warm beneath the blankets. As difficult as it was trying to sleep on a stranger's wonderfully comfortable sofa, she didn't even want to think what it would have been like out there alone in her car.

The next thing she knew the pale gray light of morning was pouring in the window and Jack was six feet away, trying to be quiet about stoking the fire.

He knew the moment she wakened.

From the corner of his eye, Jack caught movement from

the sofa. He wasn't accustomed to being quiet inside the cabin, but he'd managed to keep from waking his unexpected guest while he'd put on the coffee and let Felan out. He'd also managed to avoid taking too close an inventory of the form beginning to emerge from beneath the blankets. He'd noticed only the abandon with which she slept, sprawled on her stomach, one leg straight, the other bent and enhancing the sweet curve of her hip. Indefensible as she was while she slept, any further notice had seemed too much a violation of her privacy. As much as privacy mattered to him, the least he could do was allow her hers.

Now that she was waking, the rules changed. Flicking a splinter of kindling into the growing flames, he sat back on his haunches and watched her sit up. As she did, the blankets slipped to her waist.

She'd slept in her clothes.

"Morning," he said, watching her push the fall of burnished sable hair from her eyes. Mussed as they were, the shining strands looked invitingly touchable. So did the rest of her. With her arm raised, her sweatshirt molded to her shape, its hem slipping up to reveal a glimpse of creamy skin above the waist of her jeans.

He met her eyes, soft from sleep. He'd spent half the night trying to forget how good she'd felt in his arms. Thinking now of how it would feel to ease his fingers through her hair and himself onto her body guaranteed he'd spend the morning engaged in the same exercise.

"Hi," she returned. Pulling the blanket back up, her glance darted over his shoulder.

"He's outside."

A sheepish smile flirted with the corner of her full mouth. "Are you always so good at reading people's minds?"

"It's not hard when something's so obvious. As afraid as you are of Felan, it stands to reason you'd want to know where he is."

"I'm sure he's a good dog."

"No, you're not. If you were, you wouldn't be afraid of him."

His bluntness killed her smile. It also arched the soft curve of her eyebrow. "I was referring to how you must see him."

"No. You were placating me."

The other brow went up. "Is that possible?"

He looked away when the smile resurfaced in her eyes. He had no strength for tests this morning. He needed coffee. He needed food. He needed the sleep she'd stolen from him last night.

The sputter and hiss of the coffeemaker sounded over the crackle and snap of the fire. Jack headed for the cupboard, aware of the quiet sounds she made moving around behind him. The rustle of the blankets as she folded them. The soft padding of her footsteps on the carpet.

He usually downed his first cup of coffee in front of the window, watching the elk come across the meadow to drink from the creek. When the weather turned cold, he drank it hunched in front of the fire, gathering its warmth in the early-morning chill. It was colder this morning than it had been in months, but he'd pass on the little rituals he'd learned to cherish. The fire would heat the room soon. With her in the house, it seemed wiser to warm up by doing something physical.

He was on the back porch, listening to the weather report and eyeing the stack of wallboard he had to hang when she opened the kitchen door a few minutes later. She'd brushed her hair back, tucking it behind her ears and traded the purple shirt she'd slept in for a loose, pink sweater.

Seeing the faint line of worry furrowing her brow, he dipped his head toward the frost-trimmed window behind him. "I take it you've looked outside."

She nodded, missing the edge in his voice. "It's gorgeous. But there must be an inch of ice out there.'' The radio occupied space at the far end of the pressboard workbench, its volume low but audible. ''Have you heard a weather report?''

''Not yet.'' Gorgeous, she'd called it. Were he inclined to sit back and enjoy the view, he supposed it was. All he cared about was that the thick coat of ice glazing everything didn't bode well for her immediate travel. ''All I've caught so far is that cars are stranded everywhere from Missoula to Casper.''

''What about the roads around here, the passes? Are they open?''

''The passes are bound to be closed.'' He lifted his mug, watching her over the steam rising around its rim. ''The only way to find out about the roads is to call the highway department, but I can't imagine they're not closed, too.''

''Do you mind if I call?''

''The phone's out.''

He wasn't sure, but it sounded as if she muttered, ''Of course it is,'' just before she shivered. The house was still cool. With only half the insulation up on the porch and no heat there at all since he hadn't turned on the portable heater, the porch was plain old cold. He thought about offering her his down vest.

''There's coffee in there if you want it.''

''Thanks,'' she returned, too preoccupied to care about the chill. ''What I really need is that road report. If this goes clear into Montana, it's going to take me longer to get to Seattle than I'd planned.''

Jack's mug stalled halfway to his mouth. ''I thought you said you were going to Moose Creek.''

''I did. I was going to spend the night there. Actually I'd planned to be there by noon yesterday so I could spend the day looking around. I'm supposed to spend tonight between Missoula and Spokane.''

She shoved her fingers through her hair, the motion suddenly agitated. According to the schedule she'd prepared for herself, she should have left Moose Creek an hour ago. "I'm starting a new job in Seattle on Monday," she told him, her mental wheels spinning. "That gives me today and the weekend to make a little under a thousand miles, but I'm losing time today and if the weather's this bad the rest of the way, I'll never get there in time.

"I've got to get in touch with the paper," she decided, talking more to herself than to him as she hugged herself tighter. "I spent nearly every cent I had getting that job. On airline tickets," she explained when she noticed his sudden frown. "For the interviews. I had to fly up there from Dallas twice. And that was after I'd blown what I'd saved for a new car on tickets for interviews in Philadelphia and Boston. You can't believe how fierce the competition is on the big dailies."

The thought of being delayed clearly upset her. Jack barely noticed. "The paper?" he repeated, his voice deadly calm.

"The paper I'm going to work for. I'm a reporter," she told him, though she was too preoccupied with her predicament to notice that the information did nothing to soften his expression. "I'd like to still be one after Monday."

It wasn't lack of comprehension that knitted Jack's brow and put the tension in his jaw. He understood perfectly. About reporters anyway. As a life-form, he ranked the esteemed members of the press just below plankton. They possessed no conscience, no soul and fewer scruples. As far as he was concerned, all that mattered to them were the allegations, the headlines. They didn't care what sort of damage they did to a life.

Watching the animated woman in his doorway, his knuckles went white around the handle of his mug. If he'd had to guess, he'd have thought her a teacher. A counselor, maybe. He wasn't sure why. Maybe it was because she seemed so...nice. He'd just never have considered a reporter. "And you just happened to pull over here?"

At the flatness of his tone, she mirrored his frown. "There wasn't anywhere else to stop. You said yourself last night that there isn't anything else around."

It was as clear as the flecks of gold in her eyes that she couldn't figure out what his problem was. Even less pleased with her presence than he'd been before, he didn't bother to enlighten her.

"Which newspaper are you going to work for?"

The frown turned to confusion. "The *Seattle Sun*. Why?"

Jack felt his stomach clench. The newspapers in the northwest had crucified him.

"Let's just say I'm curious." Suspicious was more like it. "What kind of reporter are you?"

"Better than some. Not as good as others."

"I mean what do you write," he muttered, not wanting to be impressed by the blunt assessment of her skills. "Society stuff? Sports?"

"Hard news."

His jaw jerked. "How long have you been doing that?"

"The news? Three years," she replied when he gave her a tight nod. "Two with my own byline. I'll have to prove myself at the *Sun*, so I'm sure it'll be awhile before I get one there. But I'm more into feeding my body than my ego. Do you have a cell phone?" she asked, suddenly hopeful.

"No."

"I have one in my car. I'll just have to go get it."

She turned on the heel of her sneaker, a pink blur of purpose as she headed inside. He hated to stop her.

"It won't do you any good," he called, catching the door

before she could swing it closed. "We don't have cell service here. All you'll get is dead air."

The steam left her stride, bringing her to a halt beside the pine table and the box she'd opened so her plant could get light. Despite her bafflement over his sudden interest in her occupation, she'd answered his questions with the openness of someone who has nothing to hide. He couldn't help the defensiveness that had taken hold of him, though. He was certain no one could have found him. But he'd believe in the tooth fairy before he'd believe her presence mere coincidence.

"Who did you call last night? After I told you where you were," he expanded, trying not to sound impatient when she looked as if she had no idea what he was talking about. "Who did you talk to? Someone at your paper?"

"I didn't call any..." She caught herself, turning away as her glance skittered from his. "I called my friend in Dallas. She—*he* knows I'm here."

Jack watched her hug her arms to herself, her slender shoulders stiffening. She was lying. And badly at that. She couldn't even meet his gaze. She hadn't called anyone. No one even knew where she was.

It occurred to him, vaguely, that there should have been someone waiting for her somewhere. Someone who would be worried about her not having checked in last night when she'd reached wherever she was supposed to have been. A woman traveling alone should be in contact with *somebody*. But he was more concerned with her reaction just then, than he was with any threat she might feel in being alone with him, or with the fact that she seemed to lack any close connections. Her unguarded response told him their concerns were miles apart. She was far more interested in getting to a phone and getting out of there, than she was in getting information out of him.

Last night, the only questions she'd asked had been about his dog.

Thinking his isolation must be making him paranoid, he told himself to back down and back off. If he didn't, she'd get suspicious even if she wasn't already.

"Look." He took a step toward her, then swore to himself when she backed up. "I'm sorry. It's just that the guy who owns this place has had trouble with reporters before." It was the truth, as far as it went. The man Jack worked for was as obsessive as Jack himself about keeping his private life from the press. It was just that Jack had no life other than his private one anymore. "I just wanted to make sure you weren't here trying to get a story or something."

Some of the starch slipped from her shoulders. Still, she seemed more cautious than she had before. There was also a spark of interest in her eyes that hadn't been there until now. "Who owns this place?"

"I thought you wanted to get the highway report."

"I do. But you've got me curious. Why were reporters giving him trouble?"

"Because that's what they do best. I'll make you a deal," he went on, ignoring the droll look she shot him. "You make breakfast while I chain the pickup. There's a phone at the lodge. As soon as we're through eating, I'll take you there to see if it's working."

The woman seemed as transparent as crystal. He could practically see the wheels spinning in her mind as it changed gears. "The lodge?"

"It belongs to my boss."

"The man you won't tell me about," she replied flatly.

"You got it."

"Not even his name?"

A touch of cajoling entered her eyes as a little more tension left her shoulders, but her wheedling was wasted. Her scent drifted toward him, soft, clean, impossibly erotic.

It was like breathing pure oxygen. The rush went straight to his brain, heightening his senses, threatening his judgment.

"Not even."

"Can't blame a girl for trying." She shrugged, seeming to shed the rest of her tension. "Thank you, Jack," she said, her smile soft as she touched his arm. "For what you're doing. For what you've done. You're a very generous man."

He felt like a fraud as she turned away. Self-protectiveness motivated him. Not generosity. He was just as anxious to be rid of her as she was to be on her way.

Chapter Three

Jack didn't go straight to the lodge. He wanted to check the phone line first. Getting his phone service back was as important to him as having the woman beside him in his truck depart. Without the phone, he couldn't use his computer to monitor his investments, and those investments were the only means he had of repairing some of the damage he'd so unwittingly done. If need be, he'd drag himself out in the dark every morning to use the computer at the lodge if he had to, but the one in his room was infinitely more convenient. With the time difference between New York and Wyoming, he got up early enough as it was to log on when the exchange first opened.

He told Carrie only that they were taking a little detour, then turned the radio up to catch the weather report and turned his attention to the road. Driving wasn't bad on the gravel. The ice broke under the weight of the tires and the uneven surface allowed good traction. The highway was a different story. The going was slower there, even with chains.

The defroster ran full blast, the rush of air competing with the rumble of the truck's workhorse engine. Still, the air in the cab was sharp with cold. His breath puffed white vapor when he spoke.

"There it is."

"What is?" Carrie asked as he reached over and turned the radio down.

"The break. I hoped it would be this feeder and not the main line. It's come down along here before."

He slowed even more, bringing them to a stop while he rolled down his window. The defroster was already working overtime. Now, arctic air blasted into the cab, refogging the windows and annihilating the work the heater had done.

Oblivious to the shocking cold, Jack thumbed up the brim of his Stetson, glancing from the line dangling across a bed of frozen fireweed to a tree branch leaning against a creosoted phone pole. "Looks like the weight of the ice pulled it down." The window went back up with a protesting squeak. "I can fix it, but the cable I need is in the maintenance building by the lodge."

Carrie sent a worried glance back toward the dangling wire. "Does that mean the phone at the lodge won't be working?"

"The line to the lodge comes off the main line farther south. Over that ridge." He pointed a gloved finger to the distance. "Just hope this is the only place it's down."

His hand landed back on the wheel, clenching with a tension that was mirrored in his jaw. Seeming to absorb that subtle agitation, Carrie leaned back, rubbing her arms over her jacket to ward off the chill.

"Is the lodge very far?"

Telling her the lodge was a mile from the cabin, and that the only way to get to it was from there, he turned the pickup around to head them back in the direction they'd come. Not sure what to make of the faintly brooding quality settling over him, not wanting to add to it, Carrie rubbed the fog off her window and tried to concentrate on something other than the now silent man beside her.

They passed her car and trailer, bumping along the lane she'd walked twice last night, then headed through the caretaker's compound, passing between the cabin and the large garage. As they did, Carrie caught sight of the window she'd first looked out that morning.

"Why is there a bar across the kitchen window?"

Without sparing her a glance, he said, "A bear came through it."

Her voice remained commendably calm. "Recently?"

"Three years ago. Maybe four." Beneath his rawhide coat, his broad shoulders rose and fell in a shrug. "That's what I was told, anyway. I wasn't here then."

"Have you had any problems with them? Bears, I mean."

His eyes remained steady on the gravel road when he told her he hadn't. Relieved to know that, Carrie would have shared that thought, and asked where he had been before coming here, but he turned the radio back up, filling the interior with the strains of an old cowboy lamenting the loss of his lady. Or, maybe, it was his horse.

Taking the hint, she settled back to ponder just how wild this place was—and to consider the fact that the thermometer outside Jack's back door read twenty degrees. With the forecast for more of the same, the ice out there wasn't going to melt anytime soon.

The road to the lodge led into the woods, curving only where it had to in order to avoid the creek, a hill or a particularly thick stand of trees. It crossed the creek twice, on narrow bridges railed with lodgepole pine. Carrie eventually found herself leaning a little more forward on the seat, peering through the clear spot on the foggy window. The ice that glazed every tree, rock and blade of grass, made the world look as if it were coated in crystal.

They crossed a meadow, entered another woods and emerged at the top of a hill to the sight of a sprawling lodge on the valley floor below. Even shuttered for the winter, the huge log building with its studied and rustic lines looked to Carrie like something out of an architectural magazine. Every window seemed to sport a veranda and every veranda had a view of the mountains or the beautiful, hidden valley guaranteed to steal a person's breath.

"Wow."

Beneath the brim of his hat, Jack's glance slid toward her. "It's big," he agreed, pulling to a stop at a rear entrance.

"I mean the views. This is incredible."

Surprised, curious, he watched her slide from the truck. She was taking in the panorama like some city kid visiting the country. The breeze was forcing down the air temperature, but she didn't seem in any hurry at all to escape the chill. She simply rubbed her arms as she turned full circle, her expression one of quiet fascination as she took in the mountains and woods surrounding them.

"What are those?" Her eyes narrowed on the brown specks at the far end of the small valley. "Are they moose, or elk? They don't look like they have antlers, though."

She stood with her face to the breeze, the wind toying with her sleekly styled hair. Wondering how someone could appear as innocent as she did sophisticated, Jack followed the direction of her gaze.

"You'll never see that many moose together. You'll see one. Maybe two. But that's it. They're loners. Those are bison."

"Buffalo?"

"Buffalo," he repeated.

"Wow," she said again, the sound quieter, almost reverent.

He would have expected a broader vocabulary from a journalist. He would also have thought she'd be more impressed with the massive building than with the scenery. The lodge was the size of a small hotel. Impressive by any standard. The fact that it was used only as a summer home would have made it even more so, to some people. But then, she'd caught him a little off guard with that houseplant of hers, too.

He glanced toward the gunmetal gray sky, an edgy feeling clawing his gut. With the wind coming up again, he didn't want to think about what that sky meant. "Let's get going."

In the stillness, the slam of his door sounded like a gunshot, scattering magpies from the trees behind them. The birds' raucous chatter filled the air as he headed toward the overhang sheltering the doorway. Carrie was only seconds behind him, using the sides of the pickup bed for balance as she rounded the truck. With one eye on her, Jack unlocked the door, flipped on the light and disarmed the security system that was wired to his cabin. He was relieved that the electricity was still on. There were backup generators, but messing with them wasn't something he wanted to do just then. Get in, get out, get her on the road. Those were his priorities at the moment.

He'd just turned to see if she was going to need help on the slippery walkway when he found her right behind him.

She smiled. "It's slick."

"Yeah," he muttered, feeling his gut tighten, and motioned her inside.

The main level of the lodge was upstairs. This level was, for all practical purposes, the basement. He mentioned that much as he led her through a foyer lined with custom-made wooden benches and ski racks that never saw use. Little excesses were evident everywhere. In the wine room, with its oak monastery table and a collection of vintages that might well turn to vinegar long before their owner would get around to consuming them. In the small theater with seating for thirty, in a house that never saw more than ten guests at a time.

Aware of the journalist nosing around behind him, certain her brain was cataloging everything in sight, Jack turned into a room the size of his entire cabin.

He'd taken half a dozen steps inside when he heard her chuckle. The sound was throaty, unexpected and far too appealing.

"This is terrific. Absolutely terrific," she repeated, gawking like a child in a candy store as she entered the arcadelike space. "It looks like a game room for ghosts."

He supposed it did. Everything from the oversize sofas to the old-fashioned pinball machines and the billiard table in the middle of the room was covered with white sheets. The dartboard above a draped game table even had a white dustcover hanging over it.

"Are you sure you won't tell me who owns this?"

Jack motioned to the curved, carved mahogany bar. "The phone's over there."

"You're not very subtle, you know?"

"I'm not trying to be."

She cocked her head, struck again by the vague familiarity of his compelling features as he held her glance. She remembered what he chose to read, and the almost deliberate austerity with which he surrounded himself. "Jack," she began, hesitating. "Is this yours?"

"What?"

If he wasn't going to be subtle, neither would she. "Are you a broker?"

"What makes you ask something like that?"

"The books on your shelves. You seemed to really be

into stocks and bonds and commodities. All that stuff that's Greek to those of us who barely manage passbook savings accounts.''

"I'm not a broker," he pronounced flatly. "I'm a caretaker. And no," he added with a look that said she might as well stop digging. "This isn't mine."

"Well, you never know," she murmured, defending the possibility. "There are all sorts of eccentrics running around. You might live in the cabin because you got sick of all this and decided you wanted a simpler life."

"I live in the cabin because it's provided with my salary. If I had this kind of money, I wouldn't waste it on conspicuous excess." He lifted his hand toward the bar, the motion impatient, his expression closed. "See if the phone works."

She'd met reticent people before, but this man topped the list. When he didn't want to talk about something, he simply didn't. But what he didn't say, spoke volumes. She'd have bet every possession in her ice-covered trailer that he knew exactly what he'd spend such money on.

Curiosity was what made her so good at her job. But remembering her job was what made her put the questions in her mind on hold and reach for the phone.

The instant she heard the dial tone, she turned to ask Jack if he knew the number for the highway department, but it was just her and the sheets in the room. So, she called information, then the highway department, spent two minutes getting busy signals, two more on hold and finally got a harried clerk who told her she probably wasn't going anywhere before midafternoon.

The next call went through quicker, but the nerves in her stomach had knotted themselves into a neat little ball by the time she found Jack pacing near the door they'd entered. She'd thought for sure that she'd be relieved once she'd made her call. She wasn't relieved at all.

It must have showed.

"What happened?"

Carrie let out a long, low breath. "The man I needed to talk with was in a meeting, so I told his secretary what was going on." Her new boss's secretary was to efficiency what Gatling was to the gun. The woman even spoke in a sort of rapid-fire manner that economized time by wasting none of it on breathing between sentences. "She told me she appreciated 'my difficulty,' but that it would definitely be in my best interests to be no later than Tuesday. She suggested taking a plane if I have to. Mr. Hawthorne has little tolerance for people who don't make deadlines." Her nose wrinkled. "Nothing like getting off on the right foot, is there?"

"So, what did you tell her?"

"That I'd be there by Tuesday. And I will," she added. "I'll rent a sled if I have to." She couldn't take a plane. Even if she could afford a ticket, she couldn't leave her car and trailer. "Seattle is two days away. With the extra day I just got, I now have three and a half to get there."

"You shouldn't have sounded so definite." He reached past her to punch numbers into the security pad, the motions as abrupt as his statement. "Remember that front they mentioned on the radio?"

"The one that's coming in tonight?"

"That's the one."

"What about it? I'll be gone before it gets here."

For a moment, he said nothing. He simply flipped off the light and opened the door. Meeting her eyes, he dipped his head in the direction of the cold air blasting inside. It was snowing.

"You might be gone," he agreed, nudging her out. "But you won't be heading north. Come on. Let's get the cable and get out of here."

"It's just flurries," Carrie pointed out, edging her way

around the fender of the truck to the passenger door. "Maybe it'll stop."

"Yeah. About April. We average twelve and a half feet of this stuff a year up here. It starts with 'flurries.'" He jerked open his door. "You might as well forget going through Moose Creek. Even if they don't go ahead now and shut down the road through Yellowstone for the winter, the roads north could be impassable for days. Your best bet is to head south a couple hundred miles and pick up the interstate."

She scrambled into the cab, the slam of her door echoing his. Even under the best of circumstances, it would take an entire day to go that far out of her way. "Twelve and a half feet?"

"The way it blows around, it'll be twenty feet in some places, six in others." He backed up, slid, swore and tried again, giving the truck a little less gas. "Why didn't you just stick to the interstate to begin with? Moose Creek isn't exactly on the beaten path between Dallas and Seattle. It would have made more sense for you to go through Salt Lake City. Or California."

He kept his scowl on the road behind them as he backed up to a large log building hidden from the main house by crystal-coated trees. She didn't need to see his eyes to catch his irritation, though. It was in his voice, and the rigid set of his jaw.

She was feeling a little tense herself. He had no business insinuating that she hadn't thought her plans through.

"I'm well aware of the more direct routes." If she could claim any redeeming trait at all, it was practicality. Act now, think later was definitely not her style. "I wanted to go through Moose Creek because I was born there," she informed him, not that that was any of his business, either. "The detour only added a hundred miles to my trip, which isn't much at all when you consider the whole distance. I might be guilty of sentimentality, but I'm not stupid.''

Having been born in the area apparently gave her a right to be there that he hadn't been prepared to accept. Or, maybe he went silent because he was debating the merits of her last statement. Whichever it was, a heavy hint of annoyance smoldered in the glance he shot her before he pulled under a large carport and, leaving the engine running, got out.

She was right behind him, leather sneakers crunching on blessedly dry and unslippery gravel.

Metal clanked when he unlocked a barn-size door and jerked it back on its rollers with a mighty shrug. ''I don't care if it was only fifty miles out of your way,'' he muttered at her. ''The weather turns this time of year.''

''Well, this 'turn' wasn't in the forecast when I left four days ago. When I checked, all the passes were open and there wasn't a single bad storm on the weather map.''

''Whose?''

''Whose what?'' she insisted, scowling at his back on their way through the crowded maintenance building. Gardening tools hung on walls. Saws and axes hung next to them. Shelves held cans of paint, putty and plumbing parts. He headed for a row of huge spools. Barbed wire. Electrical wire. Heavy black cable.

Her glance swung back to Jack. Jack of all trades.

''Whose weather map?'' He lifted one of the hip-high spools onto its side, then gave it a shove to roll it toward the workbench. ''I haven't heard of one yet that you can rely on. Up here, you figure that if it's October, it could snow. If it's November, it will.'' His expression grim, he surveyed the array of tools on the Peg Boards. Snatching off a pair of large wire cutters, he handed them to her. ''It's November.''

It was *early* November, but she didn't waste her breath

pointing that out. Taking the coil of rope he also handed her, she headed out ahead of him, tossed the rope in the bed of the pickup, then went back to get the ladder he'd propped against the outside wall while he rolled the spool out.

"A woman shouldn't be traveling out here alone, either."

The glare she aimed at him was glorious. It was too bad he missed it.

"Well, I am alone," she muttered, fumbling with the latch on the tailgate. "I tend to operate fairly well that way, too. I've had a lot of experience at it." Her knit gloves were no match for the cold and her fingers were freezing. Even with that minor handicap, she should have been able to get the latch open. But it was either stuck, locked or broken.

She rarely swore. But she did now. She rarely lost her cool, either. But this man was pushing all the wrong buttons. He could hoist the damn spool over the tailgate, or lower the blasted thing himself.

She'd just slid onto the passenger seat when she felt the truck buck under the weight of the cable being dropped into the bed.

"Damn," he muttered when he got in, then started to get out again.

"What now?"

"I forgot the electrical tape."

"It's right here." She pulled the roll of black tape from her pocket. "You'd set it on the ladder."

She placed the roll on the seat between them, but when his glance jerked back to hers, his only response was to jam the truck into gear. Outside, snow was falling faster, thicker and the scenery was rapidly disappearing.

"I don't know why you're acting like I'm responsible for this. I don't want to be here, either, you know."

Her expression was pure exasperation. So was her tone. Had Jack felt at all charitable just then, he'd have sympathized with the feeling. But charity had been drained out of him a long time ago, along with every other decent trait or emotion. Anger. Now that was something he had no trouble conjuring. At himself most of all.

"I didn't say it was your fault." It was some perverse quirk of fate that had dumped her in his lap. It had to be. Either that, or she'd been inflicted on him as further punishment. "You should just always expect the worst from both people and the weather. That way you'll never be caught unprepared."

She'd been picking at the frays on the knee of her jeans. Now, her head swung toward him, her hand catching the corner of her hood to keep it from blocking her view. "I could never do that."

Sure you could, he thought, you're a reporter. But he kept the conclusion to himself. She'd already picked up more about him than he liked simply by perusing his bookshelf. There was no sense raising more suspicions on her part about why he'd just as soon see all reporters strung up by their thumbs.

Muscles tensed, he slowly negotiated the rapidly disappearing road. The last thing he wanted was to spend another night in the confines of his cabin with *this* particular journalist. That was what had him so edgy. He was already far too aware of her, of her quick mind, her feminine shape, her impossibly soft and erotic scent. He didn't want her reminding him of what he couldn't have. He didn't want to be responsible for her, or for her to expect anything from him, count on him in any way. He wanted her gone.

The back tires slipped.

Years of experience had Jack turning into the skid, rather than jerking the wheel the opposite way. An instant later, feeling the tires grip, the quick tension eased in his shoulders. Some of it, anyway. The snow was giving them better traction than had the ice. As hard as it was coming down, it was also making it nearly impossible to see the road.

Carrie relaxed her death-grip on the armrest. Concentration etched Jack's features, magnifying the strong, angular lines of his profile. There was more to his irritation than simply being inconvenienced by her presence. She was sure of it. He'd been different ever since he'd learned that she was going to Seattle instead of Moose Creek and he'd given her the third degree about her job. Before that, he'd only seemed distant. Since then, he'd been edgy. Now he was plain old irritable. She'd liked him better silent.

She had more on her mind than his inexplicable mood. Her own irritation had taken a dive the instant she'd felt the back of the truck break free. They'd just missed a granddaddy of a pine tree. She hadn't even seen it until it popped into view by the front bumper.

The wind picked up, driving the curtain of flakes sideways.

"Are we in trouble?" Carrie asked, gripping her seat belt as the wind battered the truck.

"Not yet."

"Will you let me know when we are?"

"You'll be the first."

As treacherous as driving had been for Carrie yesterday with the wind and the ice, at least she'd been able to see. Now, it was like driving with the white sheet fluttering over the windows. Jack knew what he was doing, though. She felt as sure of that as she had his protection when she'd let him lead her to his dog last night. If he said they weren't in trouble yet, then she wouldn't worry.

They were crossing the second bridge when he rolled down his window and flipped off the crust of ice and snow from the tireless windshield wipers. The wind tore through the cab, driving the chill air straight through her jacket, jeans and sweater. Gooseflesh sprang up everywhere, shivers chasing themselves from the back of her neck to her knees. Carrie didn't say a word. The heater was barely keeping up and, though Jack's expression was impassive, and his coat heavier, he had to be feeling the cold, too.

Minutes ago, her greatest concern had been how she was going to drive her own car if she couldn't see the road. Huddled into herself as they bounced over what felt like a small boulder, she prayed that they wouldn't be forced to spend the day—or worse, the night—stuck in a snow drift in Jack's truck. As small as his cabin was, it had at least offered them some escape from each other. There would be none on the bench seat of a pickup. Not with those shoulders taking up half of it.

She was thinking that the only way the situation could be worse was to have the beast-dog occupying the two feet of dark gray fabric between them, when they slowed, then stopped moving completely.

The engine was still running, the defroster still blowing. The windshield wipers still dragged with a fingernail-on-chalkboard screech across the ice on the window above the defroster vents. Beside her Jack, stripped off a glove.

"Stay put," he ordered, flipping up his collar. He tucked the right lapel under the left before he buttoned it with an expert flick of his fingers and tugged the glove back on again. "I have to open the door to pull into the garage. You can't see the cabin but it's there."

She couldn't even see the garage. The defroster on Carrie's side of the front window barely worked, which meant her visibility had been even worse than his. Between that and the fact that the view out the passenger side window was blurred with breath-fog and snow, she hadn't even realized where they were.

He reached for the door handle, yanking down the brim

of his hat. As he did, Carrie tossed the tape she'd set on the seat onto the dashboard and scooted into no-man's land.

Jack didn't get out as she'd thought he was going to do. Instead, just as she slid over, he pushed down the handle, then looked back at her as if he were about to say something. Her eyes were dead-even with the cleft in his chin when her knee hit his thigh and her shoulder bumped his.

She went still, startled to find herself so close. Beneath the brim of his hat, his dark eyebrow slowly arched and his glance locked on hers. He made no effort to move. No effort at all to give either one of them any more space.

She could feel the heat of his thigh where her knee pressed hard muscle. "I thought I'd pull the truck in when you opened the door."

He watched her mouth as she spoke, then pulled his unnerving glance back to hers. There were flecks of silver in his eyes. Quicksilver that grayed the deeper blue, cooling the heat. Or, perhaps, merely masking a molten core.

"I was just going to ask if you could do that." His voice grew softer. Or, maybe, the rush of the wind only made it seem that way. "Can you handle this?"

Awareness shimmered through her, shaking her all the way to her shoes. He was talking about driving the truck. About the fact that it was a stick shift and the ground was slick, a combination she might not be familiar with. She knew that.

"I think I can."

"Just go easy."

"I will."

She thought he'd turn away. She wanted him to. If she backed up herself, he'd know how he affected her and that would be like handing a match to a man with a stick of dynamite. He stayed right where he was, the arctic blue of his eyes deepening when his gaze narrowed. His expression was too guarded to guess his thoughts, but her own were decidedly disturbing as his glance drifted slowly over her face.

When his eyes settled on her lower lip once more, her heart bumped her ribs. But he seemed to find his own thoughts disturbing, too, if not simply unwanted. A heartbeat later, the hard line of his mouth pinched and he pushed his door against the wind.

Snowflakes swirled inside the cab, dusting the seat, the dash and Carrie's gloved hand where it flattened over the pulse pounding in her throat. Her heart jumped again when the door slammed shut and Jack faded into the blurring wall of white. Only seconds had passed, but in those seconds, she'd completely forgotten about the cold, the snow and the fact that she could barely feel her fingers.

A lump of uncertainty settled in her stomach. She didn't know which unnerved her more: the man she could barely see rolling back the garage door three feet in front of the truck, or the fact that she might well be stuck in a blizzard.

A minute later, she'd pulled the truck next to a covered snowmobile in the double garage and Jack was pulling the door closed.

"Stay right with me," he ordered, stepping sideways through the opening he'd left.

From that narrowed doorway, Carrie could barely see beyond Jack's shoulder. Since she couldn't see the cabin at all, she had no intention of letting him out of her sight. The garage felt like a meat locker. Wishing for some of the heavier clothes packed in her trailer, she moved toward him, but that thought was lost when she followed him through and she was nearly knocked over by the raging wind.

The wind had tugged at the truck all the way back from the lodge, prodding and pushing it around like a child with a new toy. Carrie hadn't been prepared to meet it full face. Nor had she been prepared for its effect on her lungs. She heard Jack yell at her to cover her nose. But her breath had already caught when she'd breathed in and the frigid air hit the back of her throat. In the second it took to tuck her chin and nose under her jacket collar, Jack's arm landed hard around her shoulders.

She didn't hear what he muttered at her. But he apparently wasn't going to waste time checking behind him to make sure she kept up. His own head ducked, he braced his shoulders against the wind like a blocker set to tackle and headed them into the blinding snow. As she recalled, it was only twenty or so yards to the back door, but she could barely see where she put her feet, much less where they were going. Which meant Jack couldn't see, either.

Snow clung to her lashes, the frozen flakes stinging her skin as the wind whipped and snapped around them. They'd taken less than a dozen steps, but already her lungs ached, her fingers were numb and her body was practically vibrating from the cold. Two more steps and a sharp bark sounded ahead of her. She heard it again, only it seemed to come from the other direction now as the wind tossed the sounds around, then tore them away.

She felt Jack's big body press her to the right. She moved with him, her shoulder beneath his arm, her hip to the top of his thigh. She responded to the slightest shift of pressure or pace, letting him lead her like a partner in a dance, matching each step, flowing with him.

The ground had turned solid white. The ice covering the pine needles and dirt had grabbed the flakes and held fast—except for the snow that swirled from the ground, making it impossible to tell what was falling and what had already been dumped from the sky. Carrie could have sworn that they should have already reached the cabin, but when she uncovered her mouth to ask Jack if he could see it, the wind froze the words in her throat and she ducked her head again.

She felt his arm brace her tighter, his free hand coming up to nudge her head into the protection of his shoulder. Still, they didn't stop moving, even though every step was like trying to move through a wall.

She was wondering if a little panic might not be in order when the corner of the porch emerged ahead of her. Then, steps. A moment later, she stumbled up them and Jack reached past her, pulling open the glass storm door. She reached for the knob of the wood door herself, but the knit surface of her glove only slid over the smooth metal instead of turning it open. Jack's grip was firmer. He'd scarcely pulled her hand away before he was pushing her inside.

Seventy pounds of gray fur blocked the threshold.

Carrie froze.

Jack swore. Still pushing, he made the dog back up. Felan gave another guttural bark and knocked a roll of duct tape from a sawhorse with the excited wag of his heavy tail.

Carrie, knee to nose with the canine sniffing at her jeans, nearly fell over the sawhorse backing away.

"For God's sake," Jack muttered, catching her by the arm while he used his free hand to pull the storm door closed. "Are you trying to break your neck?" He tugged her forward to keep her from doing a back flip over the bar of the sawhorse, closing the inner door with his booted foot at the same time. The hunk of snow jarred from his heel landed on the planks. "He's not going to hurt you. If it hadn't been for his barking, we could still be out there trying to find the back door."

Jack let her go, refusing to meet her eyes. He didn't want to know if she was worried or frightened or cold. Mostly he didn't want to see the haunting fear he'd seen the first time he'd laid eyes on her, or the vulnerability that made him want to take her into his arms because she was trying not to be afraid of something she feared very much. That more than anything.

"Go on, Felan," he muttered, opening the door to the kitchen. He dug a piece of jerky out of a jar on his workbench and slipped it to his buddy, substituting the treat for the affectionate roughhousing that was their standard greeting when he'd been gone for a while without him. "Go lay down. We'll play later."

As if he knew that the woman who stood as still as Lot's wife was the reason he'd been relegated to the hearth mat, Felan eyed Carrie on his way past, the treat hanging from the corner of his mouth like a flat cigar. The big beast looked as displeased with her reaction as Jack seemed himself.

"I'm sorry," Carrie murmured. "I didn't think when I saw him. All of a sudden, he was just there..."

Jack said nothing. He just peeled off his gloves and tossed them onto the workbench, then whipped off his hat to whack off the snow. White powder dusted the floor, and clung to the edges of his boots and her shoes.

Carrie had yet to move. She stood where he'd released her, between the workbench and the sawhorse, arms crossed and shivering. Jack had his coat off and was shaking the snow from the ochre colored hide when he finally met her eyes.

There was no way she could leave. Not until the snow let up. They both knew it. It was a toss-up who was unhappier with the idea.

He finally nodded toward the kitchen door, necessity warring with preference. "You might as well take off your coat and go on in. You'll warm up faster by the fire."

Chapter Four

Carrie took a deep breath, exhaled to the count of ten and breathed in again. Concentrating on her breathing was supposed to release anxiety and relax tense muscles. She'd read that in an article on stress reduction. Or maybe it had been in an article on natural childbirth. Whichever it was, the technique usually worked for her. At the moment, battling nerves, the shivers and the lingering remnants of the fright the dog had given her, the effects of the exercise were negligible.

She stood on the kitchen side of the long, pine table, her movements stiff as she tucked her numb fingers under her arms to warm them. If she were ever asked to describe her idea of a nightmare, she'd be hard-pressed to come up with anything more unsettling than what she'd experienced in the past twenty hours. She'd been treed by a wolf-dog, stranded in an ice storm and blinded in a blizzard. Granted, her last little adventure had only given her a taste of what being in a blizzard was like, and she truly wasn't the sort to panic easily, but she had no desire to repeat the experience. What bothered her most, however, was the nagging feeling that her situation was only going to get worse.

Hugging her arms tighter, she eyed the fanged canine hogging the heat she craved. Felan had staked out the hearth rug. Though the animal's eyes now appeared closed, she suspected that he was aware of every move she made—much like the man at the end of the table.

Jack snagged a chair, its legs scraping against the scarred linoleum, and sat down to pull off his boots. A size eleven hit the floor with a dull thud.

"You said his barking led you to the door." She spoke the reminder quietly, her attention divided between the dog and the tension radiating in waves from Jack's big body. "I wondered how you could see when I couldn't," she admitted, wanting badly to fill the strained silence. "I've heard of farmers getting lost in blizzards between their house and their barn, but I'd never understood how that could happen." She certainly did now. It had occurred to her ever so briefly that it might very well happen to them, too—that they'd miss the cabin and be unable to find shelter. "Has he done that before? Led you here with his barking?"

The other boot hit the floor. "I don't usually leave him here. The only reason I did was because you were with me and he scares you."

"I appreciate that," she returned mildly. "But that isn't what I asked."

He shot her a level glance. "He's led me back a couple of times, and I knew he'd bark when he heard the truck."

"Then you weren't worried? About us overshooting the cabin, I mean?"

Jack wasn't sure what he heard in her voice. It was more than the curiosity in her expression, but far less than the anxiety anyone else might have expressed. What it sounded like most was a need for reassurance.

Even if he'd been inclined to tell her that he wouldn't have let anything happen to her, reassuring her about the weather was both arrogant and foolish. "I didn't say that. I've counted the steps between the cabin and garage," he told her, rising to strip off the fleece shirt he wore over dark blue flannel. "And I know the land around here." He knew it nearly as well as he'd known his own. He knew the roads, their bends and turns and the distances between them. He knew the trees that marked his routes once the roads disappeared under the snows that would come.

"I think I know Felan, too," he continued, carrying his boots to the hearth before heading for the kitchen again. "But in a whiteout, when the snow comes down so fast that it erases the landscape and the wind blows so hard that it distorts everything from temperature readings to the direction of sound, a person's senses can become distorted, too. It's a crapshoot every time a person finds himself in one."

A cupboard squeaked when he pulled it open. A moment later, a heavy brown mug hit the orange counter and he filled it with the coffee he'd left on. "You ought to know that."

"I should?"

"You said you were born here."

"I was," she returned, not sure what to make of the frown he shot over his shoulder before he slipped the carafe back into the coffeemaker. "But we left when I was eight. As far as the weather is concerned, I have a vague memory of a green snowsuit I absolutely hated, but that's about it."

"That explains it."

"Explains what?"

His frown slid to the quarter-size hole above the knee of her jeans. Specifically to the bare skin visible through it.

"Why you don't know how to dress." His jaw clenched as his gaze worked its way to her sweater. "What have you got on under there?"

There wasn't a shred of male interest in the demand. He was looking at her as if she were a small child who couldn't be trusted to dress herself on her own. Not appreciating his tone or his implication, and not about to describe what she did have on under the hip-length cotton sweater, Carrie's chin went up.

"I'm warm enough."

"Sure you are. That's why you're standing there with your shoulders around your ears." He moved in front of her, mug in hand, a mountain of solid muscle and intimidation. "And that isn't what I asked," he muttered, deliberately turning her own words back on her.

Faced with the solid wall of his chest, her chin went up another notch and she forced her shoulders down, arms still crossed. She'd chosen to stay in the kitchen because the table provided a barrier of sorts between her and the dog sleeping in the living room. At that moment, seeing the glint in Jack's eyes, the dog actually seemed less dangerous.

She no sooner heard his mug hit the knotty-pine surface behind her, than she felt his fingers wrap around her forearms. His eyes steady on hers, he pulled her arms apart, almost daring her to stop him, and picked up one of her hands.

"Those gloves of yours are fine for driving," he informed her, his touch far gentler than his expression as he held up her cold and reddened fingers, "but they're way, way too thin to do you any good outside. You need insulated ones here. Mittens would be even better. And slick surfaced or leather. Snow sticks to knit."

With the disgusted shake of his head, he dropped her hand. Before she could question what he was doing, or why she allowed it, his hands slipped under her sweater and flattened on the sides of her hips. An erratic heartbeat later, she felt his big hands on her waist.

She was aware more of weight than warmth when his fingers curved around her ribs. Her nylon teddy separated her from the calluses she'd seen at the base of his fingers. Yet, he might as well have splayed his hands on her bare skin. A heated, liquid sensation gathered where his thumbs met above the snap of her jeans. That sensation slithered slowly downward, shocking her senses, enlivening her nerves and threatening the stability of her knees.

His thumb and index finger pulled at the silky fabric. "This is it?"

She wanted to believe it was his height and the fact that she had to tip her head back so far to see him that made her feel dizzy. But she knew it had more to do with the accusing intensity in his eyes and the blatantly proprietary way he touched her. That same sense of possession had been in his hold when he'd tucked her against his solid body a few short minutes ago.

"I packed for five days in a car, not for a ski trip." By some miracle her voice was steady, even though her insides were jumping. "It was eighty and clear when I left Dallas. The temperature in Seattle was in the high forties and it was raining. I didn't think I'd need anything more than a waterproof jacket and gloves."

She felt his thumb graze the curve of her rib below her breast. The motion seemed unconscious, prompted more by reaction than thought. Not by the twitch of a single black eyelash did his expression change. He was that controlled. That deliberate.

"It's no wonder you're cold," he muttered when a tremor ran through her. "You're not wearing anything under your jeans. This sweater," he added, nudging at it from the inside, "looks warm, but the knit's too loose to hold any heat. You need more layers in weather like this. Especially now that it's snowing.

"Next time you go out there," he told her, cutting her off before she could remind him that she hadn't planned on the weather, "you put on whatever you brought in with you. Even if you just plan on being in your car. Look what happened to you last night. And just now. You never know when you'll get caught. If I'd paid closer attention to how you were dressed, I'd never have let you leave here this morning." His fingers flexed in agitation, tightening at her waist. "That wind out there is gusting at thirty and forty miles an hour. The thermometer's reading less than twenty. Don't you know what can happen to you in weather like this?"

Jack felt the smooth muscles of her stomach shift with her deeply drawn breath. From the way her expressive eyes flashed, he had the feeling she was either counting to ten or preparing to tell him off. He wasn't concerned about her reaction to his lecture. Every breath he drew brought her soft scent with it, reminding him with each jolt to his groin that it was a mistake to be this close to her.

All he'd wanted was to make sure she understood what she was up against. He wasn't going to be responsible for her freezing that sweet little backside of hers the next time she went outside. But he wasn't going to be responsible for what happened if he didn't take his hands off her, either. She made no effort to move away and that made it impossible for him to think of a single reason why he should let her go.

The thought had no sooner registered than she curled her fingers around his wrists and pulled his hands from under her sweater.

"I've heard about hypothermia," she assured him in her best I've-got-this-under-control voice. "And I promise, I'll be careful."

She stepped back, gamely holding his glance as she tugged her sweater over her hips.

He moved with her, canceled the step she'd taken and snagged her hand again. It still felt like ice. "You don't have to promise me anything," he told her, forcing her to back into the table to avoid the press of his body when he picked up his mug of coffee. Placing the mug against her palm, he took her other hand and wrapped her cold fingers around the warm ceramic. "All I'm doing is telling you what you need to know while you're traveling through here. What you do with the information is up to you."

He gave her a few seconds for his message to sink in, then left her clasping his brown mug and moved away. His motions deliberate, he took another mug from the cupboard and filled it with steaming coffee, seeming every bit as disinterested in her as he'd just proved he was. She'd been treated with indifference in far less subtle ways. She'd even been told outright that her presence was unwanted because she was in the way. But this wasn't a long-ago complication with family, or an interview situation where she'd been protected by the professional armor that wasn't always as impervious as it seemed. Totally unprepared, his dismissal stung with a fierceness that nearly stole her breath.

"I appreciate the information," she told him, working to hide the hurt. It was unexpected, that pain. That was all. He was the man who'd held her, who'd made her feel safe. Because of that she'd somehow forgotten to protect herself, to keep her guard in place. "I'll see to it that I don't inconvenience you any more than I already have by freezing while I'm stuck here."

It wasn't sarcasm Jack heard. It was defensiveness. The kind that surfaces when an emotional bruise has been bumped. Telling himself he didn't want to know what sort of bruises she harbored, fighting the thought that he'd just added to them, he focused on his more immediate concerns.

"It could be hours before this lets up. By then, it'll be dark."

He saw her shiver just before she nodded again. "Maybe the storm won't last that long. The radio said there's another front behind this one, but if this lets up by midafternoon and if the break between storms is long enough, I could probably make it to Jackson."

He knew she was worried about her job. She was worried about being stuck another night. She was worried. Period. So was he. There were too many "ifs" in her plan to allow any probability to her departure.

He took a sip of the bitter brew, already resigning himself to what he couldn't change while he concentrated on the heat flowing into his chest. He'd have suggested that she drink up, too, since he'd learned that the quickest way to get warm was by drinking something hot. Except he didn't want to concern himself that much with her.

He was concerned anyway. He had more insulation than the woman standing with her back stiffly to him—an easy seventy pounds anyway, and he'd been dressed for the weather. She had to be freezing. She was just too stubborn to admit it.

He looked from her to the dog sprawled in front of the fireplace. She was also too uneasy about Felan to go anywhere near the fire.

"Are you hungry?"

"Not really."

"Well, I am." One more swallow of coffee and the mug hit the counter. "Why don't you fix us something to eat?"

The sharp sound caused Carrie to jump. Annoyed with the betraying reaction, she cupped the mug with both hands to keep from spilling its cooling contents and straightened her shoulders.

"I'd be glad to." The snow would stop soon, she told herself, and she'd be on her way. In the meantime, she'd simply handle the man bearing down on her the same way she would a hostile interview subject and act as if nothing he said or did could rattle her. She'd show no sign of weakness. No sign that he affected her at all. "Just tell me what you want."

Jack's eyes narrowed on her face. He'd never known anyone who could shrug off defensiveness as easily as she just had. One moment her body had been rigid, self-protection written in the set of her shoulders and the starch in her back. Now, her head was tilted, exposing the gentle curve of her neck. There was something in her eyes, though. A wariness beneath the bravado that made her look more vulnerable than she could have possibly realized.

He didn't want her vulnerable. He wanted her to be hard-edged and abrasive. He wanted her to be as cold and calculating as the reporters who'd dissected his life and magnified the parts that had made the best press. He didn't want her to be awed by the mountains, or to have a smile like sunshine, or to fit his body as if hers had been made just for him. She'd been totally fluid against him as they'd made their way in from the storm. She'd matched his every step, his every movement. He didn't doubt that she'd be just as fluid beneath him in bed.

His glance moved from the lushness of her mouth to the gentle swells of her breasts. Her vulnerability aroused an unwanted compassion. Who she was fanned his distrust. But what she stirred in his loins was a far different hunger than the one they were talking about.

She'd asked what he wanted.

At the risk of making a bad situation worse, he didn't think it wise to tell her.

"Surprise me." He lifted his hand, then snagged his fleece shirt from the runged chair back to keep from brushing his fingers against her skin. The temptation to touch her was far too strong. Too much like a need. "But if you feel like baking something, I wouldn't mind."

"Baking?"

"Sure. There are some mixes over there somewhere." He nodded toward the stack of grocery boxes at the end of the counter. "I don't know if I've got what you'd need to start anything from scratch."

Fabric wadded in his fist as he turned into the living room. A dozen steps later, he'd crossed the carpet and disappeared into the hall.

The breath leaked from Carrie's lungs like air from a slowly deflating tire. She'd stood her ground. She hadn't let him rattle her.

Right, she mentally muttered, rubbing at the nerves jumping in her stomach while she poked through a box of canned goods. He'd stood close enough for her to feel the heat radiating from his body, looked her over as if he couldn't decide whether he wanted to kiss her or toss her out in the snow and she hadn't let him affect her. In a pig's eye. The thought of him touching her again had rattled her so badly she'd forgotten she was freezing.

She remembered now. So she turned on the oven and was standing beside it savoring its heat when Jack came back out wearing a pair of dry boots. He didn't look directly at her when he passed. He merely glanced at the box of brownie mix she was reading, but she assumed the satisfied look on his face was because he approved her choice.

"You're not going back out there, are you?"

His eyebrow sketched upward at her quick concern. "I'm bringing in more wood. It's right out here," he added, finding that concern either surprising or unnecessary.

There was a square hatch in the wall at the far end of the porch. Carrie remembered seeing it, and the bin on the outside of that same wall. Apparently wood was loaded into the bin outside and retrieved from the inside. If a person didn't give too hard a tug on a jammed log and get an arm caught in an avalanche of firewood, she could see where the setup had its advantages.

She could also see that her thoughts were running a little too close to the surface. She hadn't liked the idea of him going back outside, but she didn't care to consider her reasons for that while he went out to bump heavy things on the porch and she moved around his kitchen opening drawers in search of utensils. Most of the drawers were empty. One held a pot holder. Another held only a spatula and a large spoon. Pickings in the cupboards were just as lean. They bore only the essentials and then the bare minimum of that. It was the kitchen of a man who thought of food only as fuel, one who undoubtedly took little pleasure in the meals he ate alone.

The suspicion would have made her feel bad for anyone else. Where Jack was concerned, it only made him seem more of a loner, more impervious. She wondered if he took pleasure in anything.

She shook her head, physically shaking off the thought. As soon as the snow let up, she'd be out of there. She'd never see the man again and the entire episode would simply be a brief, bizarre encounter that wouldn't even seem real once she settled into her new apartment and buried herself in her work. Her reactions to him were simply due to the uncertain circumstances.

Relieved by her rationalization, she heated canned soup and grilled cheese sandwiches in a frying pan while Jack carried split logs into the living room and stoked the fire. Every minute or so, she glanced toward the barred window across from the long pine table. All she could see was white. The snow hadn't let up by so much as a flake. Over the snap of the fire in the other room she could hear the wind whistling through the rafters in the attic.

Jack sat back on his haunches, taking his time about

picking up the bits of bark from the hearth and tossing them into the flames before he closed the glass and metal door. Behind him, he was aware of Carrie setting the box with her plant on the floor and setting the table with utensils. She glanced out the window, then checked her watch, seeming more agitated than she had before. Or, maybe, just less adept at hiding it. Agitated himself, he said nothing. She'd figure out soon enough that she wasn't going anywhere today.

He stayed out of her way, absently scratching Felan behind his ears and wondering if he'd ever realized how small the cabin was—until the smells from the kitchen had his stomach rumbling.

"That about ready?"

She stood motionless at the stove, chewing on her bottom lip. Caught stewing over her situation, her head jerked up, her dark hair nudging her cheek as she turned. Giving the shining strands an absent swipe, she murmured that it would be in a minute and slipped sandwiches onto plates and dished soup into bowls.

She was on her way to the table, glancing out the window for the umpteenth time when he decided to offer them both a reprieve.

"I wouldn't count on much of a break out there, today," he told her, scraping a chair back. "But if there is one, maybe I can get you to Moose Creek on the snowmobile."

She looked at him in honest confusion. What he noticed most was that she'd seemed to have finally warmed up. She'd pushed the sleeves of her pink sweater to her elbows.

"You said the road will be closed north of there. I need to go south. And I can't leave without my car and the trailer. Everything I own is in them."

"So whoever you were going to see there can bring you back when the weather clears."

Comprehension slipped into her eyes, along with a hint

of apology for the false hope she'd given him. "I know I said I was born there, but I wasn't going to visit anyone." She sat across from him, smoothing the white paper napkin in her lap as if it were fine linen. "I don't know anyone in Moose Creek."

"No relatives? No family friends?"

"No one."

He had the good grace to hide his disappointment. Either that or he was too hungry to indulge it at the moment. He picked up half of his sandwich, looking more puzzled than critical. "So why go a hundred miles out of your way?" he asked, before half of what he held disappeared in one bite.

"I just wanted to see it."

"That's it?"

She nodded.

"Why?"

She submerged a carrot into her soup, her own, normally healthy appetite supplanted by the knot in her stomach. She rarely spoke of her vagabond childhood. Rarely thought of it anymore, actually. And her reasons for wanting to see a place that could never be what it was in her mind would undoubtedly sound very foolish to a man who didn't appear to have a single sentimental bone in his body. "Because I don't remember what it looks like."

The other quarter of his sandwich went the way of the first, his eyes on her while she toyed with her lunch, his mental gears shifting.

"What's the rest of it?"

"What makes you think there's more?"

Because you won't look me in the eye, he thought. Except for when she'd tried to pretend she'd called someone last night, she'd never hesitated to meet his glance head-on. "Isn't there?"

She shrugged, then smiled. "I suppose there is," she

said, her voice as soft as the snow obliterating the woods and mountains beyond the window. "But I don't expect to find it there. What I remember about it is a state of mind that disappeared a long time ago." She paused, studying the fine, dark hairs on the back of his hand. "It's the only place I ever really felt secure. Really safe." She raised her glance to his, the delicate arches of her eyebrows knitting over the quiet inquiry in her warm eyes. "Do you know what I mean?"

It had been Jack's experience that women wanted information pried out of them. They hinted and evaded then expected their minds to be read. Carrie apparently wasn't that manipulative. Or that complicated. He knew exactly what she was talking about, too. This cabin was like that for him. At least, it had been.

"Yeah." The acknowledgment came with an ease that surprised him. "I do. Why did you leave?"

"It wasn't my choice. My dad left when I was eight," she said, drawn by his quiet admission. "Mom isn't the sort of woman who deals well with life on her own, so we moved from Moose Creek to stay with my aunt in California. After that we lived with a guy she'd met at work, but that didn't work out with me around, so I went back to my aunt's while Mom stayed with him until they broke up. Then she met Stewart. It was about then that I started wanting to come back here. Just to see it again. I just never had the opportunity before now."

Jack couldn't help himself. "What happened with Stewart?"

"Same thing. Only I went to another set of relatives that time."

Her aunts and uncles had always been kind enough to her, but they'd had their own families, and stretching tight budgets to include another mouth had caused more than one marital battle. She knew. She'd overheard the arguments, usually late at night and always after her mother had come by for a visit.

She didn't mention that to Jack, though. Nor did she tell him how hard it had been to just get settled into a new place, a new school, then have to start all over again. Something was always shaking her sense of security, it seemed. She'd learned to land on her feet, though. She'd had to. Mostly because there'd never been anyone else around to catch her when she fell. Sheer stubbornness had played a factor, too. No way was she ever going to be as dependent and needy as her mother.

"Mom finally got married again, and when I was sixteen my first half sister came along." Jack's sandwich was already gone, so she handed him the half of hers that she wasn't going to eat. She had the feeling all of his appetites were huge. "Mom and Archie had two more after that. All blond and blue-eyed like her."

His glance moved from the dark eyes she'd inherited from her redheaded father to the brown hair that had been a throwback to heaven only knew where.

"So how did you fit in?"

"I was the baby-sitter." Her smile made her shrug look vaguely philosophical. "Fortunately they were good kids. For siblings." The curve of her mouth deepened. "At least they didn't make me swear off having my own someday."

"I take it you've never been married."

"I'm not in any rush. You?"

"Once was enough," he said, then when her eyebrows arched he added, "It was a long time ago. And no," he continued because he could tell it was coming, "we didn't have any children." He wouldn't have been able to stand it if he'd lost them, too.

She tipped her head, something beyond curiosity in her eyes. "May I ask what happened?"

Jack leaned back in his chair, dropping his glance from

the quick concern in hers. He wasn't sure how the offer to take her into Moose Creek had worked its way to the demise of his marriage. He had been the one asking the questions, his curiosity grudging. Now, wondering at the lack of bitterness in her, he could feel that too-familiar feeling rising in him.

He didn't know how she did it. She had once felt secure in her world, as he had. Then, she'd been abandoned, palmed off and pushed aside until a use for her had been found. He didn't doubt for a moment that she'd felt like an outcast. Yet, she spoke as if the way she'd been treated by people who should have cared about her had been of little consequence, as if she harbored no ill at all against the mother and the men who hadn't wanted her around.

He pushed his empty bowl aside, the food in his stomach settling like lead. No one knew better than he did how it felt to be cast out by those he'd thought had cared. He'd lost everything he'd always thought he could count on. His reputation, his entire sense of who he was. He'd once been a respected member of the community. He'd had a wife, a business, friends. He'd contributed to charities and coached Little League and planned for sons of his own someday. Then, an error in judgment had cost him everything.

This woman had been a victim. However unwittingly, he'd brought his fate on himself. Still, that she could be familiar with his loneliness held as much threat as solace. He didn't want her that close.

"I blew it," he finally said, his tone ruthlessly even. "That's what happened." He kept his glance steady on her, recrimination warring with defense. "So why a journalist?"

For a few moments, her head remained tipped, her eyes narrowed as if she were debating whether or not to push. Then, her soft smile returned.

"Because I don't sit still very well," Carrie said, wondering what he'd done to place such blame on himself. "I thrive on the chaos. There's always a detail to chase down at the last minute. A deadline to beat. You never know what to expect on any given day, and I like that, too. I must," she added, wryly. "I've had to move three times in the four years I've been at this. Twice to get better positions and the last time because of downsizing. I'm hoping Seattle will be it for a while."

She didn't want to think about where she was supposed to be headed at that very moment. "Would you answer a personal question?" she suddenly asked, more interested in him just then, anyway.

"Depends."

"Did you have an affair?"

Indulgence marked his tone. "No. I didn't have an affair."

She didn't know why it relieved her to hear that. "When you said you blew it, I thought maybe that was why you came here. Two women in the same town. Big scandal. That sort of thing." A hint of apology slipped into her eyes. "Blame it on a reporter's imagination."

There'd been a scandal all right. The muscles in his shoulders tensed. So did those in his jaw. His voice sounded tighter than it had even moments ago. "I came here because the town I lived in isn't what it used to be."

As if a door had slammed, he closed up right in front of her, his manner turning cool and distant as he rose with his dishes.

Carrie's instinct was to prod. There was more to his attitude than the failure of a marriage, difficult as that would have to be. That suspicion kicked her curiosity into overdrive, but she couldn't bring herself to poke for clues about whatever it was. He'd protected her. He'd offered her shelter. And she'd invaded enough of his privacy already. His past had clearly cut him deeply. She could almost feel his pain and his bitterness when he told her he was going to work on the porch, then closed the door solidly behind him.

At two o'clock the wind was still blowing and the snow had buried the top step of the cabin. At three, Carrie poked her head out the kitchen door to ask Jack if he'd heard a weather report lately. He didn't even look up from the shelf he was installing. He merely told her the radio indicated that the two weather fronts had merged and there would be no break in the snow before morning.

Being an optimist, she hoped for a break anyway. But by the time five o'clock rolled around and dark had settled around the cozy little cabin once more, she'd accepted what Jack had already known and finally resigned herself to staying put for another night.

Jack came in twice to stoke the fire. On his last trip through, he asked if she'd mind doing the meal thing again. Then, just as he had last night, he ate his dinner on the porch while he worked and she spent the evening pacing and learning how to avoid hypothermia from a book she found on his shelf.

"Make sure you read chapter three" was all he said to her when he finally came in for the night and disappeared with his dog into his room.

Chapter Five

Morning broke with a sky of battleship gray and air so frigid it hurt Carrie to breathe. She really wasn't accustomed to cold. Not the bone-chilling, face-numbing kind. She wasn't accustomed to indulging herself, either. Not when it came to physical discomfort, and definitely not where her personal longings were concerned. It was easier to deny a need than to long for something that just wasn't possible. But she was dealing with both the cold and an often-denied desire as she trudged through the snow toward her car.

Just once she wanted to have everything under control. Just once she wanted to be settled in somewhere and know that she belonged right where she was. The way Jack seemed to belong here, in this wild and rugged place. He was as enigmatic and compelling a man as she'd ever met, and one of the most frustrating, but she envied him the control he seemed to have over his life. Over himself. But here she was again. Starting over. Or, at least, trying to. Seattle was still nearly a thousand miles away.

At least the view was pretty.

Snow blanketed everything, looking as pure and pristine as bridal satin. It sloped in two-foot drifts against anything solid enough to have blocked the wind from carrying it farther, and sat like puffs of whipped cream atop the exposed rocks in the creek she paralleled. The limbs of the birch trees had been blasted nearly free of their brilliant leaves and left encased in coats of pearl. Deep green branches of fir drooped beneath the snow's weight. Breathtaking as it was, what impressed Carrie most was the fact that the wind had stopped blowing, and that none of the white stuff crunching under her shoes was falling from that very threatening sky.

As far as she was concerned, she was home free. Or would be as soon as she cleared the layer of snow off her car and cracked through the crust of ice that welded her door shut.

Snow flew as she swept it from the roof and windshield of her little beige sedan with the broom she'd borrowed from Jack's back porch. She didn't know for certain where Jack was, but she suspected he'd taken off to repair his phone line. She'd been asleep when he'd come out to put on the coffee, and since he'd been so careful not to wake her by being more quiet than she'd have thought a man his size could be, she'd stayed put until he and his beast-dog had gone out. She'd figured out where he'd gone while standing at the window with a cup of coffee a few minutes later and seen the two black lines of tire tracks cutting through the snow from the garage to the road.

Those parallel tracks took a sharp right from the driveway and disappeared around the bend.

She attacked the back window, wincing when the snow flew back at her. The powdery white stuff was already caked to her shoes and to the bottoms of her jeans. Now it clung to her knit gloves, too, as she swept great swaths through the accumulation on her car. Her fingers and toes were already cold, but the activity kept her muscles warm, warding off the worst of the chill. As long as she kept moving, she was fine. Or so she was thinking when the drone of an engine encroached on the winter silence.

The drone grew louder as Jack's black truck rounded the bend, the truck's heated exhaust vaporizing in a gray plume in the freezing air. By the time she'd cleared the snow from the taillights on her trailer, he was close enough that she could see Felan eyeing her from the passenger seat.

She was leaning on her broom when Jack pulled up behind her. Leaving Felan in the truck with the engine running, he got out and headed toward her.

He wore his heavy, rawhide coat, and the black hat that made him look like a cowboy, even with the ponytail. Worn jeans hugged his powerful legs and he tugged at his heavy gloves as he strode toward her. He would have looked right at home on a horse, riding his own land.

The image drew her, as it had before. The ruggedness of it. The way it suited him so well. And, as before, she dismissed the tug she felt in her midsection as nothing more than a normal female response to an abnormally attractive male. Jack was cynical and remote. He clearly preferred his solitude. And they couldn't be in the same room for more than ten minutes without him getting edgy, or irritated or clamming up and her wanting to either tell him off, or ask him to please talk to her. Just because she couldn't seem to forget how safe she'd felt in his arms, meant absolutely nothing.

Liar, her conscience prodded, but, since she would never see him once he disappeared from her rearview mirror, she didn't worry about why it seemed harder to breathe when he met her eyes.

"Morning." Beneath the low brim of his hat, his glance slid from her to her rented trailer and back again. "Decide to go for it?"

"As much snow as you said you get here, I don't imagine I'll have a better chance." She smiled, then felt the expression falter when his own features remained as still as stone. She leaned the broom against the side of the car, crossing her arms to fight the sudden chill now that she wasn't so active. "I heard on the radio that the interstate is being plowed, and that the road south of Jackson should be open by this afternoon. As soon as I get the car turned around and my things from inside your cabin, I'll be out of your hair."

She didn't wait for his reaction. She'd yet to see him smile and the thought that her imminent departure would bring on the apparently rare event didn't do a thing for her ego. Turning to her driver-side door so she wouldn't have to see his relief, she curled her gloved fingers under the layer of ice on the recessed handle.

Her fingers were colder than she realized. They didn't want to bend much and when she tried to pull up, she couldn't seem to get any leverage at all. She tried again, with both hands this time.

"There's an easier way to do that."

More than happy to hear what that way might be, she pulled her hands back to curl them against the front of her jacket. A minute ago, she'd actually been comfortable. Standing still, she was freezing.

She was really beginning to hate being cold. But all she said was, "How?"

Jack's expression was as bland as oatmeal as he picked up the broom and turned it upside down. Holding it with one hand near the bristles and his other back from the rounded end, he used the wooden handle like a battering ram to give the door a series of quick, sharp taps around its perimeter, crazing the ice. He did the same with the car's handle, then tossed the broom aside to open the door with one mighty yank. Ice shattered like broken crystal, shards slicing into the snow.

"Thank you," she murmured, reminding herself that, when all else failed, to try brute force. Fumbling her keys from her pocket, she stepped past him to slide onto the tan cloth seat.

Though her dexterity was hampered by the cold, she managed to get the key into the ignition. She could not, however, make it turn. She was about to mention that to Jack when she saw him hold out a red plastic lighter.

"Flame your key."

"Do what?"

"Hold the tongue-end in the flame," he explained, looking unusually patient when he crouched down next to her. "When the key is hot, the heat should thaw the ignition switch enough for it to turn."

Jack thought she looked a little skeptical when she took the lighter from his leather covered palm and pulled off her gloves. Some of the snow clinging to them fell into her lap, dusting her jeans, but she was concerned only with getting the lighter to light.

"I'll do it," he said, seeing how stiff and red her fingers were.

He reached for the lighter. Carrie pulled it away, determination etched in her features. Two seconds later, an inch-high flame sprang from the wick. Despite the fact that the flame was shaking because her hands were, she flashed him a triumphant smile and murmured, "Got it."

He'd have bet the farm that her car wouldn't start. Or that she'd flood the engine trying. The engine balked a little, but it kicked in with a rattle and a chug that indicated it would do just fine once the oil warmed up enough to circulate. Apparently, like its owner, it wasn't going to let a little cold slow it down.

She had the defroster going full blast and her useless gloves back on when she stepped out and nudged the door closed with her hip.

"Did you get your phone line fixed?" she asked, picking up the broom again. Holding it the way he had, she stepped past him, fighting another shiver on her way.

"I got the line spliced, but I won't know if the phone works until I get to the cabin and see if there's a dial tone. Hey!" He reached out, grabbing her wrist, suspending the broom midair. "What are you doing?"

Incomprehension swept her features. "Breaking the ice."

"That's a good way to break your windshield." He lowered his hand, bringing her arm with it. "Let the defroster work for a while then use your ice scraper."

The look she gave him was admirably even. She'd lived in Dallas. She doubted they even sold ice scrapers there. "I don't have one."

"You can have one of mine. Come on, I'll help you get your chains on."

"I don't have any of those, either."

His eyebrows slammed together like lightning bolts. "How do you plan to get anywhere? You're probably thirty miles from the nearest plowed road. Even then, you're going to need 'em."

"You said yourself that traction is better on snow than on ice," she returned reasonably. "And I bought new tires just before I left. I hated spending the money on them, too," she muttered, thinking of a dozen other things she could have used that money for, "but I got the all-weather kind. The guy at the tire store said I'd need them for the rain in Seattle."

"They may work fine for the rain in Seattle, but they're not going to do a damn thing for you on the snow and ice in Wyoming.'' He frowned at one of the tires under debate. It was buried up to the stem of its air valve in what was likewise being discussed. ''You need chains. In some places you'll be pulled off the road if you don't have them on...if you don't slide off it first.''

''Fine,'' she muttered, preferring not to think about the sliding off part. She planned to drive slow. *Very* slow. ''So I get pulled over. If that happens, I'll ask the officer to give me a ride to whatever town he or she works out of and I'll buy chains.''

Carrie had no idea what was going on behind Jack's arctic blue eyes. He wasn't happy about something, though. Not the way the muscle in his jaw was jumping. That made no sense at all to her, either. She was only trying to do what he'd wanted her to do since she got there.

''Wait for me inside your car,'' he finally said. ''I have a pair of chains I think I can cut down to fit. And here.'' He peeled off his gloves and held them out to her. ''Put these on before you lose your fingers.''

She stared at the buff-colored leather, then looked up at him. ''I'm okay.'' Hunching her shoulders, she tucked her hands under her arms. ''They're not that cold.''

''You're only saying that because you can't feel them.'' That wasn't true. But it was close. ''What about you?''

''I have another pair in the truck.'' He nudged them toward her. ''Come on. Take them.''

He had that look about him. The same one he'd had last night when he'd asked what she was wearing under her sweater and she'd balked at a reply. He'd put them on her himself if he had to.

Wondering how he thought she'd survived for twenty-eight years without him, refusing to acknowledge that, two nights ago, she might not have, she murmured a quiet ''Thank you'' and accepted his offer.

His strides were eating the distance between her car and

the cab of his truck when she slipped them on. The fleece lining still held the warmth of his big, capable hands, but any consideration she might have given that little intimacy was canceled the moment Jack opened the door of his truck. Felan bounded out, danced around Jack's legs, then bolted in the direction of the cabin, snow flying like a rooster's tail in his wake.

Jack automatically glanced toward Carrie. She was standing with her hands encased in his big gloves, pressed to the base of her throat. "He probably saw a rabbit," he called out to her, then swung himself behind the wheel and slammed the door.

It didn't take a rocket scientist to figure out that Felan still scared the daylights out of Carrie. It didn't take one to know that she definitely was not accustomed to this kind of weather, either. He could tell that she had on more clothing under her jacket than she'd had yesterday, just by the bulk. But he didn't care what she put on, how good a trouper she was, or how unfazed she pretended to be by the cold. He seriously doubted that she'd ever encountered winter in the wild at its raw and unforgiving worst.

The weather wasn't bad at the moment, though. Last night's storm had only left about eight inches of snow on the flats, and he'd had no trouble at all on the road himself. In theory, she ought to be able to make it to the interstate—*if* it didn't start snowing hard and *if* her car and trailer didn't slip on a curve and wind up jackknifed in a ditch, or over the edge of a hill. The road saw little traffic this time of year as it was. Conditions being what they were that day, there might be none at all heading this direction. No one to help her.

With a ruthlessness that had once been totally foreign, he cut off the thought, chains rattling as he pulled an old pair from a box in the garage, checked them over, then tossed them in the bed of the truck. She was not his responsibility. She was simply a stranger who'd become stuck in front of his cabin and would soon be on her way. Just because he suspected she might be a little too stubborn for her own good was her problem. That he couldn't help wondering if she always pushed herself so single-mindedly, was his.

Jack was back in minutes, seeming a little edgier than when he'd left, but Carrie figured that was because he had things he needed to be doing other than helping her. Had she known a thing about snow chains, she'd have thanked him for the pair he said she could have and put them on the car herself. She might as well have attempted to build a nuclear submarine. She hadn't a clue where to start. She told him that, too. But all he did was mutter, "Don't worry about it," and hand her a shovel.

It took them the better part of an hour to do what, to Carrie, had sounded fairly simple. While she removed snow from around the front tires, he cleared the snow from around the ones in back and laid the chains out like little railroad tracks in front of them. He then told her she'd need to drive the car onto the chains, *slowly,* then he'd pull them around the tire. She didn't catch what he was going to do with the needle-nose pliers he'd pulled from his coat pocket or the little neon green elastic gizmos he tossed onto a spot he'd cleared down to hard-pack. As cold as she was getting, she didn't care. All she wanted was to get in her car, crank up her heater and get moving. She had two days and sixteen hours to get to Seattle. If it hadn't been for some silly, nostalgic need she'd had to see Moose Creek, she'd have been there by now.

She couldn't get the car to budge. The back tires simply sat there and spun their way down to glare ice. Jack hollered at her to ease up and try rocking the car by putting it into reverse and then forward again, but she couldn't get that to work, either. That little failure only increased her irritation with herself.

The edgy feeling doubled when Jack pulled her door open and told her to get out so he could do it. It was her car. She ought to be able to get it to move. But he was only trying to help her out of the mess she'd gotten herself into, so she turned her car over to him, then stood back, wiggling her toes in her shoes to make sure they were still there, and listened to the engine rev as it strained to pull the heavy trailer through the snow and gain traction at the same time. She felt just like that car sometimes, struggling and working like fury and getting absolutely nowhere.

Groaning, she blew a foggy breath. It was truly pathetic that she could identify with a piece of mechanical hardware that was not only boringly practical, but about six payments away from being replaced.

Jack finally got the car to do what she couldn't, and eventually got one of the chains on and tightened. He mentioned, almost too patiently it seemed to her, that the things had a habit of loosening or coming off at the least opportune times, so he had her secure and tighten the other one herself to make sure she'd know how to do it. She approached the task with as much enthusiasm as she would have an assignment to cover a dog show. Crouching in the snow with nothing but a layer of denim covering her bare legs was bad enough. Having to abandon Jack's warm gloves seemed like cruel and unusual punishment. They were six sizes too big, though, and she couldn't handle the pliers wearing them. So she pulled them off and reached for the metal chains that had been chilling under the tire and the pliers that felt as if they'd been dipped in ice. In the time it took for her first resigned breath to crystalize, her fingers felt as stiff as Popsicle sticks.

She was beginning to think the whole business of putting on chains was enough to make a saint either cry or swear when Jack declared the barbaric-looking things tight enough. After hauling himself to his feet and giving her a hand up to her own, he had her pull her car a few dozen feet forward to see how well it braked. The car braked fine. It was the trailer that slid into the ditch.

Despite her slip because of Jack yesterday, Carrie really wasn't into swearing. Not since it had cost her over twenty bucks the year she'd resolved to donate a quarter to the bag lady outside her apartment building every time a curse passed her lips. Crying was out, too. Her tears would freeze to her cheeks and the thought of ice next to her skin was more than she could bear. Doing what she always did when there was nothing to do but get something over with, she refused to consider the matter further and pushed on. Shoving open her door, she tucked her chin into the collar of her jacket and tromped up to Jack.

She would forever think him a gentleman. He didn't say a word. "Would you mind pulling me out?"

Her voice had a faint huskiness to it that hadn't been there before. Hearing it, Jack straightened from where he leaned against the front of his truck and shifted his attention to the impossible calm in her expression. It was either the cold affecting her vocal cords, or plain old frustration. The way the last hour had gone, his money was on the latter.

He glanced toward the trailer. The right back tire had slipped down the eighteen-inch slope to the ditch that ran along the highway. The left tire turned slowly in the air, the axle high-centered by the edge of the road.

He'd pretty much expected something like that to happen. She'd hit the brakes too hard, typical of someone inexperienced in driving in such conditions. But now, he was also interested in seeing how far she'd go before she gave up.

"No problem," he assured her. Setting his hat more firmly on his head, he sauntered back to his truck.

Moments later, he was back with a huge chain he'd pulled from the box mounted behind the cab. Getting the trailer back on the road wasn't that big a deal. Turning the trailer and the car around in eight inches of snow when the only place to back it into was the six-foot-wide driveway twenty feet behind them was more of a challenge. The trailer, weighted as it was, didn't want to stop when the car did, which made it want to slide—usually sideways. Between the two of them, they managed to keep everything on the road, though; Jack, behind the wheel, the driver's window down so he could see her. And Carrie, standing in the snow in the middle of his driveway directing him.

By the time her car and trailer were both back on the road and headed in the right direction, Carrie was so cold and so frustrated with how long everything was taking that she wasn't even talking unless it was absolutely necessary. It hadn't occurred to her to take a break, much less to quit. Jack was beginning to think the word wasn't even in her vocabulary when she asked in a voice as tight as a watchspring if she could borrow the ice scraper he'd mentioned before.

With her window down, the inside of her car hadn't had a prayer of heating up. The best the defroster had been able to do was to melt two circles the size of tea saucers on her windshield. The rest of the window gave a distinctly glazed and distorted view of the snowfield and powerline disappearing over the ridge.

Wondering how much longer she thought she could keep this up before the cold chased her inside, Jack reached under his truck's seat for one of the black plastic scrapers that were free with a fill-up at Chapman's Gas & Go. He should tell her to go inside himself, he thought, handing it to her, then canceled the thought. Her cheeks were still ruddy from the cold, so she was probably okay. Once they began to pale, he'd let himself be concerned.

A few tiny snowflakes were spitting from the sky as she tucked her chin deeper into the collar of her jacket and started chipping at the ice at the edges of the melted circle. Even wearing his gloves, her hands were too cold to get any leverage. The scraper slid over the ice, then slipped through the gloves like a bar of wet soap.

He heard her mutter a curse. An instant later, she hit her hand on the fender in pure frustration and promptly winced at the pain.

"That's it." Taking her by the shoulders, he turned her around. "Go inside and warm up. You've been out here long enough."

"I can't go inside. I have to finish this so I can leave."

"Not this very second, you don't. You can't hold onto an ice scraper. How do you expect to drive a car?"

"I'll warm up once I get going."

Exasperation sliced through him. "Have you always been this stubborn?"

Her chin tipped up. "Yes," she told him, but if she was trying to look as competent as she undoubtedly was under most circumstances, she failed miserably. At the moment, looking like a Botticelli angel with her white hood framing her face and frustration pooling tears in her eyes that she would undoubtedly blame on the cold, all he could see was the vulnerability she seemed hell-bent on denying.

If she truly was as independent as she seemed, Jack suspected it was because she'd always had to be.

He let his hands fall. He had the urge to either shake her or pull her into his arms, but it seemed safest to swipe the ice scraper out of the snow and hand it back to her. He'd have offered to clear the window himself, but he had the feeling she'd just tell him that he didn't need to go to the trouble for her. She was almost obsessive about not wanting to put him out. What he couldn't understand was why something he should have appreciated, irritated him so much.

"You're right. You do need to get going. You have a long way to travel," he added, softening his agreement. "Drive carefully."

She murmured that she would, scrambling to move from frustration to the realization that they were saying goodbye.

"Remember not to brake too hard."

"I won't," she replied, still struggling.

"Check those chains every now and again, too," he continued, finding it safer to focus on the car than on the woman who would be driving it alone. "One of them breaks loose and it'll chew the daylights out of your fender well."

"I'll remember."

His glance drifted over her face, her pert little nose, the curve of her cheek, the lushness of her lips. A wisp of soft hair brushed the delicate wing of her eyebrow. She was stronger than she looked, he reminded himself. She was used to handling things alone. She'd told him so herself. She'd be okay.

Despite the self-serving assurances, the qualifying "ifs" still nagged at him as he watched the corner of her mouth curve up. Her expression seemed suddenly very earnest. To him, very forgiving.

"Thank you, Jack. For everything." She paused, the beguiling smile fading. "I know I've put you out. But I don't know what I'd have done if you hadn't been here."

She searched his rugged features, the weathered lines around his piercing eyes, the hard line of his mouth. She needed to thank him for the chains he'd given her, and the food and the shelter. But he'd done so much more for her than providing things. Or advice. She needed to thank him for rescuing her from his dog when she'd been too terrified to think, and for allowing her the sense of safety she'd found in his arms. That sense of security, however fleeting, had been so profound that she would never forget it. She who had begun to believe she would never experience that particular feeling again. But she knew now that it did exist. And, somehow, that gave her a sort of hope she hadn't had for a very long time—along with a sense of loss she couldn't begin to explain.

She couldn't tell him that, though. He wouldn't want to hear it, and the knowledge that she might truly need something she'd learned to live without was too unsettling to consider. Almost as unsettling as the other feelings he'd elicited every time she found herself faced with his impossibly wide chest.

He was less than an arm's length away, his big body partially blocking the breeze that kicked up the top layer of snow and sent it skimming across the road. He didn't seem interested in elaborations, anyway.

His eyes were locked on hers, his expression still and intense as he lifted his gloved hand to nudge her hair from her eyebrows with a leather-covered finger. She truly didn't know what she'd have done without him.

"I have the feeling you'd have managed somehow." His finger trailed from her temple to her jaw, lightly so it wouldn't scrape her cold skin. He resented the barrier insulating his touch. He resented, too, the loneliness he would now again be left to face. "Don't forget your plant."

Her heart jerked against her ribs at his touch. "I won't." She knew he wanted her gone. Everything he'd said and done had made that abundantly apparent. Everything but the bleakness shadowing his eyes at that moment. She'd glimpsed that desolation before, felt it touch her as it did now. It made her want to reach for him, even as it warned her away. "I'll get it and my bag as soon as I finish here. I have everything ready inside the front door."

"Then, I'll say goodbye now. I have to break the ice on

the ponds before the stock start wandering up this way looking for water.'' The unexpected glimpse into his soul was already shuttered, masked by his ruthless control. That control firmly in place, he tipped up her chin and lowered his head. ''Knock 'em dead in Seattle.''

The man didn't play fair. That was her only thought when she felt Jack's warm breath on her face. His mouth settled over hers, cool, firm, deliberate. It had scarcely registered that his lips were softer than she'd thought they'd be when she felt his hands slip up to cradle the sides of her head.

It didn't occur to her to pull back. This was just a kiss goodbye. She'd kissed men goodbye before. A couple, anyway. She'd even felt the faint pull of regret, relief and the stirrings of desire. What she'd never felt was the heady scrambling of senses that caused her to grip Jack's lapels, or the deep tug of longing that made her open to him with no hesitation at all.

She heard a faint moan come from deep in his chest. Or maybe the aching sound had come from her own. Her breath caught at the feel of his tongue touching hers, startled as she was by the shock of hot and cold. The contrast was the very essence of him. Fire and ice. Pulling her with one hand, pushing with the other. But all she cared about at that moment was the feel of his hands moving over her, and the urgency threatening beneath his control.

He kissed her deeply, angling her head to better suit him, sliding his hands down her back to get as much contact out of her body as he could. Wanting that contact, craving it, she leaned into him, letting him pull her as close as he could with their bulky clothes between them. She'd felt security in his arms before. What she felt now was something that spoke to the very core of her being. But it didn't feel safe. Not at all. He was filled with too much hurt, too much anger. Yet, what she sensed in him now was the same raw need that threatened what little common sense he hadn't already destroyed.

She was in the middle of nowhere kissing a total stranger, and feeling more reckless, more vital, than she had in her entire life.

The thought had her pulling back her head, the unevenness of her breathing betrayed by foggy puffs. Stunned, her eyes locked on his.

Jack felt as if he were coming out of a fog as he eased his hold, but he didn't let her go. His eyes glittered over her face, his breathing as ragged as her own. He had wanted to kiss her since the first moments he'd held her in his arms. Now that she was about to leave, he'd seen no harm indulging himself.

That was before she'd opened to him and her heat had strafed through him like wildfire. He drew her closer, hating the barriers that kept him from feeling the softness of her body, her shape. She'd kissed him back with the same hunger he'd felt. Only he hadn't realized how hungry he'd been until he'd tasted her.

"It's a good thing you're leaving," he murmured, searching the awareness and confusion mingled in her eyes. "Keep that up, no telling what time you'd finally get out of here." The corner of his mouth quirked, hinting at how devastating his smile would be. "I can't honestly say I've ever been kissed goodbye like that before."

They were even. She'd never been kissed that way before, period.

He stepped back, jaw working, and gave her shoulder a squeeze. "You be careful out there."

Totally disconcerted, Carrie nodded. She was usually pretty good at covering her reactions. At least, she was around everyone else. Jack just seemed to catch her at her weakest moments. "I know not to step on the brakes too hard," she assured him, determined to sound as unaffected as he did. "And I've got enough gas to get to Jackson. I'm sure I'll be fine."

Taking another step back, he gave her a nod, then glanced toward a herd of elk wandering in the distance, their dark tracks dotting the side of the distant hill. He immediately dismissed the sight, familiar as it probably was to him, but Carrie's attention stayed where it was. Not on the herd. They were too far away to be much more than mobile black specks against a blue-white landscape. As she willed her heart to stop racing, her attention focused on the landscape itself.

Ahead of her, the land was nothing but a huge snowfield. The road itself was little more than a slight dip in that endless white blanket, broken only by the tire tracks made by Jack's truck. The sky was starting to leak snow again, too.

She was miles from anywhere.

Jack seemed to be reading her mind.

"If it starts snowing hard, keep your eye on the poles along the side of the road. Use them as markers and keep moving slowly and you should be okay." It was a trick people from the area had always used. Nonlocals tended to panic and stop when visibility got bad, a move that either got them stuck or caused an accident when someone happened along and plowed into them. "You need to keep an eye out for the wildlife, too. They use roads and cross-country trails for travel corridors. Hitting an elk or moose is like hitting a boulder."

Still taking in the winterscape before her, Carrie gave him a decidedly hesitant nod. Headlines were popping into her mind like flashes from an old newsreel.

Skiers Stranded: Girls Lose Feet to Frostbite.
Two Missing in Winter Storm Feared Dead.
Arctic Cold Claims Lives of Four.

Every winter, stories came across the wire about the

weather up north and its effect on those living in or caught by it. And every winter, she read the stories, then promptly dismissed them because they didn't affect anyone she knew. She'd lived in the southwest. It got down to freezing every once in a while, but the only snow she'd ever encountered was what she'd deliberately sought in the mountains on a couple of less than brilliant attempts to master something other than the bunny hill.

The stories applied to her now.

"How long do you think it will be before they plow the road to here?"

Jack's shoulder lifted in a shrug. "I have no idea. This road isn't a priority. They'll get around to it eventually, but it could be days."

Carrie finally looked over at him. Jack wished she'd kept her attention right where it had been. She was worried, but trying very hard not to be. The unguarded concern in her eyes made him want to reach for her, to tell her she would be all right, but he knew he couldn't do that. Touching her again would be downright dangerous.

"I gotta go," he said, and handed her the scraper that had once again wound up in the snow. "If you think you should, you'd better get moving, too."

He didn't even look at her before he climbed into his truck and followed his tire tracks through the scattering of trees around his driveway. *If you think you should,* he'd said, and offered no recommendation of his own.

An odd, empty sensation settled in Carrie's chest as she watched Felan, barking his deep, guttural bark, emerge from behind the cabin to follow the truck into the garage. She was on her own. Much as she'd always been. Nothing had changed there. So it shouldn't have mattered at all that Jack didn't care what she did, as long as she wasn't his problem. But it did matter, because the knowledge made her feel very lonely all of a sudden and that was a feeling she studiously avoided acknowledging.

It only took one swipe through the new flakes dusting her windshield for her to acknowledge something else she could no longer avoid. She was face to face with a drive she had no business attempting on her own. She considered herself fairly adventurous. She always had been, which she figured accounted for everything from her ability to adapt to the frequent moves she'd had to make, to her instincts as a reporter. The timid did not survive when it came to dealing with the general public. It wasn't that she was into taking risks for the thrill of an adrenaline rush. She valued her neck too much to take overt chances with it, but she did tend to forge through unfamiliar territory without balking too much.

She balked now.

She had no idea what the land was like heading south. She'd come in from the east. What she did know, was that she could barely make out the road ahead of her. Then, there was the matter of the trailer. She'd managed it all right in the rain. But control had been getting pretty iffy in the sleet. In the snow, the thing seemed to have a mind of its own.

Two different forms of survival pulled at her while she stood with the snow falling softly around her. She had to get to Seattle. If she wasn't there when she'd said she'd be, she might well lose her job—which meant she'd also lose the apartment she'd leased because she wouldn't be able to afford it and she'd be out her nonrefundable deposit. If she did lose the job and the apartment, she could go back to waiting tables until she could find a position on a paper somewhere else, but the thought of living out of her car held all the appeal of yesterday's blizzard.

Since standing there freezing her fanny in the wilds of Wyoming didn't hold any appeal, either, she did the only thing a sensible woman could.

Chapter Six

Jack ruffled the thick fur behind Felan's ears and rubbed the snow from his white muzzle. Whatever the dog had been chasing had either won the round or was now buried somewhere beneath the snow. It didn't matter that Jack provided food for his companion, a bowl of kibble was no match for the thrill of the hunt.

"Just don't bury anything under the back stairs," Jack muttered, giving the big dog one last scratch. "I don't want to find a grizzly rooting around my back door trying to get at it for one last meal."

Like a child placating a doting parent, Felan cocked his head as if to say, Who-me? and promptly wheeled off to terrorize some other hapless critter. Rising from his haunches, wishing the dog had stuck around to keep him company, Jack turned to his chores. It wouldn't be long now before the bears would head into their caves until spring. They'd been on a feeding frenzy all autumn, pre-

paring for their hibernation. They had a long winter ahead
of them. Every creature living there did.

Already edgy, thoughts of the long nights to come only
made the feeling worse. Snagging one of the red cans of
gasoline from the long shelf at the back of the garage, he
topped off the tank on the silver-gray snowmobile, then
checked its oil. Survival was never taken for granted once
winter came to this corner of Wyoming. As harsh and cruel
as a jealous lover, nature rarely forgave those who weren't
prepared for her. Animal or human.

He was dead certain Carrie didn't have a survival pack
in her car.

"Jack?"

The sound of her voice was decidedly uneasy. That was
how she looked, too, when he turned to see her standing
in the wide, open doorway of the double garage, her arms
tightly crossed. Snow fell steadily behind her.

"I was just listening to the radio. I wanted to check the
weather report again before I left," she explained, masking
her distress as best she could. "They're predicting another
six to eight inches of snow today. I don't imagine that
sounds like much to you, but I don't want to get stranded
out there.

"If you'll let me stay until the plow comes through,"
she went on, reluctantly because his silence was hardly en-
couraging, "I'll do what I can to repay you. I don't have
much money right now, but I can send you some in a few
weeks for room and board. In the meantime, I can help you
with your chores on the property, if you'll tell me what
they are."

It took a lot of courage for her to ask to stay. As much
as it would have to leave, Jack figured. She knew how he
felt about having her around. He'd hardly been subtle about
it. He'd hardly been subtle about that bit of spontaneous
combustion out by her car, either.

He stopped by the truck's tailgate, hands on his hips and his expression carefully blank. Nothing about him revealed the tension knotting his gut, or the relief he felt to know that he wasn't going to have to go after her. He would have. He hadn't wanted to admit it, but he'd known even before he'd left her to ponder her plight, that he couldn't let her leave until the road had been plowed.

"You aren't going to pay me." He moved closer, forcing her to tip her head back to see his face. "But it's not going to work the way we've been doing it."

"What do you mean?"

"The sleeping arrangements," he clarified, his voice as flat as the tire propped against the far wall. "You're not sleeping on the couch."

Caution washed over her features. "The couch is fine."

"Not as far as I'm concerned."

Her guarded glance swept his face, her entire body stiffening. "I said I'd repay you. Just because I kissed you back out there doesn't mean—"

"I'm not talking about you sleeping with me." The thought hardened more than his voice. "If that happens it won't be because I expect it for letting you stay here. If we wind up in bed together, it'll be because you want it as much as I do, and it definitely won't involve either one of us owing the other anything...before or after.

"I'm talking about us both needing more space," he informed her, watching the color heighten in her cheeks. "I'll clear out the spare room. There's a bed buried somewhere in there. You can sleep there tonight."

That would give her someplace to be other than in the main part of the cabin. He would have told her that, too, but he had the feeling she now understood him perfectly. He'd never seen her look quite as disconcerted as she did just then.

"I'm sorry," she murmured to the middle button on his

jacket. "And thank you. I don't usually jump to conclusions like that. I guess I'm a little more rattled about all of this than I thought."

"I'm surprised you'll admit it."

Carrie's glance jerked up, but Jack's expression betrayed nothing beyond the same hardness she'd seen when he'd informed her what sleeping with him would and would not involve. She should have been totally put off by how he'd regard making love with her. Or maybe grateful for his bluntness. He certainly didn't leave a girl with any illusions. But she didn't feel either put off or grateful. What she felt was confused, aroused and as restless as Jack looked.

He started for the cabin, leaving her in the doorway. "I'll clear out the room."

"I'll help."

"That's not necessary."

Undeterred, she hurried after him, loath to let him go any more out of his way for her than he already had. "I can't let you go to that trouble. If it's just a matter of clearing off a bed, I can put whatever's there wherever you tell me. I know you've got other things to do."

He turned so quickly she bumped into his side. Catching her by the shoulders, he set her back. He didn't want her in that room. Not yet.

"Do you have any clothes in the trailer? Anything warmer," he expanded, frowning at the bare skin peeking through the hole in the knee of her jeans. "And any boots?"

"Sure…"

"Then get them," he told her, and left her with the decisive bang of the cabin's storm door. He didn't want her in the room down the hall from his until he'd removed the boxes that had come from his old office, along with the records his attorney had returned to him after the trial—the boxes that were labeled Exhibits A Through Infinity and which any reporter worth her press pass would take one look at and question.

He wouldn't lie. He never had, and he had no intention of starting now. But he was no longer under any obligation to answer any questions from anyone, and he sure as hell wasn't going to volunteer anything to Carrie. He had no desire to wade through the muck of that devastating year. It was over, even though he'd be paying for it one way or another for the rest of his life.

He shouldered his way into his room, past the neatly made double bed he'd tossed and turned in most of last night. He wouldn't have kept the papers at all, had he not needed them to make what restitution he could.

Other than his bed and a nightstand, there wasn't much in the room. The only other furniture was an old armoire that held his clothes. He'd converted the closet that ran the length of the far wall into an office of sorts. A computer sat in there on a small desk, its modem near the phone jack he'd run to it. Two file cabinets filled the other end of the long space. The whole area could be closed off so he didn't have to look at it unless he was using it. It was bad enough that he faced it all first thing in the morning, five days a week. He didn't want to see it when he came in at night.

Corded muscles tensing, he hefted the heavy boxes in the spare room two at time, carried them down the hall and stacked them in the empty corner by the armoire, labels facing the wall someone had painted hospital green. The charts, pictures and certificates that had once graced his office, he stuffed under his bed. Boxes of old yearbooks and memorabilia from a life that no longer existed, went into another corner in his room. As for the rocking chair holding the fussy yellow chintz curtains the previous caretaker's wife had chosen, and the starving-artist quality wildlife paintings he'd taken off the walls, Carrie would just have to work around those.

He'd closed his bedroom door with a solid click, and walked into the living room to find Carrie dumping a small armload of clothing on the end of the sofa. A maroon sleeve dangled near the collar of something hot pink. A pair of brown hiking boots had been dropped by the coffee table.

Since she'd shed her jacket and shoes on the back porch, she headed straight for the fire.

"Where's Felan?" she asked, trying to sound more curious than concerned.

"Out indulging his wild side."

"Still chasing rabbits?"

She started to smile, but she'd barely met his eyes before her glance skittered away. He recognized uneasiness when he saw it. The disquiet he sensed in her wasn't only because of what had happened between them, though. She was feeling more than a little lost just then, alone and unsure. He was positive of it. He'd felt that way himself when he'd first come here, and he'd deliberately chosen this isolated place.

Not wanting that empathy with her, edgy with it, he motioned toward the hall. He had no patience for small talk.

"The room's all yours. Just ignore the stuff piled in the corner. If you want to help out around here, you can take over the cooking. You can clean, too, if you want. Just leave my room alone. I'll take care of that myself."

"Sure," she returned, thinking she'd have left his bedroom to him anyway. Bedrooms were personal space and Jack was as private a man as she'd ever met. But thinking about his bedroom in any context didn't seem wise just then. Not with him watching her the way he was now.

He moved closer, the muscle in his jaw jumping, and stopped an arm's length away.

"What I said before," he began, his deep voice low and

faintly husky, "I meant every word." He lifted his hand, touching the hair curved at her ear so lightly she wasn't sure he'd really touched her at all—until she felt his thumb graze her cheek. "Remember that."

It was the gentleness of the touch that was so disturbing. Strong as he was, rugged as he was, that touch spoke of a man capable of as much patience as passion. He almost seemed to promise as much while his eyes held hers.

The thought sent awareness shimmering through her.

"Are you reassuring me?" Her breath hitched when his thumb brushed her bottom lip. "Or warning me?"

Jack's glance shifted to her mouth. "Both."

He met her eyes again, just long enough for her to think he wished he'd kept his hands to himself, before he let his hand fall. He turned away, tension flowing in his wake.

"The phone's working if you want to call the paper again."

He'd made it halfway across the room before she pulled herself together enough to stop him.

"When will you be back?"

He wasn't accustomed to advising anyone of his schedule. She was certain of that. Yet something about the way he paused when he snatched his hat from the peg made her think he was even less accustomed to the idea of anyone caring what his plans might be.

"Before dark. I'll have Felan with me."

In a motion he'd undoubtedly repeated a thousand times, he swept his hair back with one hand and settled the battered black hat on his head with the other. He had his back to her and his hand on the doorknob when she saw him pause again.

He turned his head slightly to the side, his profile as rigid as the set of his shoulders. "Did you get everything you need from your trailer?"

"Everything that was warm."

"Then, don't leave sight of the cabin. This snow will have the bears going into hibernation, but there could be a few out there looking for a last meal."

"I thought you said you hadn't had a problem here."

"That doesn't mean there can't be one."

The door closed behind him, ending the conversation before Carrie could tell him that she knew what she was supposed to do when bears were around. She'd spent her first night reading all about how a person was not to run when faced with a grizzly, how she was to back away, speaking loudly and waving her arms. She knew to avoid surprising bears by making noise when she was outside. She'd also read how to avoid a moose attack. Not that she cared to ever put her theoretical knowledge to the test. She just wanted Jack to know that she wasn't entirely unaware of the dangers beyond his walls, and to have him clarify a couple of the more confusing points she'd read. Like how any sane person could suppress the urge to run when every instinct screamed to do just that.

Her instincts were screaming now. Jack had made it clear enough that he wanted her. He'd made it just as clear that he had no interest in a relationship beyond sex. *We'd owe each other nothing. Not before. Not after.* Remembering how shamelessly she'd responded to him, running was what she should be doing at that very moment.

The problem was that there was nowhere to go.

The day had turned the deep blue of a snowy evening by the time Jack shoveled off the back steps and stamped the snow from his boots. Stepping inside to the newly insulated porch, he slapped his hat against his thigh to knock the snow from it, and shook the wet white stuff from his jacket. Beside him, looking for all the world as if he wasn't about to let his master outdo him in this little competition, Felan gave a shake that sent snow flying in all directions.

Jack was cold, tired, hungry and sore. He'd spent the last three hours repairing a section of Cyclone fence that something—a moose probably—had run through and torn down. Even wide-open spaces had a few limits. At least his boss's bison were foraging at the south end of the huge property and hadn't found the six-foot-wide gap.

He unlaced his boots, still caked with snow despite his efforts. All he wanted was to thaw out in the shower and fill his belly. He wouldn't let himself think beyond that point. The possibilities were too frustrating. Normally, after he cleaned up and ate, he'd settle in for the evening with either a book or whatever project currently held his interest on the workbench. Tonight was not normal. Tonight, there was a woman on the other side of the door who had completely destroyed his peace of mind.

He'd have been fine if he'd just kept his hands to himself. It had been one thing to wonder about her, to fantasize about those soft little hands of hers roaming his body. But to actually know how she tasted, how artlessly she responded to him, had him feeling like baying at the moon.

Since he couldn't relax with her around, and the thought of closing himself up in his bedroom again held all the appeal of spending the night in a cell, he could only hope she'd decided to hole up in her room for the rest of the evening.

That hope was lost within seconds. He'd barely opened the door before he saw her sitting on the sofa. An instant later, he caught a whiff of something wonderful cooking on the stove and his stomach growled.

"Smells good," he conceded, watching her set aside a book when he and Felan walked in. Her glance immediately fell to the dog heading for his empty dish. Stifling the urge to tell her, yet again, that she didn't need to worry about the animal, he muttered, "How long before it's ready?"

She rose with the grace of a doe, her attention already

back on him. "I just need to mix the biscuits. I didn't know when you'd want to eat, so I made stew." She cocked her head, studying him as she crossed her arms over the faded red A on a gray University of Arizona sweatshirt. She'd changed her clothes. He couldn't help noticing that both knees on her jeans were intact.

"I was wondering what had happened to you." Looking as if she wasn't sure she should admit that to him, she lifted her shoulder in a shrug. "You said you'd be back before dark."

"I got busy" was all he said, not wanting her quiet concern to matter to him. Clamping his hand over his shoulder, he dug his fingers into the sore and knotted muscles there. "Hold off on the biscuits. I need a shower first."

He'd taken two steps in that direction, when he noticed the phone on the lacquered fir end table. He hoped it still worked. The last thing he wanted to do was repair the line again. "Did you call your paper?"

"I didn't try. I'm sure the executive offices are closed for the weekend. I did reach my new landlady," she added, relieved at having accomplished that much. "She was great. My being a few days behind schedule won't be a problem for her at all."

"I'm sure it won't."

His flat pronouncement left her puzzled. "Why do you say that?"

"She can afford to be sympathetic. She's already got your money."

For a moment, Carrie said nothing. She simply stared at him while he unbuttoned his shirt and tugged its tail from his jeans. The tail of the undershirt he also wore came with it.

He'd entered the room like a blast of arctic air, his presence a physical force that swept through her like a chill. Being so easily affected by him made her feel oddly threatened, and being dependent on him for shelter had her feeling threatened enough as it was. She was accustomed to taking care of herself. To coming and going as she pleased. To depending on no one. She was already vulnerable enough where he was concerned. So she'd tried to ignore the rigid set of his jaw, and the forced patience in his voice. She tried, too, to overlook the fatigue etching the lines more deeply around his eyes, the discomfort tightening his features as he kneaded his shoulder, and the fact that she'd actually started to worry about him. What she couldn't overlook was how little faith he seemed to have in anyone.

"Have you always been so cynical?"

Her quiet question caught him entering the hall. "There's a difference between cynicism and being realistic."

"Like it's realistic to expect the worst from people and the weather?"

She saw his hand fall from his neck as he faced her. What he'd said to her yesterday must have bothered her more than she'd realized.

He simply seemed surprised that she'd remembered it.

"Pretty much," he returned, easily accepting what she innately fought. "Doing what you do for a living, you know there's always more than one way to look at something."

"But do you always take the most negative?"

"Don't you?"

Despite the ease of his question, the tension in his big body was almost palpable. It radiated toward her, stiffening her back as the cool blue of his eyes bore into hers.

"No. I don't," she returned, knowing she'd never given him any reason to think such a thing. "And I don't appreciate being judged by whatever rotten experience you've had with a reporter. There are certainly moments when it would be easier to believe that every man is out only for himself, but I can usually find redeeming qualities in most people. It's a struggle sometimes, but it's not one I'm willing to give up.''

The steel in his eyes belied the mildness of his voice. "Then I envy you your generosity. That's something I just can't seem to manage anymore. And by the way, I never said I'd had a bad experience with a reporter.''

"You haven't had to," she returned, carefully matching his tone. "Your reactions are too knee-jerk to come from secondhand experience. I don't know what happened to you, but whatever it was didn't happen because of me.''

He couldn't deny her assertions. Nor did he seem willing to deny that he'd been victimized, exposed or exploited by some member of the press. That the experience might also be responsible for more than a lousy attitude toward reporters was a possibility she didn't question. She just didn't question him. She wasn't about to ask him what had happened and have him shut her out as he was so adept at doing.

"Don't let me keep you from your shower," she said, knowing she'd found redeeming qualities in him but unable to recall what they were at the moment. Wondering at the effect he sometimes had on her, determined to overcome it, she turned away. "I'll make the biscuits.''

She left him standing there, the concerns she'd felt when he'd been late melting away with the heat of her irritation. No self-respecting bear would have any interest in someone with such a tough hide. Any concerns she'd had about him being out in the weather were history, too. The weather couldn't possibly bother him, not as cold as he could be. And he was just plain too ornery to get hurt and lie out there unconscious or in need of help. She doubted he'd accept help if his life depended on it. Or so she was thinking as he strode off, working at his shoulder and mumbling something she suspected she was better off not hearing anyway.

* * *

He was working at that same shoulder when she opened the door of her room to his knock a half an hour later.

The narrow little hallway didn't have an overhead light. What light there was filtered around the corner from the living room, but most of that was blocked by Jack's body. Specifically the wide shoulders filling the doorway.

Needing to see more of his face than dark shadows, she swung her door wide to let the lamp she'd found illuminate his rugged features. A blue thermal henley stretched over a chest of solid stone and turned his eyes the color of an arctic wolf. His dark hair looked damp, and was combed straight back from his forehead and pulled into its usual ponytail. He looked very big, very male and very unhappy to be standing there.

"Aren't you going to eat?" His frown darted from her to the book on the double bed, then to the plant sitting on a box by the window. Its leafy vines draped over the pile of yellow curtains obscuring the rocking chair. One pair of curtains had been hung over the window to give her some privacy from the local zoo and her overnight bag sat by the wall.

"I thought you'd prefer to eat alone."

The frown returned to her. He opened his mouth, looking for all the world as if he were about to ask whether that meant she had, or had not, eaten dinner. But when his hand fell from his shoulder, the movement caused him to wince and the scowl that threatened to etch permanent lines into his forehead changed quality.

"Look," he began, not quite terse, but close. "I didn't mean to insult you before."

"Don't worry about it."

"Wait a minute," he muttered, catching the door when she started to close it. "I need to ask you something."

The admission sounded grudging, which was rather how

he looked as he shifted uneasily and tried to assess her receptiveness.

"I've pulled something in my back," he finally said, apparently finding her expression more agreeable than she'd realized. "I thought the shower would help, but it didn't. And I can't reach to get this on it." He held out a tube of analgesic cream, the giant, economy size. "Would you rub it in for me?" He paused. "Please," he practically growled, clearly hating that he had to ask.

"Is that why you apologized? So I'd do this?"

"I apologized because it was necessary. Now, are you going to do this or not?"

"You have such a charming way about you," she muttered, swiping the tube from his hand. "If this is how you ask for a favor, I'd hate to think how you'd sweet-talk a girl." Considering all he'd done for her, she didn't see how she could refuse his request. He was in pain, and she could help. She just didn't know if she should rub his neck, or wring it. "Show me where you want this."

She could have sworn she saw relief in his eyes. But she was far more conscious of the quick flutter of nerves in her stomach. With one elbow aimed at the ceiling, he gathered soft blue fabric in a wad at the back of his neck and dragged the shirt over his head.

The move took mere seconds, which was all the time it took for the air to leave Carrie's lungs. By the time he'd peeled the shirt down the dark hair dusting his forearms, she'd breathed in the clean scents of soap and shaving cream clinging to his skin and was seriously debating the wisdom of doing what he'd asked. Jack's chest looked as solid as hammered bronze, each ripple and plane delineated in the pale, golden light. Taut muscle and sinew roped over his broad shoulders, flowing like a sculpture into the thick biceps she'd once clung to. Thinking it best to avoid that particular memory, her glance slid over his corrugated stomach, following the line of dark, silky hair feathering beneath the beltless waistband of his worn jeans.

She was in trouble here, she thought. She was twenty-eight years old, reasonably sophisticated and the veteran of one not-so-steamy, six-month relationship with a sports editor and a lot of first dates. She'd seen men's chests before. She'd just never stood next to a half-naked man and felt as if she couldn't breathe.

His shirt was dangling from one hand when she swallowed hard and jerked her focus back to his face.

Jack had just started to turn. She wasn't sure what he saw in her expression, but whatever it was made him stop, his eyes locking hard on hers. The air felt charged all of a sudden, dangerous and expectant, the way it did when a thunderstorm was building. But the thunder was only in the low rumble of his voice.

"I just want this." He tapped the tube in her hand. "That's all. I promise I won't touch you."

Her chin came up. "I didn't say I was worried."

"You didn't have to."

"Are you going to answer me?"

"By my left shoulder blade."

She nodded, her heart pounding at the intent way he watched her. She didn't fool him. He was a big man—a big, half-naked man—and he had to know his masculinity intimidated her. He probably knew she was intrigued by it, too. "Turn around," she said, trying to remember how little he truly thought of her.

He let another second pass, then two, but he finally did as she asked. The breath that had threatened to explode her lungs slowly slithered out.

He's beautiful, she thought, her glance sliding from the dark ponytail flowing down his strong neck. His tapered back seemed a mile wide at the shoulders, and was as exquisitely carved as his chest. But his wasn't the body of a man shaped to impress others with his prowess. She didn't doubt for a moment that every angle and plane had been honed by the work and sweat of physical labor.

Clearing her throat, she uncapped the tube of cream. "What did you do to yourself?" she asked, thinking it best to focus on what had him in knots, since she already knew why she was.

"I'm not sure when it happened. Might have been while I was trying to reset a fence post. Or maybe when I was moving hay. It just starting seizing up on me."

The sharp sting of menthol hit her nostrils when she squeezed the white cream onto her fingers. The preparation was cool, but Jack stood perfectly still when she touched it to the wide muscle beside his left shoulder blade. She massaged it in, trying to not think about how smooth his skin was, how warm and supple it felt beneath her fingers. Or how knotted the muscle itself felt. It wasn't just hard, like she was certain the rest of his broad back would feel. It was so tight that it felt like stone. It was no wonder he'd been acting like a bear with a thorn in its paw.

She thought she heard him groan.

"Did that hurt?"

"Heavens no," he breathed.

"Do you want me to rub easier or harder?"

"Harder."

Splaying her hand on his back, she pushed her thumb alongside the indentation of his spine, following the flare of the muscle. Beneath her touch, knots rolled like marbles. "Like that?"

She felt him suck in a breath. With her hand still on his back, he made a quarter turn and braced himself against the wall.

"Yeah."

He spoke more quietly this time, his voice edged with capitulation. He had to be hurting to let her hear that. Either that, or what she was doing felt too good for him to fight. So she moved behind him, struck again by the thought that he seemed to take pleasure in so little, and repeated the motions that had elicited the groan.

"What about the other side?" she asked, wondering if he didn't hurt all across his back, but had only focused on the part that bothered him the most. "Is it sore, too?"

He hesitated, seeming to weigh the value of what she was doing with what his response might tell her. "A little."

The muscles banding his right shoulder felt nearly as hard as the others. They weren't as knotted, but the tension he carried in his shoulders and back was disturbingly apparent when her hands slipped along the deep ridge of his spine. She wasn't surprised that tension was there. Not with all the bitterness he tried to suppress. A person couldn't bottle up resentment the way he did and not expect it to take its toll. Or maybe what was so hard on him was the way he tried to bottle up his capacity for caring.

She had news for him, she thought, preferring to think the tingling in her palms was from the cream and not the contact with his skin. He wasn't nearly as good at the latter as he wanted to be. A man didn't rescue an injured dog if he didn't care. And he didn't lecture someone on how to dress properly in the cold, or make sure she knew not to wander too far away. Not if he was truly as indifferent as he wanted to seem.

"What about here?" She slid her hand up to the taut muscles at the sides of his neck, her fingers slipping into his hair. She was surprised at how soft it felt, and wondered if he wore it long simply because there was no one to cut it.

"Hurts" was all he said.

"Easy or hard."

"Easy."

"Okay," she whispered, and began stroking there, too.

She didn't bother to question what she was doing. She didn't have to. She knew. She was taking care of him, because, at that moment, that was what he needed. Rather like he'd taken care of her, assured her, when she'd been unable to help herself. Stroking his back, feeling some of the tension leave his body, she couldn't help but wonder how long it had been since he'd allowed anyone close enough to do that.

Jack edged forward to rest his forehead against the wall. Her hands felt like heaven. Surprisingly strong, wonderfully soft. When he'd asked for her help, he'd only been thinking that he'd be in worse shape tomorrow if he didn't do something about his back tonight. All he'd truly wanted was for her to smear on the cream. Now, he felt as if he'd die if she stopped. Not because she aroused him, but because he couldn't remember the last time he'd been touched.

He hated acknowledging that he needed the contact. Hated remembering how long he'd gone without feeling another human being's skin against his own. But what had him swallowing hard was Carrie herself.

There was nothing deliberately provocative about the movements of her small, surprisingly strong hands over his back, the way she stroked and kneaded, asking every once in a while if she was rubbing too hard, or not hard enough. She was simply relieving pain, making sure he felt better. He couldn't remember the last time anyone had wanted to do that for him. And that felt far more dangerous than the sensations starting to build now that the heat of her hands and the cream were loosening the knots in his back.

He raised his head, listening to the cabin creak and settle as the wind picked up. The fire was burning down in the other room, and the air inside was cool, far too cool to be standing there bare-chested. With her fingers slipping so intimately over his skin, he didn't really care about the layer of gooseflesh that had just raised itself. What he did care about was ending what could easily turn into pure torture.

At the thought of how her hands would feel slipping around to his stomach, he reached behind him with his right arm. An instant later, the heel of her hand brushed his waistband and he snagged her wrist.

"That's enough."

Jack's voice sounded rougher than he'd intended. As if his skin had just turned to hot coal, she drew back, but she couldn't go anywhere with his fingers locked around her wrist. Before she could try, he twisted around, his fingers sliding around her fragile bones.

Instantly he loosened his grip, and softened his tone. "Your arms must be getting tired."

Carrie didn't care about the tightness she could feel in her own shoulders from reaching up so far. What she saw in Jack's eyes was totally unexpected. Pure need. The kind of raw hunger that is born in the soul, and causes the soul to die if it's left unfed. In one sweep of his dark lashes, he'd blocked it so effectively that she might only have imagined it. But she knew what she'd seen the scattered moments before his gaze dropped.

His shirt was still wadded in his hand. But it was the one holding her wrist that had his attention.

"I promised," he said quietly, reluctantly releasing her. He took a step down the hall, backing away as if he didn't trust himself to stay. "Thanks, Carrie."

She thought she said he was welcome. All she knew for sure was that it was the first time he'd called her by name.

Chapter Seven

Jack was up and gone when Carrie ventured into the kitchen the next morning. He'd stoked the fire, put on a fresh pot of the ever-present coffee, then, from the looks of the tracks outside, headed for the garage, Felan bounding alongside him.

The evidence of their departure was in the new path that had been shoveled from the back door to the garage, and the four-pointed depressions in the fresh snow. Judging from the depth of the snow on either side of that path, she figured another foot had fallen since yesterday morning. And it was still coming down.

At least the wind wasn't blowing, she thought, trying to not panic at the thought that she seemed to be getting more stuck by the second. If the wind wasn't blowing the snow, then the plow had a better chance of clearing the road. Grasping that thought like a talisman, she headed for the shower.

Half an hour later, blown-dry and dressed, she checked to see if Jack had hooked the dryer back up. Finding that he'd not only hooked up the dryer, but that he'd finished the porch walls, she dumped all the bathroom and kitchen towels into the washing machine and started cleaning the shower stall. She usually approached housework with the same enthusiasm she did a ringing alarm clock, but at the moment, she simply felt grateful for the tasks. She couldn't stand not having something to do. Inactivity made her restless—and thoughts of how drawn she'd felt to Jack last night had her restless enough as it was.

The bathroom was finished, the clean towels folded neatly over their oak towel racks and she'd just taken a load of her own laundry from the dryer when she caved in to her growing curiosity. The dollhouse she'd noticed before had been pushed to the far end of the workbench. Wondering why Jack would build something so fanciful, she clutched her small batch of underwear to the front of her sweater and stepped over to take a closer look.

The white sides were up, but the unfinished structure had no roof. Tiny green shutters with tinier black hinges graced arched and paned windows. Perfectly turned newels anchored the steps to a wraparound porch and the oval window in the carved front door was etched to look like frosted glass. Stacked beside the three-foot-wide structure were strips of Victorian gingerbread that had been marked to cut but not yet carved.

She'd just noticed a small collection of little wood statues, mostly of children at play and gnarled old people, when the back door opened.

Frigid air swept in, snowflakes swirling over the bare planks and the brown mat in front of the kitchen door. She turned to see Jack pause when he saw her, the realization that she was there stalling his movements before he looked away and shut out the cold.

The shiver that raced through her was from more than the sudden drop in air temperature. After last night, she'd actually harbored the hope that they might get along a bit better. That hope faltered. He did not seem pleased to have found her there.

"I was just looking at your dollhouse," she said, refusing to act as if she'd been caught snooping. Everything was out in the open. She hadn't touched a thing. "Did you carve the figures, too?"

He pulled off his hat, more of his attention on the snow he shook to the floor than on her. "Yeah. I did."

"Your detail is incredible." She glanced back to the polished, wooden shapes. Lined up under a low shelf, they were nearly hidden by the dollhouse. "Do you sell your work?"

"It's just something I do at night."

"It's too good to just let sit here."

The depth of feeling in the little statues was truly impressive. She could almost hear the children's laughter, feel the contentment he'd carved into an old woman, the pride he'd carved into an old man. Hearing the hesitant note slip into Jack's voice when he murmured a quiet, "Thanks," she couldn't help wonder if he'd etched those emotions into the figures so he wouldn't forget them himself.

Disturbed by the thought, she tried again. "Is the dollhouse just something you do at night, too?"

His back remained to her while he peeled off his coat. "That's for the granddaughter of the people who own the store in Moose Creek. The little girl wanted one," he added, sounding as if he might as well explain because he knew she'd ask, anyway, "but Bert's arthritis won't let him do detail work, so I told him I'd do it. It's just a way of filling time."

The flatness of his tone told her he saw no kindness in his gesture. The touch of impatience in that same tone made it clear that he didn't appreciate her being out here in his space. His displeasure faded to something less definable, however, when his eyes moved to the scraps of pastel-tinted lace panties in her hands.

Suddenly feeling a little exposed, wondering if that was how he felt just then, she clutched her garments a bit tighter. Pretty underwear was her one, true indulgence. She preferred sleek satin and lace even when she wasn't wearing a suit or dress, which Jack probably wasn't even aware she owned from what she'd been wearing around him.

"I hope you don't mind," she said, referring to her use of his appliances. "But I'd run out of everything."

The glance Jack darted down her slender frame was deliberately quick. Just long enough to prompt his imagination before he headed for the back door. "Use whatever you need."

Carrie stepped toward him. It could be another day or two before she got out of there and the last thing she wanted was to spend more time pacing between four hospital green walls and a chair full of buttercup yellow curtains.

Determined to keep the chill outside the cabin's walls, she kept her tone even as she strangled a pair of satin and lace bikinis the shade of a blush. "How's your shoulder?"

He didn't even break stride. All he said was "Better," before the kitchen door opened with a squeak and he disappeared inside.

Carrie blinked at the closed door and blew a breath. That was effective, she silently muttered, but she scarcely had time to wonder at how handily he'd reclaimed the emotional space she'd somehow invaded last night when she heard a bump against the storm door. It was followed by the scratch of something hard and impatient against its metal panel.

She knew what was making the racket. She also knew

the sounds would be followed by an insistent bark and that as soon as Jack heard it, he'd come back and open the door.

She didn't know what it said for her state of mind that she'd rather face the beast than its owner at the moment. At least Felan didn't growl at her anymore.

Still clutching her laundry, she opened the inner and outer doors. Bracing herself against the cold, she then held her breath as the large, furry creature bolted inside, stopped, shook, then planted himself by the kitchen door.

This wasn't smart, she thought, watching the dog cock his massive head as if to say, "Well?" She was now alone with the hound from hell in a twenty-by-eight-foot room. But, she reminded herself, Felan truly hadn't shown her any ill intent since their first, rather inauspicious meeting. Since she also had to coexist with him for another day or two, she might as well see if she could have any better luck getting along with him than she had his master.

Felan lifted a gray paw and put another line of scratches in the white wood door. The moment the paw hit the mat, he looked back at her with his amber eyes.

He can smell fear, Jack had said.

Great, she thought, putting a death grip on the cup of her favorite ivory, scalloped lace bra as she edged forward. He really had been awfully good, she reminded herself. Whenever she'd been around, he'd just gone about his own business, hogging the hearth rug, sticking close to Jack. And he really did look kind of sweet, sitting there with his massive head cocked and his fangs retracted. If there were just some way to open the door without having to stand directly beside him.

Carrie didn't have to get that close. About the time she'd decided to just hold her breath and do it, the door swung in.

"Hey, boy," Jack murmured, his eyes on Carrie while he patted the dog brushing past his leg.

"He wanted in."

"Yeah. I know. I'm just surprised you let him into the porch."

His glance narrowed, moving from the white knuckles visible between tantalizing bits of fabric to the relief washing the apprehension from her features. "Why are you so afraid of dogs, anyway?"

"I was bitten when I was a kid."

"Where?"

"In California."

"Where on your body?" he clarified, his expression as droll as his tone.

"The back of my thigh. I was running from it, when it caught me. What I remember most is the way it shook me. I felt like a rag doll," she added, with a dismissing little laugh. "It's strange how you can remember something like that after so long."

He knew that soft smile, the one that was so accepting. He'd seen it when she'd told him about leaving Moose Creek and how she'd never fit in with her family. She knew how to forgive, forget and move on, and if she couldn't forget, she braved what bothered her. He didn't know whether to envy her the ability, or think her foolish. What he did know was that he couldn't stand the thought of an animal tearing into her soft flesh.

"If it had that kind of grip on you, it's no wonder you're afraid."

The smile grew pensive. "It was almost twenty years ago. You'd think I'd be over it by now. But I'm working on it," she assured him. "Today, the door. Tomorrow, who knows?"

"It looks like you're almost finished out here," she went on, thinking he seemed more receptive now than he had a few minutes ago. "Are you converting this into a workroom?"

She was wrong. Jack was no more interested in making polite conversation now than he'd been two minutes ago. "It's always been a workroom. I just insulated it." He rubbed his nose with the back of his hand. "How long are you going to be out here? I'd kinda like to get the shelves up so these groceries in the kitchen can be put away."

It occurred to Carrie that she could point out how she wasn't stopping him from doing that just because she was doing laundry. It also occurred to her that she could ask to help. But Jack had refused her offers to work with him too many times already, something she found grossly ineffi- cient on his part because, even arguing, they worked sur- prisingly well together. So she told him she was through and while he worked on shelves, she vacuumed the rug, mopped the kitchen floor and fixed lunch. He ate his on the porch. She ate hers reading about the mating habits of elk.

The afternoon passed into evening with him still on the porch, and her flipping through books, watching snow fall and thinking that the day had to be the longest in her life. Any other time, she might have enjoyed reading by a cozy fire. She could have handled the quiet for a while, anyway. But the faint undercurrent running between her and Jack robbed the day of its potential. That faint tension was ev- ident every time he came inside, every time she met his glance. Neither had forgotten the explosive moments by her car, and she couldn't forget what she'd seen in his eyes when he'd moved away from her last night. But Jack made no attempt to act on the pull between them, and Carrie was too afraid of what her heart might tell her if he did. So they both tried to pretend the other wasn't there. That only added to the strain. Which was why, the next morning, she was so determined to not spend the day that way again.

Carrie had no idea how Jack always managed to be up first. Not on the little sleep he seemed to get. It had been

nearly midnight before she'd heard him go to bed. She'd
heard him again in the early-morning hours, his footfall on
the floor, the sounds of a door or closet opening and closing. Since it had barely been six a.m. and far too early for
a snowplow to come through or to call Seattle, she'd
promptly fallen back to sleep. She wakened two hours later
to the rhythmic thwack of something heavy hitting something solid.

Jack was chopping wood.

The sound of that activity punctuated the winter stillness
for most of the morning. Every so often, Carrie would hear
the creak of metal hinges when Jack raised the lid on the
wood box outside. The groan was followed by the thud of
logs, then the lid would slam closed forcefully enough to
rattle the jars she lined up on the two walls of deep shelves
he'd finished hanging yesterday.

By the time she had a winter's worth of paper products
and canned and boxed goods neatly arranged—a task she
made last until she called Seattle—Jack had returned to his
chopping under the carport at the side of the garage. That
was where she headed within minutes of getting off the
phone. She didn't believe for an instant that he'd find her
news as exciting as she did, but she had to share her relief
with someone.

She was trying not to grin when she pulled her jacket
collar up against the icy air and headed down the freshly
shoveled path. Twenty yards away, she could see Jack.
Bare-headed and wearing his heavy coat, he raised his ax,
then brought it down in a powerful arc that split the log
like a hot knife going through butter. Without looking up,
he picked up each of those halves, split them in turn and
tossed the quarters with amazing precision onto the stack
growing six feet behind him.

In the time it took her to reach the garage and follow the
path he'd dug to the carport, he'd hefted a large chunk of

tree onto his shoulder with an ease that belied the pain he'd been in only two days ago and turned back to face her. In a glance, he took inventory of everything from the flakes scattered in her hair to the frayed hole in the knee of her favorite jeans. Instead of skin peeking through, she knew he saw black legging.

Jack shrugged the log to the ground, only then letting himself meet the sparkle in her eyes. He'd seen her coming, but he only now realized that she was fighting a full-blown smile. "What's going on?"

"I just got off the phone with my editor's secretary. Mr. Hawthorne was sent by the paper's managing editor to some conference he couldn't attend, so he won't be in the office this week. His secretary, the one that talks like a machine gun," she reminded him, sounding a little rapid-fire herself, "said that with him gone, she wouldn't know what to do with me anyway. He left in such a hurry that he forgot to assign me to anyone and with one of the assistant editors out sick, no one would have time for me even if she did know where he'd wanted me to start."

He'd missed something. He was sure of it. "That's good?"

"It's better than good. I can stop worrying about the job. With him gone, I've got a whole week to get there."

Carrie looked more animated than he'd ever seen her. She was grinning like a little kid, the expression totally unrestrained. That smile lit her eyes, erasing the strain that had been hiding there even when she hadn't been talking about how badly she needed the position. He'd known she'd been concerned. He just hadn't realized how much that job meant to her until that moment. Or maybe, he had noticed and, until that moment, it just hadn't mattered.

He didn't get a chance to tell himself it didn't matter now, either. Something about her soft smile prevented it.

"The plow should be through long before then," she

went on. "Even if it takes another couple of days, that'll give me plenty of time. I called the Highway Department before I called Seattle, but all I got was a recording asking people to stay off the roads and to stay on the line if I was reporting an emergency. They'll get here eventually," she insisted, refusing to let anything interfere with the best news she'd had in days. "So." She shoved her hands into her pockets. "Since I don't hear a plow coming, what do you want me to do now? I've put away your supplies."

"Do whatever you want," he told her, pulling his ax from the chunk of wood near his foot. "I'm going to chop kindling, then check on the herd."

"The herd of what?"

"Bison."

Interest sparked, changing the quality of the light in her eyes. "May I go?"

That stopped him.

"Come on, Jack. I've never seen bison up close before. The nearest I've ever come was at the lodge the other day. They were way across that field. Remember?"

He certainly did. He'd yet to forget the pleasure she'd taken in what he regarded simply as part of the land. "You don't want to get close to a bison. They're dangerous."

"I didn't say I wanted to pet one," she muttered. "The last thing I want is to see one charging my knees. I'd just like to get closer than half a mile."

It had only been half that distance. "How did you know that's how they attack?"

"I've been reading. After we came back the other day, I remembered that you had a book on them in your book-shelf."

"You're honing up on the local wildlife?"

His disbelief nudged her chin up. "Why not?" she insisted, faintly defensive. "It's interesting."

"I didn't say it wasn't." She was a city girl, accustomed

to dogs on leashes, cats with collars and fish in bowls. He'd be willing to wager that the only other animals she'd ever encountered were of the two-legged variety. "After the way you've been around Felan, I just didn't figure you'd care much about animals at all."

"I was bitten by a dog," she reminded him, looking ever so patient. "Not a buffalo. And it's just big dogs. Not little ones. So are we going or not?"

He'd thought it would be easier outside, away from her. Inside, he was too aware of her tempting presence, and the air of caution she wore beneath her natural friendliness. As good as it would be to feel her in his arms again, his sense of self-preservation kept him from trying to break through her defenses. She had a knack for getting far closer than he liked with her questions.

She seemed to realize that the longer he hesitated, the worse were her chances. "I'll stay out of your way," she insisted. "I promise. You won't even know I'm there."

That was like saying he wouldn't be aware of the snow.

He blew a breath and gave his glove a yank. He couldn't avoid her completely, but it might be easier to be with her if she had something other than him to be curious about.

"We'll need a Thermos of coffee and whatever you were going to fix for lunch." He slid his hand to the neck of the ax. "There's a backpack under the workbench on the porch. Pack it in there. And dress warm."

"In layers. I know," she returned, backing toward the shoveled path before he could change his mind. "Give me twenty minutes. No. I only need fifteen."

"There's no need to rush. I want to get this done first."

It looked like a struggle, but she slowed down even as she turned. He had the feeling she was accustomed to running full-steam ahead, to rushing from one task to the next, or juggling a dozen at once. By her own admission, she thrived on chaos and the urgency of deadlines. He didn't doubt she'd be climbing walls before the plow came through.

He sunk the ax into a log, the change of plans changing his mind about finishing the task just then. With two feet of snow on the ground and more to come, he'd already covered the truck for the winter. The early snows were soft, as fluffy as goose down and walking would be an exhausting process. Because it would be days before the snow compacted enough to use the snowmobile, that left cross-country skis and snowshoes for transportation.

He didn't have skis for Carrie, but two pair of old snowshoes hung in the garage. He checked them over, jerry-rigging one of the broken straps, then handed a pair to Carrie when she handed him the backpack a short while later. She didn't bat an eye at the paddle-shaped contraptions. She simply looked down to see how he'd secured his, said, "This is going to be interesting," and gamely strapped them on. After tucking her very touchable looking hair under the heavy blue stocking cap he gave her to wear, she headed out after him and Felan.

The sky remained a perpetual shade of gray. It snowed in fits and starts, promising more than it delivered. But, while Jack was conscious of the weather as they moved through the stillness, he was even more aware of the woman doing her best to keep her promise. Carrie didn't say a word as they followed the road to the lodge. And when the trees gave way to the meadow, she stayed back, skirting the edges of the woods while he took a pole to the ice that threatened to cover large sections of the creek. He couldn't help noticing how the tracks crisscrossing the snow drew her attention, or how her curiosity about them grew each time she spotted something different. So, as they tramped on through trees to the next spot he wanted to check, he began identifying the footprints of deer, ermine, porcupine and mice for her, as much to keep her from following the tracks off into the woods as to let himself be near her without feeling he had to guard himself.

For an hour they walked, their footsteps muffled, their breath expelled in foggy puffs. She wanted to know how the smaller creatures survived such harsh conditions, so he explained how squirrels stashed mushrooms in tree branches to dry, and how little, rabbitlike pikas dried grass all summer long to consume under the snow. He told her, too, how much warmer it was beneath the snow, but that the burrows and dens that protected the little animals from the elements were often invaded by their predators. Her only response was to tell him she found it sad that such beauty should be so difficult to survive, and when she then fell silent, he found himself trying to look at the snowscape as she did—and wondering when he'd stopped appreciating its beauty.

"When did you first become interested in all this?" she asked, pulling him from that disturbing thought.

Snow shimmered to the ground in a little white cloud when he pushed back a low fir branch. "I can't remember a time when I wasn't," he told her, holding the branch until she could take it. "I grew up in the mountains, so we played in the woods when I was a kid."

"We?"

The question drifted toward him as he moved on. "My friends and I. I didn't have any brothers or sisters."

"What about when you were older? Did you spend time in the woods then, too?"

"I spent summers in college working logging camps."

He didn't say that his father had owned the camp, or the mill the logs had been processed in. He didn't tell her he'd inherited half the interest in that mill after his father had died, or that his friends had worked in the mill for him. He just answered her questions, hating that he suddenly felt so guarded again, but knowing no other way to be.

"That explains why you seem like such a part of all this."

Since she was behind him, he couldn't see her face. But he could swear there was a smile in her voice.

"So which was your major? Forestry, or game management?"

The guard that had once been so foreign to him, slipped more firmly into place. "Forestry," he replied, then deflected the personal shift in their conversation by pointing straight ahead of them. They had come upon the meadow where he'd known she would see her bison.

Two more steps and he moved to the side. "There," he said, and watched her go utterly still.

He'd stopped her at the edge of the trees, a hundred yards from where the massive, shaggy animals grazed. For a moment, she said nothing. She simply stood with her gloved hand at her throat, staring at the snow-blasted spruce standing silent guard over a huge pool the color of a cornflower. Steam billowed in a feathery plume from its surface, creating thousands of crystal fingers where it settled and froze on the rocks behind it. The underground warmth kept the snow from clinging to the tufts of yellow grass. Around the pool itself, twenty or so bison milled about with their bearded heads bent to the earth.

The awe in her expression was echoed in her quiet voice. "What is this place?"

"It's a thermal pool," he told her, not wanting it to matter that she found the place as awe-inspiring as he had the first time he'd seen it in winter. "There are a couple of them on the property. The water isn't drinkable, but the heat keeps the snow melted so they can get to the grass. This'll be picked clean in no time, but they'll still come for the warmth."

Her glance moved over the snowbanks to a shaggy old

bison that had separated itself from the others. "What'll they eat when that's gone?"

"Sage." He pointed off to the side, toward the frosted branches emerging from the undulating snow. "That's that stuff over there. And other grasses. They'll root through the snow to get what they need. Except for that old bull over there," he added, since she still watched the frost-coated animal. The old bison's ribs were already starting to show. This early in the season, that was not a good sign. "I don't imagine he'll have the strength to forage for very long."

His dark blue stocking cap covered her ears, hugged her face. Jack was studying the fine grain of her skin, thinking her more pretty than beautiful when his words washed the animation from her features and robbed the light from her eyes.

Surprised at how acutely he felt the loss, he touched the sleeve of her jacket to draw her attention to a flock of honking geese heading south.

By the time she'd glanced back down and caught sight of two squirrels racing up a tree, some of the light had returned.

"I don't understand the man who owns all of this," she said, truly at a loss. "Was he born around here?"

"You looking for a story?"

"I'm always looking for a story," she admitted with a little laugh that did strange things to the base of his spine. "It's the nature of the beast. But I'm really not now. I'm just curious about why someone would own a place like this, then spend so little time here."

"He has businesses to run."

"Then it's just a vacation home?"

"One of a few. But I think he looks on this one as more than that. He wants everything beyond the lodge kept as natural as possible, and he has the bison because he wants to help replenish their numbers."

There was respect in Jack's voice for the man's intent. But it was the intention itself that hinted at the identity of the land's mysterious owner.

"Does this belong to that guy who owns all those television stations? And a few hotels and maybe the crown jewels by now?" She searched his face, her tone quiet. "I remember hearing about some enormous spread he bought to put bison on. Is this it?

"It's okay," she assured, when his silence provided her answer. "I'm not going to say anything to anyone. I write hard news. I wouldn't know where to begin with a story about bison."

She turned away, suddenly subdued as she watched the old buffalo.

"Will you feed it?"

Anyone in Moose Creek could have confirmed who owned this land. But that didn't matter to Jack when he saw the look in her eyes. Hers was a request, not just a question. She'd been bothered about the animal's welfare ever since he'd mentioned its fate. That concern had been too quick to be forced, too constant to be faked.

He hated that he'd come to the point where he actually had to rationalize simple human kindness.

"I'll watch out for him," he told her, more drawn by that concern than was wise, "but I won't feed him. That would only delay the inevitable. It's not easy for any animal here. There's not one that's guaranteed to make it through a winter. A perfectly healthy squirrel can become dinner for a marten. The marten is attacked by a mountain lion. That bison will feed the birds and a few coyotes."

"I understand the food chain, but that doesn't mean I like the way it works. It all seems so cruel."

"At least there's no duplicity in the wild." For once the thought filled him with more resignation than bitterness. She was probably right about him, he decided. He had become a cynic. And he hated that, too. "Every animal knows its enemies. With people, someone you believe to be a friend can do you the greatest harm." He looked out over the land. "All this is...is survival."

As if the weight he carried had grown too heavy, Jack slipped his gloved hand under the strap on his shoulder, adjusting his backpack. "We'd better get going," he said, suddenly sounding as subdued as she felt. "It's going to take us awhile to get back to the cabin."

Her only response was to fall into step behind him. She didn't know what to say to him anyway. She'd always had a hard time with the cold-blooded aspects of nature, but it was clear Jack found that savagery more honest than what he'd experienced in civilization. She knew he thought his harsher philosophy more realistic than her own, and perhaps it was. She was hardly blind to the numbers of people who used and mistreated their fellow man. But she was beginning to suspect that his trust had been abused so badly that he didn't trust anyone at all.

They traveled in silence through the ice and snow-crusted trees. The only sounds to break that stillness were the occasional screech of an eagle soaring overhead or the bugling of a moose off in the distance. Felan would follow Jack for a while, then take off through the thickets. Moments later, a delicate mule deer would leap across their path or birds would scatter, feathers drifting back to the earth. Except for the dog's occasional exuberance, it was so quiet that even her breathing sounded hushed.

Jack remained ahead of her. As they continued on, she could almost see the tension leaving his big body. Exertion could have caused that, but she suspected the relaxing of his shoulders and his stride had more to do with the hushed surroundings. She didn't doubt for a moment that he'd found some sort of peace in this place. What she discovered as she followed his footsteps was that she could identify with that peace, too.

She'd fallen behind. Not because she was tiring, though she doubted she'd have any trouble at all sleeping that night. There was just something about the silence that worked its way into her, calming her, slowing her down all on its own.

Realizing Jack was waiting for her up ahead, she picked up her pace.

"You know," she said, reaching where he'd stopped by the clear and icy creek, "I've lived most of my life in cities, and I thrive on the craziness of my work. I should hate all this isolation and quiet."

"Maybe you're not thriving."

She stood beside him, studying his strong profile while he watched water ripple around snow-capped rocks. "What do you mean?"

"Just what I said. Maybe you're just doing what you have to do to survive. Like the animals."

Carrie didn't like the odd unease sweeping through her just then. "I love what I do," she insisted, sounding as if he'd just brushed a nerve she hadn't even known was sensitive. "If I didn't, I wouldn't be doing it." Masking defense in inquiry, her tone became hushed. "Is that what you're doing? Just surviving?"

The look he gave her made it abundantly clear he didn't buy her conviction. He didn't challenge her, though. He simply lifted his gloved hand to brush away the snow that an encounter with a low branch had left clinging to the side of her knit cap. His hand lingered there, no more than a slight impression of weight at the side of her head, while his glance moved cautiously over her face. It was as if he were searching for something. Permission. An answer. She didn't know. And she couldn't begin to guess. Then, the bleakness she'd seen before shadowed his features, immediately turning to the steely guard she was beginning to recognize all too well.

"It's enough," he finally said, and let his hand fall.

It was instinct that made her reach for him. It had to be, because Carrie didn't think she'd consciously invite rejection. She caught his arm, refusing to let him turn away.

"You don't honestly believe that."

"Yeah," he said. "I do."

"Why?"

Demand he could handle. It was her unmasked concern that invariably threatened his defenses. "I think you'd better ask that question of yourself. Come on." He tipped his head in the general direction of the cabin. "You'll stay warmer moving. We don't have that much farther to go."

He was right. It was warmer when she was moving. If it hadn't been for that, and the fact that he was already ten feet ahead of her, Carrie might have pointed out that, while his avoidance techniques were masterful, she wasn't the one who'd isolated herself in the wilderness. He might seem very much a part of the beautiful, wild land, but there was something about him that simply didn't fit the image of a man content to spend his life taking care of another man's property. Knowing he'd spent most of his life in places like this, she just couldn't imagine what that something might be.

Chapter Eight

"May I borrow that menthol cream I used on you?"

Jack turned from his brightly lit workbench to see Carrie standing in the kitchen doorway. She was in her stocking feet, her socks the exact shade of pale peach as the sweater covering the hips of her jeans.

If he remembered correctly, he'd glimpsed some tantalizing pieces of lace that same color when he'd caught her with her laundry.

"Sore already?" he asked, trying to avoid wondering if she was wearing those particular bits of lace as he set aside the snowshoe he'd brought in to repair.

"A little."

"I'm not surprised. With all the weaving back and forth we did, you put on a few miles today."

Absently rubbing the top of her thigh, she gave him a rueful smile. "Jogging uses different muscles, I guess. But it was worth the pain."

He had the feeling she'd think that. She hadn't even warmed up before she'd been at his books looking up the animals she'd seen, grilling him with questions about the thermal phenomenon of the area. He didn't know when she was more dangerous: when she looked as enticing as she did just then, without shoes and with her shining hair swinging unrestricted around her shoulders, when she forced thoughts about his life he'd truly rather avoid, or when her fascination with her surroundings lowered his guard. One thing he did know. Every time he felt the impact of her smile, he found it a little harder to remember why he needed to keep his distance.

Seeing that smile now, he told her the cream she wanted was in his bedroom and headed inside to retrieve it. He'd just entered the hall when he remembered he'd returned the tube to the bathroom, so he turned into there instead. She quietly followed, stopping at the bathroom doorway while he opened the medicine cabinet. In the cabinet's mirror he saw her eyes skim his back, the tip of her pink tongue unconsciously touching her top lip before he pulled open the door and their reflections disappeared.

"Is there an adhesive strip in there?"

"Blisters?" he asked, wondering if she had any idea what it did to a man to have a woman watch him the way she sometimes did.

"Just one."

"Need ointment?"

"If you have it."

He handed her a box of adhesive strips so she could take one out while he fished around for a tube of antiseptic ointment. A few moments later, he traded her a small tube for the box, then found the tube she'd asked for to begin with. But when he held it out to her, reaching to turn out the light as he did to get them out of the close confines, her hand bumped his, his body brushed hers and the next thing he knew, everything she'd held was on the floor.

Carrie bent before he could, grabbing the adhesive strip from the doorjamb beside her and one tube from beside Jack's scarred brown boot. She wouldn't have dropped the things at all if she'd concentrated more on what she was doing, instead of standing there wondering how long their tacit truce would hold.

Telling herself to just be grateful for it, she started to rise. It was right about then that the muscles in her legs decided to let her know how unhappy they were with the abuse she'd subjected them to. Putting her hand on her knee to give herself extra leverage, she'd just started to push up when she felt Jack's fingers close around her upper arms.

"You okay?" he asked, easily drawing her up in front of him.

The bathroom was tiny, scarcely large enough to hold one person, let alone two. Angled just inside the doorway, she found herself caught between the door frame and Jack. His body was so close she could feel his heat.

"Fine. I just... Yes," she decided, aware of his big, strong hands—and the fact that he wasn't letting go. She gave a little laugh. "It usually takes a full day to get this stiff."

"Blame it on the elevation. There's less oxygen here than where you're from. Your body has to work harder."

"Isn't anything easy about living here?"

She watched him shake his head slowly. The lines fanning from his eyes seemed more pronounced than usual, strain evident in his carved features. Or maybe, she thought, it was fatigue that etched the little furrows more deeply. He always rose early and he'd pushed himself physically all day. Just as he always did.

"I can't think of anything that is."

The shadows seemed to deepen as his eyes narrowed on

hers. She felt his hands move against her arms, his thumbs brushing over her smooth biceps. The quiet way he watched her made it seem as if he were imagining the texture of her skin beneath her sweater. Or, perhaps, wondering how her skin would feel against his bare hand.

The thought made her breath hitch.

He lifted one hand to her shoulder. "Even this seems harder than it has to be."

"This?"

"This," he repeated.

His glittering gaze fell to her mouth. His dark head inching lower, the tips of his fingers skimming the curve of her neck. The incredibly light touch altered her heart rate even before his firm lips brushed hers.

"Know what I mean?" he murmured.

Air shimmered from her lungs. "I think so," she whispered.

"So I guess that answers your question."

She'd forgotten what the question was. His fingers snaked into her hair, gathering the shining mass in his fists. She didn't understand the look that washed over the chiseled planes of his face just then, but she felt his fingers flex against her skull when his mouth settled over hers once more.

She had tasted hunger in him before, and restraint. Both were there now, battling each other as he coaxed her to open to him. He kissed her slowly, deeply, causing her knees to go weak and her bones to wilt. Flattening her hands against the wall of his chest to keep from sinking against him, she touched her tongue to his and heard him suck in a shuddering breath. A heartbeat later, she felt his hands slip down her back to her hips. In one deft movement, he aligned them so intimately he could have entered her had they not been fully clothed.

A moan slid from her throat, heat gathering in her stomach. Her hands fisted in his soft flannel shirt. She knew exactly what he meant about this being so difficult. The physical chemistry between them was too real to question. It lived with them constantly, a silent beast waiting to waken with little more than a touch. What made the attraction difficult was his need to separate lust from caring. He wanted sex. She needed more.

Her heart hammered against her breastbone. Lowering her head, she drew a breath—and drank in the scents of fresh air and soap clinging to him.

"I'm not going to bed with you."

"I'm not going to push." He touched his lips to her temple, coaxing her to tip her head. "All you have to do is tell me to stop."

The words were a brush of air over the shell of her ear. Scattered seconds later, she felt his lips move down the side of her neck and her breath feathered out in a faint, "Oh." The sound could just as easily have been a sigh. All she knew for sure was that she believed what he said. If she told him to stop, he would. She also believed that he wouldn't back away until she made it clear that was what she wanted him to do. But as her head fell back, easing his access to her throat, she couldn't for the life of her figure out why he should stop right now.

His big body pressed closer, his mouth working over hers, teasing her, testing her. She melted into him, curving her arms around his neck, and taunted him back. The heat of his chest and his rock hard thighs burned through her clothes. His ragged breaths became her own when she drank them in. Then, her senses exploded. She felt his hand cup her bottom, lifting her higher. Pressing her against the hardness, he told her in no uncertain terms exactly what she did to him.

Sensations darted through her, wild, unfamiliar sensations that were already threatening to destroy reason when he pushed his hand under her sweater. His groan vibrated through her when he encountered one of the layers he'd insisted she wear, but he didn't let the soft cotton impede his progress. His hand closed over her breast as his tongue slipped over hers. When his thumb brushed her nipple, she thought she'd go up in flames.

It was the thought that she could easily lose control with this man that kept her from completely sinking into the sensual fog he promised. But it was the thought that she actually *wanted* to lose that control that had her stiffening.

Jack felt the change in her. He wanted to ignore it. He wanted to make her relax, then carry her to her bed, get rid of the clothes that kept him from her softness and slake the need burning inside him. She had been so supple in his arms, her responses so incredibly receptive. Now, her smooth, taut muscles had gone as rigid as stone.

Before she could pull back, he gentled his kiss and eased his hand to her side.

It didn't matter that he was so hard he hurt. He'd told her he wouldn't push. Having nothing to give her but his word, he wasn't about to break it.

Feeling as tight as a wire about to snap, he rested his forehead against hers, calming himself, calming her. Never before had he experienced the flash-fire heat he felt when he kissed her. He wanted to think that was only because he'd gone without for so long, but he suspected there was more to it than that. The jolting reaction had to do strictly with her.

Not sure he liked the thought, he pulled a few deep breaths and eased back. He discovered his hand was shaking when, lowering his head, he pushed his fingers through his hair.

"You dropped something." The menthol cream was on the floor between them. Reaching for it, he willed his heartbeat to slow.

"I'd offer to help," he said, his deep voice husky. "But I think you can reach where this needs to go." He picked up her hand. Finding it even less steady than his, he folded her fingers around the tube. "You'd better get to bed before I forget what I promised and you find me in there with you."

He made no effort to move. And for longer than she should have, Carrie stood there struggling with the choices he'd given her while he traced the line of her jaw with his finger. He wanted her, but he was letting her know again that whatever happened between them was up to her. If she wanted him in her bed, he'd be there. If she didn't, well, the choice was hers. He could live with it either way.

"Good night, Jack," she whispered, wanting to hate him for the emptiness she felt at that moment.

His hand stilled. "Good night," he returned, his voice hushed, then brushed a kiss over her mouth that was so tender it hurt her heart.

In three strides he was gone.

Watching him disappear around the corner, Carrie promptly sagged against the wall. She was in trouble here. Big-time. She couldn't hate him. She couldn't even be upset with him. Jack was simply being honest about what he wanted. It just happened that she wasn't into casual encounters. People had philosophical differences all the time and, philosophically speaking, she and Jack couldn't get any farther apart. That alone should have raised a few more defenses. Unfortunately she'd found herself woefully lacking in that department since the moment she'd first laid eyes on the man. It wasn't just that he could turn her blood to steam, or even that she couldn't forget the safety she'd once felt in his arms. What worried her was how something inside her couldn't help wanting to ease the pain she so often sensed inside him.

You'll be out of here soon, she told herself, but the reminder didn't bring the relief it should have. Not caring to consider why that was, she settled for worrying about how that past several minutes would affect his tenuous acceptance of her presence. He hadn't been so edgy today, so obviously anxious to be away from her. But she knew that could change in a heartbeat.

Nothing changed. When Carrie walked into the kitchen the next morning, her movements a tad less fluid than normal from the exertion of the day before, Jack promptly handed her a bottle of anti-inflammatories and a big glass of water.

"They'll both help," he said.

Cool blue and assessing, his eyes held hers when she reached for his offerings. She didn't know what he was looking for, or even what he'd find, but the memories of last night were there, hovering between them like a physical presence.

"Thanks," she murmured, not sure which one of them pulled away first when their hands brushed. "After these and a little more of what got me to feeling this way to begin with, I'll be as good as new."

"Which is worse, calves or thighs?"

It was her inner thighs, actually, but it didn't seem wise to mention that just then. "It's hard to tell."

"Exercise is a good idea." His glance lingered a moment longer, but she could read nothing in his rugged face before he picked up the mug he filled and headed for the porch. "Don't go too far."

Thinking she'd have better luck attempting to decipher Stonehenge, she downed the tablets he'd so thoughtfully given her, followed them with breakfast, then added the layers she'd need for a temperature that hovered at a balmy twelve degrees. Exercise would be good for more than loosening sore muscles. So, even with it snowing hard enough to obscure the mountains in the distance, she told Jack on her way through the porch that she was going out to shovel off her car and trailer so the snowplow wouldn't run into them. He told her that was probably wise and went back to work scraping the bottom of a ski.

He was still working on skis, waxing this time, when she came in to warm up, then headed out again—this time to shovel the path from the back door to the garage, since Jack hadn't done it yet. She'd worked out much of the ache in her legs, but she was still too sore to jump when Felan, having been let out earlier by his master, came loping past her on her way back to the house. The only muscle that moved was her heart as it lurched a little, but she made herself stay where she was—then actually laughed out loud, mostly in relief, she suspected, when the animal looked back at her and whined so she would open the door.

"Go on," she called, watching him shake. "Jack's in there. Paw on the door."

The dog cocked his head and barked.

"Go on," she repeated, looking toward the ice-edged window beside the back door. Jack was there at the workbench, watching.

Felan apparently didn't care that his master was inside. The way he saw it, she was standing right there and she could open the door. Still looking at her, he planted himself on his haunches and gave three barks that made it clear he wasn't moving until she did.

Jack couldn't tell what Carrie muttered, but exasperation seemed to get the better of her. Shovel in hand, she headed for the back door. He lost sight of her when she neared the steps because of the way the window was positioned, but it was only a moment before the doors opened, Felan walked in and the doors closed again. Moments later, he saw her head back toward the garage with the shovel.

Except for Felan, and the sound of coyotes, he hadn't

seen her balk at much of anything. She also didn't seem to have a dependent bone in her body. It was that last quality that posed the catch-22 for him. Had she acted as if she expected anything of him, had she looked to him to take care of her in any way beyond providing a roof, he felt certain his defenses would have taken a better hold. But she clearly didn't expect to be taken care of. As it was, his biggest fear was that her independence would get her into trouble. When he returned from hanging the skis and looked out the window, he could see her trying to swing his ax.

The last thing he wanted to do was worry about her cutting off a foot. Grabbing his coat and hat, he left Felan curled up by the heater and headed out after her.

He stopped just under the overhang and planted his hands on his hips.

"What?" Carrie asked, watching his glance shift from her to the ax she'd more or less embedded in a chunk of log. "You didn't get much kindling cut yesterday, so I thought I'd do it."

"Have you ever used an ax before?"

"No, but, that doesn't mean I can't try." She pulled up on the handle. The ax didn't budge. "What am I doing wrong?"

What she lacked in upper body strength, she made up for in sheer determination. Determination, however, wasn't enough. She'd managed to get the blade a full two inches into the wood, but now she couldn't seem to dislodge it.

"For one thing," he said, wanting to smile at the frown she aimed at the offending tool, "you need more muscle behind your swing. The idea's to get the blade to go clear through. If that doesn't work, you twist the head when you pull up to get it out, or pull up the log with the ax and hit it against the ground. Tell you what," he said, not bothering to mention how much more sore she'd be if she worked this long enough to get the hang of it, "I'll take care of the firewood. You're already taking care of the house."

"There's nothing that needs doing in there." That was why she'd come out to shovel the path. All the time she'd dug around her car, trying to expose its tires, she'd kept thinking about how much deeper the snow was getting. And that thought fueled an agitation she didn't want to acknowledge. She couldn't concentrate to read. She had no desire to pace. Even if he'd had a television, she couldn't have sat still to watch it. Not as restless as she was feeling around him. That left physical labor.

"I need to do something, Jack. I can't just sit around in there while you hole up on the porch."

"I'm not holing up on the porch."

The look she gave him would have made raisins out of prunes. "Of course you are. You've been doing it since I got here. That's where you go when you want to avoid me."

"It's where I go to work on things. That's why I insulated it."

"So you're avoiding me in comfort. It's the same thing. Look," she murmured, trying to keep the focus of her agitation away from him. "I don't do well with time on my hands. I need to stay busy. Okay? If I had my Christmas cards I could get a head start on them. Or, I suppose I could get all my pictures labeled and put into albums like I've been promising myself I'd do for the last ten years, but I don't have any albums and my pictures are buried under three feet of snow."

"It's barely over two feet."

"That's not the point."

Jack blew a breath. "I know."

She hadn't expected him to understand. His admission left her staring. "You do?"

"You don't have to look so surprised," he muttered. "I

recognize cabin fever when I see it. If you want something to do, you can clear the roof. I was going to do it today or tomorrow, but the job's yours if you want it.''

Her skeptical glance shifted toward the cabin. The two feet of snow on the pitched roof had been sculpted by the wind into curving cornices on the building's south side. Icicles hung from the eaves, gleaming dully in the perpetual gray light and making the weather-grayed cabin look like an iced gingerbread house.

"Why do you clear it off?"

"So the weight doesn't break the beams. Come on," he told her, sounding as if she'd lasted about as long as he'd figured she would. "I'll get you started. I use a saw on the cornices on the lodge buildings, but all you need here is a ladder and a shovel."

She was right behind him as he headed into the garage. "How long were you here before you felt like climbing walls?"

"A couple of months."

"You lasted that long?"

He couldn't tell if it was disbelief in her tone, or admiration. "I'm not like you."

"You're saying *you* know how to relax?"

He handed her the shovel she'd already put back, letting his tolerant glance tell her he wasn't about to debate her question. He'd been a lot less tense before she'd shown up. "What I'm saying," he explained, pulling an aluminum ladder from the rough wood wall, "is that I didn't have anyplace else I wanted to be."

He heard her murmur a quiet "Oh," when he headed for the side of the cabin where snow had already drifted halfway to the eaves. She was right behind him, following his path through the unbroken sea of white.

She was up to her knees in that sea when she stopped beside him. "Pitch the snow toward the back," he told her.

"The bank will eventually be even with the roof there. When it's compacted more, you can just walk up it instead of using the ladder."

Carrie didn't bother to tell him she didn't plan to be there long enough for it to "compact." Part of her purpose for doing what she was doing was to escape such thoughts. Glancing to the edge of the roof a few feet above her head, she reached for the side of the ladder. Jack held the other side, steadying it for her.

"This could take all day," she said, sounding more relieved than intimidated at the prospect.

"Give it two." His hand cupped her elbow as her foot hit the first exposed rung. "The pace is slower here."

He was only helping her up. Still, something about the feel of his supporting hand and the rumbling tones of his voice seemed different to her just then. Not intimate, necessarily. Just less adversarial. It hadn't even occurred to her until that moment that they were adversaries. She'd never really thought of him as one. But he had her. From the very beginning. Odd, she thought, that she should realize that only because his edges no longer seemed quite so sharp.

"Are you being nice to me?"

"Not on purpose."

"Good. I was afraid we might be starting to get along."

"Not a chance," he returned, the glint of a smile stirring in his eyes. "Be careful up there."

That smile tried to reach his mouth, but the expression was too rusty to work. Liking what even the attempt did for his features, she told him she would and gripped the rungs with her knit gloves since they were easier to work in than the big pair Jack had given her.

Cold metal provided no traction for boots caked with snow. Even though she'd knocked off what snow she could, she slipped a bit on the second rung. Jack grabbed her hips, steadying her. A moment later, he slid one hand down the back of her thigh to her calf.

"Got it?" he asked, his voice oddly tight.

"Got it," Carrie returned, amazed how his touch robbed the strength from her own vocal cords.

He eased his hand away, and she continued up. When she had her footing on the roof, she reached back for the square-scooped shovel he held up to her.

His jaw was working when he moved out of the drift. "I'll be on the other side of the cabin. As long as I'm out here I'll clear the snow from below the windows."

He wouldn't say that she was to call him if she needed help getting down. But Carrie knew that was why he told her his plans before he left her there. It was almost as if he could let himself be thoughtful as long as the gesture wasn't overt. Or, maybe, she thought, the quality was simply so inherent in him that it had survived his best efforts to beat it down.

The thought teased her for the next twenty minutes, which was exactly how long she lasted on the roof. Having convinced herself that Jack's basically distrusting attitude was too all-encompassing to be blamed solely on a failed marriage, she'd stopped to flex her frozen fingers. The next thing she knew, her feet were out from under her and she was sliding down a patch of ice she'd uncovered.

Jack heard a shriek. He couldn't tell where it came from, though. When he rounded the cabin, Carrie wasn't on the roof. All he could see there was the handle of her shovel four feet back from the edge she'd cleared. The ground below was nothing but a drift and ragged little mountains of snow.

A white jacket sleeve and a navy glove popped up on the other side of a pile that looked vaguely like the Matterhorn. It disappeared an instant before he heard what he could have sworn was a giggle.

She was laughing. When he trudged around the miniature Alpine mountain, he found her sitting with one knee drawn up, the other leg out straight and both arms planted, and sinking, behind her. Snow caked and creased every square inch of her clothes and her stocking cap was nowhere to be seen. She'd even lost a glove, though he had no idea how she'd managed that. What he noticed most was the musical sound of her voice—and the sparkle in her eyes when he held out his hand.

"That was fun."

The absurdly simple statement almost had him thinking she'd slipped on purpose. The curve of her mouth had a smile threatening on his. "You're lucky you didn't break your neck."

"Don't be a spoilsport." She couldn't suppress the light in her eyes as he hauled her to her feet. Balancing herself by grabbing his arms the instant she was upright, she nodded toward the roof. "You should try it."

"Thanks, but I'll pass."

"You don't know what you're missing."

"The opportunity to see how many new and interesting places snow can get in?"

He heard her gasp when he brushed at the snow clinging to the collar of her turtleneck. Icy flakes slipped beneath soft cotton to melt against her negligibly warmer skin. Her shoulders hunched, causing more snow to fall into the gap, but the laughter stayed in her eyes until he pulled off his glove to brush the snow from her hair.

She'd yet to let go of him. It simply hadn't occurred to her that she should. Her hands were so cold they felt frozen in place, anyway. Much like the rest of her when his fingers sifted through her hair.

"You're going to have to go inside and change," he told

her, drawing her head forward to scoop snow from between her collar and her nape. "You've got it everywhere."

She felt certain his hands must have been a little cool. But as cold as her skin was, his felt as hot as a brand when his palm curved beneath her jaw. She shivered at the contact, the smile in her eyes dying when she saw the heat in his.

Her breath puffed out. His grip on her heart was taking a firmer hold. The realization that he had a hold at all stunned her, coating her in caution.

Jack slipped his thumb over her bottom lip, the warmth of her breath instantly turning icy on his skin. He couldn't believe how good her smile always made him feel, or how being near her could obscure his common sense. He was messing with fire. He knew he could lose himself in her, in the sweet oblivion they could create. But he was in no mood to torture himself with possibilities. He'd told her the choice was hers. Now he wasn't so sure that, if he had her in his arms again, he wouldn't press the issue until she caved in.

"You'd better go inside for a while."

He stepped back, catching her one bare hand in his to help her through the deep drift. At the contact, she sucked a quick breath.

His frustration found another channel. "Damn it," he muttered, when he looked from her red fingers to the flake-matted knit glove covering her other hand. "I gave you gloves. Why aren't you wearing them?"

"Because they're too big to work in."

"You won't be able to work at all if you lose your fingers to frostbite."

He switched his grip to her wrist and backed out of the drift, pulling her with him. Carrie watched his face as he did, wondering at the shadows that swept over it in the moments before he'd noticed her missing glove—the one she'd taken off so she could blow on her fingers just before she'd slipped.

She started to do the same thing now that he'd let go of her, but she'd no sooner raised her stiff fingers to her mouth than he caught her wrist again.

The scowl tightening his mouth made his voice a hard hiss. "Don't do that."

She looked at him in total confusion. "You're the one making such a big deal out of how cold they are. I'm just trying to warm them."

"Your breath will make them wet. Skin freezes twice as fast that way. Pull them up into your sleeves and get inside."

If his goal was to keep her off balance, he succeeded beautifully. No sooner had a couple of bricks fallen from his wall, than he'd shoved them back into place and added a few more. Moments ago, he'd been about to kiss her. She was sure of it. She might even have reached for him herself had he not stepped back when he had. She wanted to feel his arms around her again. She wanted him. Period. But she didn't have to wrestle with that little epiphany right now. He seemed to have changed his mind about wanting her.

He was yanking his own glove back on as if he had a personal grudge against the thing when he started for the ladder.

"Jack?" She saw him hesitate, his whole body tensing. "You're not going to finish the roof are you?"

Beneath the split rawhide, his broad shoulders lowered ever so slightly. "No," he said, no longer sounding so abrupt. "I'm just getting the shovel so it doesn't get covered up there."

He wasn't going to rob her of the few tasks she had. He made that message clear by his quiet tone, much as he'd let her know by offering her the chore that he understood how difficult it was to switch gears the way she was having to do. It was almost as if he'd had to do that very thing himself—go from full steam ahead to a near standstill and find some way to cope with the dizzying loss of motion. The books on his shelves still taunted her. The tomes on finance just didn't fit with what she did know about him.

She just wished she understood what he was wrestling with. She wished, too, as long as she was at it, that she knew what had happened in those brief moments after he'd pulled her from the snow.

Carrie changed to dry clothes, then headed into the kitchen to thaw her fingers around a mug of cinnamon-scented cider while she waited for the microwave to do the same thing to a chicken she'd brought in from Jack's freezer. She had vegetables in the sink to peel and a bag of frozen blueberries to turn into dessert, but all she really wanted to do was talk to Jack. She was dead certain they were about to lose what little ground they'd gained in the past couple of days, and she couldn't bear it if he went into full-scale avoidance again.

As if her thoughts had pulled him in, she heard the groan and slam of the outer porch doors. All but holding her breath, she listened to the heavy fall of his boots on the planks as he moved around, ridding his outerwear of snow, then heard his steps become muffled when he reached the mat by the kitchen door. He seemed to hesitate before coming in. Or, maybe, she thought, he was just waiting for Felan, until she remembered that Felan was asleep on the hearth rug.

That she'd come so far as to actually forget about the presence of the animal would have amazed her had she not been so busy trying to get through the little speech she was preparing. The lead was short and to the point, the way the best leads always were. She just didn't know where to go from there.

"Coffee or cider?" she asked when the door finally opened.

Jack's frame filled the doorway. She didn't doubt for a moment that he wished he hadn't found her right there, but he had the grace to hide his disappointment by turning his attention to closing the door and hanging his coat and hat on the pegs beside it.

"Cider, if it's ready."

"It can be in a minute. I just have to heat it."

"Don't bother." He turned, absently chafing his hand down the arm of his denim shirt. "Coffee's fine."

Carrie would have told him it was no bother at all, but he was already reaching for the steaming pot and the heavy brown mug she'd left on the burnt orange counter. His face looked raw from the cold, and he had a hat dent in his dark hair. He hadn't shaved, and the day's growth of beard added more shadows to his rugged features, making him look more intense and turning his eyes a piercing blue.

The electronic ping of the microwave bell joined the clink of the carafe being returned to the coffeemaker. "I'll have dinner in the oven in a while, but I can get you something to eat now if you're hungry. We skipped lunch."

"I'll take some of that chili from yesterday with me."

"You're going somewhere?"

"Just out to restring the basket of that snowshoe."

"I thought you already did that."

"I didn't like the way it turned out."

His tone was unremarkable. It was the set of his jaw that gave him away. That and the fact that there wasn't a blasted thing wrong with the job he'd done. The snowshoe looked perfect.

"If you'll show me how," she suggested, not willing to give up easily. "I'll do it."

"It won't take but a couple of minutes. What I really need to start on is the snowmobile engine I've got torn down out there."

She had to give him credit. He was being far more subtle than usual. Still, with his choice of task so obviously designed to discourage her from wanting to be with him, she'd have to be as dense as concrete to miss his message.

"You don't have to go out there at all, Jack." She set her mug down with a quiet clink, then opened the microwave above the stove. Chicken in hand, she crossed to the sink and turned on the water. "It won't take me long to get this into the oven. As soon as I do, I'll go to my room and you can do whatever it is you'd do if you were alone. I'm sure you'd rather go warm up by the fire before you did anything at all, so go ahead. This is your home. You shouldn't have to hide out on the porch."

He stood at the fridge behind her, a green storage container in hand. She thought she heard him blow out a deep breath.

"You're not making this easy, you know?"

"You said nothing here was." She reached for a potato. Now, she needed a peeler. "I'm just going with the flow."

"Sarcasm doesn't suit you."

"Neither does not knowing what it is I've done."

She found the peeler in the drawer.

"You haven't done anything."

"Well, there's something I do that upsets you." The roaster she wanted was in the lower cabinet by the stove. "We get along for a while, then all of a sudden you're back to avoiding me again. If you'll just tell me what it is I do, I'll stop doing it."

She felt the weight of the roaster leave her hand when she passed him with it. It landed on the counter along with the container he'd held. Taking her by the arms, he turned her around, and pinned her to the counter by planting her hands on it and clamping his on top.

His eyes glittered hard on her face. "You can't stop doing what you do. You can't stop being who you are, any more than you can make me stop wanting you." His voice lowered in sudden conviction. "I don't want to get involved with you. And you don't want to get involved with me," he growled. "You don't know anything about me."

He couldn't possibly know what she wanted. She was no longer totally sure herself. Her breath feathered out, her heart knocking wildly. "I know you're a good man. And I know you've been hurt." She knew he could be tender, and that he could be kind. She knew he was wasting himself up here alone, and that his isolation brought him as much pain as peace. There was so much she knew, but that wasn't what she needed for him to know right now. "I'm willing to listen to anything you'll tell me. I do want to know you, Jack. Very much."

Her quiet insistence nearly turned him inside out. She wanted to know him. And part of him wanted that so badly, he ached. There wasn't a man on earth who didn't want someone to accept him simply for the person he was, to care about him despite all his weaknesses, his mistakes, his flaws. But once those flaws were exposed, she would see him as he saw himself and she'd never again look at him the way she did now.

He told himself it didn't matter. He didn't trust what he could see in her eyes, anyway, because he didn't trust himself to believe it was there. He was a lousy judge of character. He also kept forgetting what she did for a living, what she would return to once she left here. Reminding himself now, he pulled back and slid his hands from hers.

He'd already let her get too close. All he'd wanted to do was push her away enough to make her keep her distance.

The fact that he was coming close to physical intimidation to achieve that goal only made him feel worse than he already did.

"There's nothing to say," he told her. "Let's just not complicate this situation any more than we already have."

The reason that he was coming close to physical intimidation.
be believe that and walk away now, they'd worse off, he already did.

"There's nothing to talk," he told her. "But there's just no complicate this situation anymore to that it's already be."

Chapter Nine

The weather didn't clear. For days, the snow came in fits and starts, adding an inch or two at a time to the ever-deepening snowpack. When it wasn't snowing, the wind blew, rearranging the drifts and making it seem as if the sky was dumping more of the wet white stuff even when no new flakes actually fell. Every day Carrie listened for the plow. She heard nothing but silence. Calls to the Highway Department met with the same recording she'd reached before, the one advising people to stay off the roads and to stay on the line only for emergencies, and the radio told of people stranded in far worse conditions than those she had to endure. She was protected from the elements when she wanted to be. She had a warm place to sleep and food to eat. Her situation truly could have been worse.

Knowing that didn't make Carrie feel any less anxious or distressed. Each passing hour had eaten away the time she had to get to Seattle. Now, that time was gone.

That situation had her nursing a knot the size of a lemon in her stomach. What magnified the knot to grapefruit proportions was Jack. The two of them had become the proverbial ships passing in the night. Like the lake on which those ships navigated, the surface of their encounters remained eerily calm, while deep beneath, strong undercurrents of tension eddied and flowed. Because those undercurrents kept threatening to reach the surface, Carrie adopted Jack's evasive approach, often opting to avoid him before he had a chance to avoid her first.

At the moment, Jack was the one making himself scarce. She had no idea where he was, either, and she really wished she did. He'd been gone when she got up, and it was now noon. As she paced between the window on the back porch and the window by the kitchen table, she wanted nothing more than to hear the dull roar of the snowmobile telling her he was on his way back. It was Monday, she'd been due in her new editor's office an hour ago and the phone wasn't working.

She paced back to the porch to watch for him there. There was nothing to see but two elk nosing tree branches and snow skimming along the ground in the breeze. Too anxious to appreciate what normally would fascinate her, she headed for the other window, wondering when the phone had gone out.

The last time she'd used it had been a few days ago, when she'd called Mr. Hawthorne's secretary to tell her she hadn't been able to leave and that she would call back first thing Monday morning. She'd been told in return to call before one o'clock or she wouldn't catch ''Mr. H'' at all. Right after that, she'd called her friend Jane at her old apartment building, since she'd promised to let her know when she arrived in Seattle. Jane hadn't been home, so she'd left a message on her answering machine telling her she'd call back when she had anything new to report. Then, she'd phoned her mom—who'd completely forgotten that the move to Seattle was taking place that month.

"You just can't imagine how chaotic it is with all the twins' activities," Beth Edmonds had explained, "I'm sorry it slipped my mind. But I know I don't have to worry about you," she added, as if that somehow excused the lack of maternal concern that had never been her strong suit anyway. "You've always had a knack for making things work out."

Carrie didn't make things work out. She simply worked around whatever happened. She hadn't mentioned that to her mom, though. Beth wouldn't have understood the difference.

Afraid to think of what she might have to work around now, she walked over to pick up the phone again and hoped for a miracle.

The line was as dead as it had been when she'd picked up the phone two hours ago. She had no idea when it had gone out. She'd never heard Jack's phone ring even once, so its silence had meant nothing.

She paced back through the kitchen, growing more agitated with each lap across the linoleum. The problem with pacing was that there was nothing to do while doing it but think. Her disquieted thoughts kept bouncing between her need for Jack to take her to the lodge to try its telephone, and the uneasiness he'd planted with his suggestion that she wasn't really happy with her life. The idea that she was merely surviving was as ridiculous to her as the idea that she was somehow as isolated in her world as he was in his own. Still, the thoughts nagged with the relentlessness of a toothache. Just like the thought that, if he didn't get there soon, she was going to have to go to the lodge without him. She only had an hour to reach Mr. Hawthorne.

On her next trip back from the porch, she reached for her jacket.

Minutes later, layered, bundled and wearing Jack's stocking hat and the fleece-lined gloves he'd loaned her, she took the lodge key off the hook where she'd seen Jack hang it and headed out on her snowshoes for the lodge. She didn't know the security code for the lodge, but if she tripped the alarm, she'd just explain to Jack that she hadn't had any choice. She suspected the alarm only alerted Jack, anyway. There wasn't anyone else around to answer it.

It was only a mile, and she knew the way. She'd taken the route twice with Jack and the road through the snow-covered trees was obvious. It was only when she emerged from the woods and crossed the first meadow that she couldn't tell where the road was, but that didn't matter. She knew it followed the creek and the creek was easy to see. Like a dark velvet ribbon dropped on smooth, white satin, the frigid, inky waters meandered through the wide snow-field. She only had to follow it to the woods on the other side and she'd be able to see where the road cut through the trees again. Once she made it through those woods, the lodge would be visible from the rise.

The air felt as sharp as glass. With her nose buried in the maroon muffler she'd borrowed from the pegs by the kitchen door, she tramped on, ignoring the few flakes falling from the sky. There had been a breeze all morning. Now, the wind picked up, cooling her despite her strenuous pace. The thermometer had registered just above zero when she'd left, but she didn't want to think about the cold. Instead she focused her attention on the sounds she heard—the scream of an eagle, the chatter of something small and furry chasing up and down the pines—and listened for Jack's snowmobile.

By the time the lodge came into view, she still hadn't heard a single sound that hadn't been filtering through the mountains for the past few thousand years.

* * *

Jack and Felan entered the cabin with a swirl of snow, a twenty-mile-an-hour wind shoving from behind and the lodge alarm going off near the electrical box. Thinking the sound must be driving Carrie crazy, he punched a code into the panel to silence the annoying racket. The wind or an animal had set the thing off, he figured. The weather had been too consistently bad for the outdoor enthusiasts to be out yet. He supposed there could be some overzealous backpackers out there seeking shelter from the miserable weather, though. In which case, they were welcome to stay where they were. With the temperature dropping and the wind blowing as it was, they'd freeze to death otherwise.

Telling himself he'd check the lodge as soon as the wind died down, almost grateful for the inconvenience because it would give him something to do other than hang out on the porch, he started peeling off outerwear. As soon as he warmed up, he'd go back out and close the shutters. When the wind started howling through the panes of the drafty old windows, it seemed he never could get the chill out of the room.

Right now, he needed to chase the chill from his bones.

He knew something wasn't right the moment he stepped inside. By midafternoon Carrie always had something going for supper. The Crock Pot stood clean and empty in its place on the long counter. The enamel surface of the stove sparkled, but was devoid of a pot or pan. The oven was cold.

There was fresh food and water in Felan's bowl, something the dog was already busy appreciating, but there was no sign of Carrie.

He wondered if she was in her room, but even before he knocked on her door, he knew she wasn't there. The cabin felt empty.

Not caring to consider why that had never bothered him before, he opened her door and poked his head inside her room. Pushing the door wider, he leaned against the frame and looked over the small and now unfamiliar space. She wasn't there, but her touch was.

Sometime during the past week, she'd tied back the yellow curtains she'd hung on the window and added one of the valances he'd left in a heap on the rocking chair. The chair itself had been cleared and moved near the window where her plant trailed from a stack of boxes she'd covered with another of the yellow curtains. She'd hung one of the pictures—the one of summer wildflowers. At the foot of her neatly made bed was a green-and-white football jersey he assumed she used for a nightshirt.

He didn't want to think about how she might have come by the jersey, if it had been a gift from some guy who'd played for a pro team, or maybe a college football coach she'd met at a press party somewhere. He didn't want to think about her with any other man, athlete or otherwise. But most of all, he didn't want to think about why he didn't want to think about it. He just wanted to know where she was.

He hadn't thought to look outside for her when he'd pulled the snowmobile into the garage. As nasty as the weather was, he couldn't imagine that she'd be out there shoveling off the roof or digging around her car. The wind-chill put the temperature in the double-digit-below-zero range. Still, he checked the coat pegs since he hadn't noticed what all was there when he'd hung his coat.

Her jacket was gone. So were the snowshoes she'd been using.

The alarm.

A burning sensation centered in his chest. It knotted in his gut when he jerked open the cupboard door to see if she'd taken the key to the lodge. He knew she needed to call her new boss today. That was one of the reasons he hadn't stopped working on the phone line when the weather started turning so lousy.

Jack's only thought when he snapped Felan into a heavily quilted, red vest and belted it to conserve the animal's body heat, was that Carrie had obviously made it to the lodge. His only hope was that she'd stayed there.

Carrie couldn't see the creek. She realized that moments after she moved beyond the trees into what should have been a snowfield bisected by a black ribbon of water. All she could see was a wall of white. The swirling snow obliterated the landscape, making land indistinguishable from sky.

Having put the brakes on her pace, she moved slowly ahead, her shoulders hunched against the stinging wind. The sick feeling she'd been dealing with ever since she'd spoken with Mr. Hawthorne was suddenly forgotten as she searched the ground for the teardrop shaped depressions she'd left a little over an hour ago. She knew they were there. She'd seen them on the road she'd just left. Thinking about it now, she realized those depressions had steadily become shallower and much less defined. Here, where the wind scoured the surface unchecked, it had erased what the blowing snow hadn't filled in.

She moved to the right, thinking that she might have followed the road in on that side and that she was looking in the wrong place. The ground gave no clue there, either. Look harder, she admonished herself, trying desperately to not think about how cold she was. The wind was blowing so much stronger than when she'd left the lodge, almost as fiercely as it had the day she and Jack had battled their way from the garage to the cabin. Her hands and feet were beyond numb.

She needed to get moving. Movement created warmth, especially vigorous movement, which was one of the reasons she'd kept her pace as fast as she had. Yet, hurrying depleted energy, and she hadn't exactly fueled up for a battle with the elements. She'd been too agitated about making her call to have more than coffee for breakfast and she hadn't had lunch at all. Having made the trek to the lodge at pretty much the same pace as the one she'd maintained until now, she was already running on reserves.

Changing direction in snowshoes wasn't simply a matter of turning around. Opting for the four-step method over the two-step since it required less finesse, she faced the other way. Her eyes were narrowed and watering from the cold and the subzero wind froze the moisture to her lashes. She pulled her muffler higher in a futile attempt to block the wind, but the wind seemed to blow straight through her, sucking the heat from her bones and causing everything from her nose to her knees to shiver. The constant, freezing blast didn't help the headache brewing at the top of her skull, either.

She figured she was half a mile from the cabin, which meant she was about that same distance from the lodge. But as she chafed her arms up and down the sleeves of her white jacket and took a couple of steps forward to head back there, she found that the road she'd just followed had disappeared. The white barked aspens that gave way farther in to pine and spruce had suddenly been swallowed by the billowing, blinding snow.

Her glance swept from left to right once more, her heart jerking in apprehension. She needed to find her tracks.

Her watering eyes made the ground a blur. Cupping Jack's big gloves at the sides of her face to fend off the wind, she searched the ground to the right of her snow-caked snowshoes. The two-inch deep depressions were still there. So were the ones beyond them. Feeling panic bubble in her chest, she retraced her steps, searching frantically for others.

If she had stayed moving in a straight line she would have found the road easily, but her search for her old tracks had thrown her off her path. She found tracks headed one way, only to see another a foot over that headed the other direction. There were no visual clues to help her out. No matter where she looked, everything was the same. She couldn't even tell if fresh snow was falling, or if it was only the snow on the ground being whipped into a frozen frenzy.

Jack had said the screaming wind and blinding snow could distort everything from temperature to sense of direction. It could even make a person hear things that weren't there. That had to be why she thought she could hear a deep, muffled drone one moment, then nothing but the rush of the wind the next. At least it seemed he'd said something about distortion, she thought, stumbling a little as her cold muscles protested the exertion. It could have been that she'd read it. Maybe that was Chapter Three of the survival guide.

That was it, she thought, trying to focus on what that chapter had been about. Jack had told her to pay particular attention to it. Hadn't it mentioned getting out of the wind whatever way possible?

Her lungs already ached from breathing frozen air and her head had gone from a dull throb to full scale pounding. It even hurt to think, but she needed to remember what Jack had said about being caught in a blizzard. Beyond getting out of the wind, all her numbing brain could recall was that he'd called being in a blizzard a crapshoot, something she thought just a little absurd because a person couldn't play craps in the snow. The dice would sink right in and disappear. Just as her feet did every time she took a step, just as her body wanted to do the longer she trudged on.

She had no idea how long she'd been wandering around

when the slender trunk of the birch wavered into view a half-dozen feet ahead. Reaching for it, she sighted another, her relief so profound that she would have cried had the indulgence not made it harder to see. She was at the edge of the woods. All she had to do was follow the trees until there weren't any more to follow. That would be where the road was.

Minutes passed as she worked her way along the tree line. Wondering if she'd gone in the wrong direction, she turned around to go the other way, stumbling more often now because lifting her legs was becoming harder as more snow weighted her jeans and her shoes and the cold drained control from her muscles.

Each time she stumbled now, she made it back up by letting herself imagine that Jack was there, lifting her with his strong arms. It didn't matter that he was only helping her because he had to. She would just let herself lean on him for a little while, just until she reached someplace warm and she could curl up in his arms and go to sleep. She felt so safe there, so protected. That was what was important. Feeling safe. She really wasn't that cold anymore anyway, she thought, stumbling again on her way to another tree. She was just tired, and the snow looked so soft and, since the trees had disappeared into a white fog again, maybe she should just rest for a while.

She wasn't inside the lodge. Jack knew that even before he reached its back door. The walkway there was completely protected from the wind, the evidence of her arrival and departure disturbed only by falling snow. There were two sets of slowly filling snowshoe prints. One set in. One set out. And not a single traceable track in sight once the depressions rounded the edge of the building.

For the past twenty minutes, visibility had varied from between twenty feet to a matter of inches, depending on the mood of the wind at any given moment. It had taken him that long to navigate from the cabin. Partially because lack of visibility put him at a snail's crawl, but mostly because he was watching for Carrie or some sign of her along the way. The narrow roads through the trees had been easy enough to follow. The clearings were the problem. But there, Felan had led the way. All Jack had to say was "Let's go to the lodge" and the dog had homed in on the building as if drawn by a beam.

Over the past week, the first snows had packed to a solid base. The new snow, though, was incredibly light, the soft powder perfect for skiing, but wearing on an animal built so low to the ground. As soon as they'd entered the woods above the lodge, the shadowed shapes of trees once more defining the road, Jack had Felan ride behind him on the snowmobile to keep him from tiring.

Now, he called the dog to him, not bothering to deny the concern for Carrie that had him as tense as a spring.

"We've got to find her, buddy. You hear me?" Jack said, hunched in front of the gray-muzzled wolf-dog. "Can you find her? Can you lead me to Carrie?"

The dog tilted his head, looking for all the world as if he were trying to understand. His keen amber eyes never moved from his master's face.

Jack tried again, but not the faintest hint of recognition registered.

That was when Jack realized what was wrong. The problem wasn't with the dog. It was with himself. Felan had never heard him call Carrie by name. He never *had* called her by name, for that matter. Except maybe once and he couldn't even be sure of that. The omission had been protective, a way of keeping emotional distance. By not referring to her by name, by rarely using it when he thought of her, she was simply a woman, indistinguishable from all others.

He figured the ploy hadn't worked past the first twenty-four hours.

"She," he tried, since he figured that was how he'd referred to her during his mumblings. But that netted the same response from Felan.

Time was slipping away. It would be dark soon. Jack had no idea what time she'd left the lodge, but he knew the weather had turned bad a couple of hours ago. She wouldn't have gone out in the storm, which meant she'd been caught in it.

People died in such conditions.

He needed something with Carrie's scent, but precious time would be wasted going back to the cabin. He and Felan weren't equipped to camp out in a blizzard, either, and each trip they made taunted the Fates a little more. Then, he remembered the glove in his pocket, the one he'd found in the snow the day she'd slid off the roof. He'd kept forgetting to take it out.

He pulled it out now, holding the blue knit glove for Felan to sniff. Repeating his instructions, he tried to not think about how small that glove was.

Felan's bark was sharp, recognition instant. As if propelled by a rocket, the dog shot in the direction of the woods at the top of the hill and promptly disappeared in the snow. Seconds later, he was back, barking at Jack as if telling him to move it.

Strapped into Jack's red down vest, Felan looked like a bouncing red ball in the blur of white. Following him, Jack traced the snowmobile's tracks back up the hill to the tree line. He pulled down his muffler, nearly choking on the bitter cold, and hollered for Carrie, hoping she would hear his voice, if not the low rumble of the snowmobile's engine. The wind whipped the sounds around him, the frigid air stinging his skin and making it impossible to breathe without the thick muffler, so he pulled it back up to warm his breath, then tried again. He didn't know if he'd missed her coming through the first time, or if she was even there to hear him. He supposed she could even have made it back to the cabin by now. But some indefinable sixth sense he didn't care to question, told him she was out there. Somewhere.

They reached the meadow. Instead of going straight ahead, Felan bounded to the left. Jack cut an arc, able to keep from losing sight of him only because the depth of the snow slowed the dog down and the red vest helped make him visible. He followed for a hundred feet before Felan angled to the left again.

Jack could barely see the woods Felan darted into. Knowing he'd never get the machine turned around in that closely growing copse, he followed until he nearly bumped into a birch, then jumped off, leaving the engine running.

The heavy snow did its best to slow him down, sucking at his thighs like an ocean wave determined to pull him out to sea. Felan had already stopped fifteen feet ahead of him and was nosing at something Jack couldn't see.

Arms pumping, damning the cold, Jack didn't know if he wanted that something to be Carrie, or if he should hope the dog was just sniffing around some animal nature had claimed. If it was Carrie, the fact that she wasn't moving with a canine poking at her wasn't a good sign at all.

"Carrie?"

Two more steps and the fear he'd put on hold for the past hour swept through him like a ghost. Jack couldn't tell if she had piled up the snow, or if the drift had already been there and she'd simply dug a hole in front of it and curled up inside. But her slumped position nearly made his heart stop beating. A snow-caked, maroon muffler he recognized as his own completely covered her face. Another step and his heart kicked into double time. Felan had nosed aside the muffler and was licking her cheek when Jack saw her eyes open. Her skin looked as pale as the snow completely covering her clothes and her cap.

It was the warmth that pulled Carrie from the sleep she craved. If she could just sleep, she wouldn't feel the cold. But the warmth burned and when she opened her eyes, she could see only the beast that chased her in her nightmares. She couldn't run. Couldn't even try. But she knew this beast, she realized, her heart pounding as she winced at the pain in her hands and feet. He wasn't like the others. And he was breathing in her face, warming it.

It registered, vaguely, that the animal had licked her. But he was warm and that was all Carrie wanted. To be warm. She was shaking so hard she didn't know if she'd ever be able to stop.

"Carrie." The deep voice came from above her, strong hands lifting her. "Come on, baby. We've got to get you inside. Can you walk? Try to walk."

The voice was familiar. The concern, the endearments were not. Certain she must be hallucinating, she tried to sink back down, not wanting to face the brunt of the wind again.

"No, you don't." The demand was sharper, more familiar. "We've got to get you up. Can you hear me?"

Jack, she thought, almost afraid to believe he was real. "You're here?"

Her words were thick, slurred like a drunk on a three-day binge. "I'm here, honey." He pulled off her snowshoes and clamped them under his arm. "Open your eyes. I don't want you going to sleep."

"Tired."

"No sleep until you warm up. Do you know who I am?"

"Jack."

So far so good. "Do you know what day this is?"

"Don't care."

He swung her up into his arms, still clamping the snow-shoes. "You do care," he told her, aiming for the snow-mobile through the swirling snow. Apathy was not a good sign. Neither was the waxy look of her face. She was suffering from hypothermia. He didn't doubt that for an instant. He just needed to know how bad she was. "Try again. What day is it?"

She didn't respond.

He set his jaw, fighting the snow, the wind and the effects of the cold on his own muscles and straddled the snowmobile as best he could still holding her. Since she was in no condition to hang on behind him, he set her bottom on the seat, draped her legs over his left one and settled her head against his right shoulder. Felan hopped on back.

"You still with me?" he asked, ducking his head where her face was pressed to his chest.

He heard a stuttered, "Yeah." Telling her to keep talking to him, he slipped the vibrating machine into gear.

The ten minutes it took to get to the cabin seemed like forever. The going was most difficult across the meadow because there were no trees to stop the wind. Between his compass and Felan, Jack found the road on the other side, then followed Felan back to the cabin. Struggling through the deepening snow, fighting the wind and the subzero temperature, the animal was pushing exhaustion himself.

Jack left the snowmobile at the back steps. With Carrie in his arms, he shouldered open the door, letting Felan in ahead of them, then snatching back the storm door before the wind could rip it off its hinges. The inner door slammed when his boot connected with it.

Snow flew in all directions as Felan dispensed with what clung to him. Knowing he had to do the same thing with them, Jack sat Carrie on the workbench. She was shivering

violently and far too lethargic when he went to work on
her snow-caked clothes.

"Talk to me," he ordered, pulling off her hat and gloves.
Her lips were nearly blue. "Tell me everything that happened today."

"Wanna g-get warm. Wanna sleep."

"Well you're not warm yet, so you have to stay awake.
Okay?"

"'Kay," she whispered, her eyes drifting closed even as
he peeled her muffler from around her neck and unbuttoned
her jacket.

Faltering over her words, she tried to tell him she could
do it.

"Sure you can," he muttered, pulling the jacket down
her arms and adding it to the pile.

After tossing his own coat in the general direction of the
washing machine, he took off her boots, then lifted her
down. Her knees immediately buckled and he caught her
to his side, holding her there with one arm while he pulled
up her sweater. "I suppose you've got the dexterity to un-
snap your jeans, too?"

She'd winced in pain when he'd pulled off her gloves,
and he could tell from the whitened tips that she was pushing frostbite on a couple of her fingers. As if in slow-
motion, she lifted her hand toward the snap, but Jack had
already unfastened it and was working on her zipper.

He knew she was trying to stand, but she felt like a rag
doll in his arms when he turned her to push her snowy
jeans and black leggings over her hips. Her coordination
was shot, her speech was thick and he wasn't all that certain
she was totally oriented. She wasn't even attempting to ask
what he thought he was doing undressing her. The only
good sign was the fact that she was shivering so hard. If
she hadn't been, she would have been on her way to a
coma.

More severe hypothermia was still a possibility. That thought clawed at the front of his mind when he set her back on the workbench and peeled off jeans, leggings and socks and let them fall in a heap at his feet. Her long, slender legs were raw red, her skin solid gooseflesh. He didn't know how much internal body heat she'd lost, but the risk of further decline in temperature always existed in the process of warming a person back up. He had no way to treat her if she went into shock.

"Hang on," he told her, and lifted her into his arms once more.

"Clothes," she murmured, only now seeming to realize that most of them were gone.

"I'll get you dry ones. Right now, we're going to thaw you out."

He knew of only two ways to effectively accomplish that. Warm water or direct body heat. If he'd had a bathtub instead of a shower, he might have opted for the former. But there was no way he could keep her standing in a shower long enough to raise her body temperature.

It took a couple of tries, because her teeth were chattering so hard, but she told him she'd never thaw out.

"Yes, you will," he promised, lowering her to the sofa. Dragging the Indian-print blanket off the back, he tucked it around her, told her not to nod off and headed back to the kitchen, unbuttoning his own shirt on the way. He knew she preferred cider over coffee, so he poured two mugs full from the jug in the refrigerator and set them in the microwave. Felan needed warming, too, so Jack hurriedly filled the dog's water dish with warm water and relieved his buddy of the down vest that had protected him, heaping praises on the animal for his help. As he did, he watched Carrie lean her head on the back of the couch and close her eyes. She was as pale as a ghost.

"Don't!"

A frown furrowed her brow as she slowly lifted her head, only to let it fall back as she curled herself into a tighter ball. Every pulse beat made her head feel as if the top was coming off. If she'd had the energy to tell him that, she would have, but even talking seemed to take too much effort. Her hands and feet felt as if hot needles were being threaded through them, and the room kept wanting to tilt first one way and then the other.

"Carrie, I mean it," Jack muttered, finding it easier to feel irritation than fear. "You have to stay awake. Here," he said, searching under the blanket for one of her hands so he could wrap it around a mug. "Drink this."

The mug of sweetly scented liquid wasn't hot, but he'd wrapped a dry dishcloth around it so the warmth wouldn't burn her chilled hands. Even with that precaution, she sucked in a gasp when he tried to gently fold her fingers around the warm ceramic. She was shaking so hard she'd just have spilled it anyway, so Jack held it for her while she took a couple of swallows, then set the mug down by the other on the coffee table and headed into his room.

He was back with his bedding within seconds. Leaving it in a heap on the sofa, he stepped over Felan to add logs to the fire. Pine snapped and sizzled, its scent filling the air as he peeled off his boots, shirt, turtleneck and undershirt. Having never warmed up when he'd first come in well over an hour ago, he sported a little gooseflesh himself.

Carrie felt the cushions at the back of the couch disappear one by one. Jack was muttering at her again, telling her she was *not* going to sleep. At least that's what she thought he said when she felt him pull away the blanket and pull her into a sitting position.

"Lift your arms," he said, skimming his hands under her long sweater and the two shirts she had on under it.

She hadn't even begun to warm up and he'd taken her blanket. She tried to take it back.

"I know you're cold," he told her, gently taking her wrist so he could ease her hand through her sleeve. "But there are only two ways to do this."

Her eyelids felt as heavy as anvils. Still, she managed to look over at Jack. All she saw was a wide expanse of muscled chest and a jaw that looked carved of flint.

"We have to either immerse you to your neck in warm water," he was saying, "or warm you up by skin-to-skin contact. I don't have a tub."

The tilting stopped. Now, the room was simply spinning.

Jack didn't know if it was lack of comprehension that caused her faint frown, or disagreement with his choice of method. He didn't care. She wasn't in a position to argue and he was going the only available route. If he offended sensibilities on the way, they'd just have to deal with it later.

Having freed her arms, he pulled her sweater and shirts off in one motion, then flicked open the catch at the back of her pale pink bra. He had that stripped away and the blanket back around her before he caught more than a glimpse of her beautiful, trembling body. He didn't want to care about her, but he did. He didn't want to want her, either, but that point had been conceded long before now. Making love with her was the last thought on his mind at the moment, however. Had this been seduction, he liked to think he'd approach it with a little more finesse.

Her eyes remained closed, but he saw her pale lips move.

"What?" he asked, fully prepared to counter any protest she had in mind.

"Sick," she whispered again.

Jack went still. She was already as pale as snow. Impossibly, more color had just drained from her face. An instant later, he had her in his arms, Indian-print blanket and all, and was rounding the door of the tiny bathroom to hold her over the toilet.

Five minutes later, having given her a glass of tepid water to rinse her mouth and holding a barely warm washcloth to her lips while she sat shivering on the edge of the sink, he was thinking about throttling her as soon as she was well.

She hadn't had anything in her stomach to get rid of. A person needed fuel in this kind of weather.

"Don't rub," he told her, when her hand came up to hold the cloth. He'd save the lectures for later. Right now, she was too sick. Too defenseless. He skimmed his fingers lightly along her jaw. "You're pushing frostbite on your cheeks. I don't think you've done any damage yet, but skin is fragile when it's that cold."

She lifted her chin ever so slightly, but the effort to acknowledge him seemed to take too much effort. Without ever meeting his eyes, she let her head fall against his shoulder.

He wasn't sure, but he thought he felt moisture gathering on his skin.

He lifted her chin and felt his heart snag in his chest.

"Sorry," she whispered, tears pooling in her red-rimmed eyes.

"Hey." Don't cry, he silently begged. Please. Don't cry. He could handle her being scared out of her wits. He could handle her being sick. He could not handle tears. "Come on. We're going to work on that shivering."

That was his only thought as he carried her back to the sofa, tucked the thick blue blankets from his bed around her and stripped himself down to his briefs. Before she could react to what he was doing, he crawled under the blankets with her.

A faint moan of surprise—or, more likely, protest—was the best she could manage under the circumstances.

"Honest, honey," he said, easing her up and stretching her out so her head rested on his shoulder and her body

contacted his wherever possible. He tangled his legs around
hers, his body reacting of its own volition as contact became intimate. "I'll show you in a National Park Service
guide where it says this has to be done naked." Thinking
that she felt like a vibrating, body-length icicle, he leaned
forward, and snagged one of the mugs. "It's got something
to do with direct transfer of body heat. Now, drink up.
Okay?"

She was already curling into him, greedy for his warmth.
But she needed to warm up from the inside, too. With his
back propped against the end of the sofa, and blankets bundled and tucked around them both, he held the mug while
she sipped and tried to not think of all the times he'd imagined holding her so close. As it was, he figured the Fates
were having a field day with this particular punishment.
While he ran his hands down her back and over the sleek
curve of her hip, gently chafing her skin to create friction
and heat, he consciously willed himself to think only of
her, and not of how perfectly her soft, slender curves fit his
harder angles and planes. The effort was admirable. Unfortunately his body paid no attention.

He needed to keep her talking. "You went to use the
phone didn't you?"

"Yours...didn't work."

"I know. I discovered that this morning. That's where I
was," he told her over the crackle and snap of flames finding fresh pitch. "Out fixing the line. The break was in the
same spot as before. Guess I didn't make a very good
splice." His breath feathered her soft hair. "So, did you
get through to the guy?"

The response was slow in coming, but she finally returned a teeth-chattering, "Yes."

"And?"

"Don't have a job anymore."

The warming movements of Jack's hand stopped. "Why? What did he say?"

Carrie knew what Jack was trying to do, that he wanted to keep her awake. But she couldn't talk about this right now. She already felt so sick she could barely think. Yet, even feeling as perfectly wretched as she did, it occurred to her, vaguely, to wonder who he'd been trying to call to have noticed there was a problem with the phone.

The thought wavered in her consciousness only an instant before she felt herself sinking. His hard body radiated the heat she craved, and it felt so solid and strong that she forgot all about how frightened she'd been out there alone in the snow. She'd wished for his arms. Miraculously she was in them. Later, she would worry about how that had come to be.

As with every other time she'd drifted toward sleep, Jack pulled her right back. "Hey, come on. You didn't answer me."

She didn't want to talk about her job now. She could only deal with one overwhelming matter at a time, and thinking about the conversation she'd had only made her feel sicker than she already did. Since it took too much energy to articulate that, she simply said, "I know."

"I see," he said, the simple words filled with more understanding than she would have thought possible. "Then we'll talk about that later. How's your head?"

From beneath the edge of the blanket covering his chest and her nose, she whispered, "Hurts."

"Does it feel like an ice-cream headache?"

She gave a slight nod, her hair tickling his chin.

He smoothed it down, torturing himself by breathing in the clean scent of it, then went back to stroking her arm, her back. "That's part of it. So's the nausea. It'll be better soon." He nudged her chin up a minute later, drawing the mug close again. "Have some more."

She was as complacent as a child, sipping when he suggested it, opening her eyes when he asked her to. When she'd finished the cider, he set the mug aside and concentrated on warming her hands by having her tuck them between his. He hissed in a breath with that one, but the air under the blankets was warm and the bone-rattling tremors shaking her body were finally beginning to ease.

Thirty minutes passed before she stopped slurring her words. Another ten before she stopped shivering. When he asked how she was feeling now, she said only that her head still hurt and that she wanted badly to go to sleep.

Finally, still slowly rubbing her back, he let her.

Chapter Ten

Jack felt a distinct, prickling sensation in his arm. Flexing his hand, careful to not disturb Carrie, he glanced toward the fireplace.

He must have fallen asleep. Instead of a roaring fire, a few desultory flames flickered above the embers. Outside, the wind whipped around the cabin, whistling between the gaps in the storm windows and putting a decided chill in the room. He vaguely recalled having planned to close the shutters, but there was no way he was going out there now. He'd just add a few more logs to the fire.

Carrie hadn't moved. She still lay with her head tucked against him and her legs tangled with his. She was warm now, her breathing rhythmic.

He hated to get up. She felt good in his arms. Better than good, he thought, drawn by the downy softness of her skin. Beneath the thick covers, she felt smaller than he would have imagined, fragile, more delicate. Yet, he could never think of her as frail. Even if he hadn't known how relentlessly she could push herself, there was a supple strength to her long, fluid limbs that he found incredibly arousing.

He'd awakened hard. Now, he felt himself pulse against the scrap of lace covering her hip. It didn't help matters that he lay half over her. The position had originally been intended to give her more of his body heat. His intentions now weren't quite so clear. Where his hand curved around her ribs, he could feel the tantalizing fullness of her breast. He knew from one brief glimpse that her nipples were small and a shade of deep, dusky rose. All he'd have to do was move his thumb and he could acquaint himself with their texture.

Refusing to complicate their already uneasy alliance, he slipped his hand from her side. With his hand on the sofa back, he pulled himself up on his other elbow and started to ease his arm from under her head. She stirred, her brow furrowing slightly in her sleep. She still looked pale. The burnished hair fanning over his forearm and the dark crescents of her lashes contrasted starkly with her skin. But the frightening, waxy quality was gone from her cheeks and a blush of color had returned to her full mouth.

The furrows faded, but Jack didn't move. In her sleep, she reached for him, only to draw a quick breath and waken with a moan when her hand bumped his chest.

A quiet "ow" preceded the flutter of her lashes when her eyes opened.

He should have moved away then. Instead he caught her wrist and drew her hand from beneath the covers to see what had so rudely wakened her.

The first thing to pierce Carrie's consciousness was the stinging sensation in her fingers. Beyond that, particulars were a toss-up. She knew Jack's head hovered little more than a foot from hers and that he was scowling at her hand. She knew she could feel the weight and heat of his muscular legs tangled around her own. She remembered being lost and cold and, as mortification joined a host of less definable feelings, she remembered being sick in the bathroom. She just didn't want to believe any of it.

"I don't know if I should thank you, start apologizing or just bury my head under the covers."

Her quiet admission drew his glance from the small blisters on two of her fingers. "You don't have to bury your head. Just tell me if it still hurts."

His voice was a low rumble of demand, his dark expression inscrutable. He lay half over her, holding his weight on his elbow as if he'd been in the process of sliding his arm from beneath her head—or preparing to lean down and kiss her.

The thought jammed her heart against her ribs. They were already curled around each other like lovers, their bodies so intimately aligned she'd have to be comatose to not notice how aroused his body was.

Her throat felt as dry as dust. She swallowed, trying to reconcile the remoteness in his face with the intimacy of their position while she sorted through the various sensations wakening between her head and her toes. "It doesn't."

"Good." Arms flexing, he pushed himself up, his hairroughened legs slipping from around hers. "I'll get some gauze for your fingers."

Carrie didn't get a chance to ask why she needed gauze. When Jack rose, the bedding slipped from his broad shoulders, exposing her to the cooler air. In those same moments, his glance skimmed down her throat to the soft swells of her bare breasts. His glance darted back to hers, so shuttered that it almost belied the tension in his jaw when their hands collided pulling the blankets over her.

The single ceiling fixture in the kitchen cast the dim edges of its light into the room. The embers in the fireplace glowed bright orange. In that soft, peach-tinted light, she watched Jack turn from her. His low, white briefs molded his beautifully lean hips, and the powerful muscles in his thighs and back rippled when he scooped his discarded clothes from the floor. Moving past Felan sleeping on the hearth mat, he headed into the hall.

Carrie's breath shuddered out as she tucked the blanket around her neck and leaned into the corner of the sofa. It was part of the nightmare. It had to be. She'd been lying in Jack's arms, naked except for an eighth of a yard of lace, and he hadn't been able to get away from her fast enough.

It wasn't humiliation taunting her, although she figured she might as well add that to her mortification over the bathroom thing. What she felt was hurt—which made no sense at all because she already knew that he didn't want anything from her. It made no sense, either, that all she wanted just then was for him to come back and hold her again.

Closing her eyes, she rested her head on the back of the sofa. She was just a little overwhelmed at the moment. That was all. Between her bout with the snow and trying to cope with the bomb Mr. Hawthorne had dropped, rationality was bound to be skewed.

Her common sense might be shaky at the moment, but her other senses were working just fine. She had no trouble at all recognizing the tension that returned to the room with Jack. Feeling it curl around her like smoke, she kept her eyes closed and listened to the muffled sounds of his movements; the soft plop of something landing on the coffee table, the metallic groan of the fireplace doors when he opened them, the heavy thud of logs landing in the grate, the snap of flame meeting fresh fuel. Then, suddenly, the movements stopped and the sounds faded to silence.

Several seconds passed and still she didn't hear him move. The silence grew, taunting her, denying her the escape she'd sought by concentrating on what he was doing until, reluctantly, she opened her eyes.

Jack stood over her, his carved features shadowed. He hadn't bothered to snap the jeans he'd pulled on, or to button the flannel shirt exposing his chest. If his tight expression was any indication, he was interested only in doing what he felt he had to do for her, then getting himself to bed.

What she'd heard land on the coffee table was a pair of gray sweats and a handful of supplies from his medicine cabinet.

"What time is it?" she asked when he sat down by her knees.

"A little before two."

"In the morning?"

With a nod, he reached under the covers for her left hand. "It was probably around five o'clock when we got back here. It took a while for you to warm up, but I imagine you've...we've—" he corrected, frowning at the tips of her stinging fingers "—been asleep for six or seven hours."

Paper crackled as he tore the wrapper from a roll of inch-wide, white gauze. His touch far gentler than his tone, he turned her hand over and began wrapping the tip of her left index finger.

"You finally got yourself a case of frostbite," he told her, sounding as if he figured she'd do it sooner or later. "This isn't as bad as it could have been, but you don't want to break the blisters. Just keep it clean and dry. It should heal fine."

His dark head was bent, his manner a study in banked frustration while he tended the tip of her left middle finger and secured it with white paper tape. She now knew why he bought economy-size boxes and tubes of first-aid supplies. Between the splinters, blisters, cuts, pulled muscles and heaven knew what else a person experienced living in such a rugged place, he probably had to completely restock every spring. What had her attention, though, was how gentle he was, considering that he probably wanted to throttle her.

"I'm sorry you had to go to so much trouble for me." He'd gone from avoiding her to taking care of her. And taking care of her was not something he wanted to do. He'd made that clear in more ways than she could count. "The wind was blowing a little when I left, but it wasn't snowing that much."

For a moment, he said nothing. He just gave her a glance that seemed to say *I don't want to hear it* and picked up her right hand. Finding that one all right, he whipped the blankets from her lower legs, hesitating when he saw her cherry-colored toenails, and checked out her feet. His warm, strong hands would have felt wonderful had she not been so concerned with his tense silence. He was like a bomb with a hair-trigger trip wire and she had no idea what she might say or do that would set him off.

"Well, you're not going to lose any toes," he finally informed her, whipping the covers back over her feet. "But you sure as hell could have. I told you not to leave the area of the cabin."

"I didn't have a choice." Her voice matched his, just as quiet, just as tense. "I had to make that call."

"I know that. If you'd just waited awhile, you could have made it from here. I was out fixing the line."

She stared at him, incredulous. "How was I supposed to know that? It's not like you left me a note. You stopped telling me where you were going days ago."

He sat at her knees, his own spread wide and his hands on his thighs. The muscle in his jaw jerked when he looked from her. Being this close to her made it impossible for him to forget how she'd felt in his arms. Touching her, breathing her scent only added to the torture. His body still felt as tight as a stretched rubber band. Yet, physical need wasn't solely responsible for the frustration burning in his gut. Now that he knew she was all right, it was easier to be irritated than to admit how worried he'd been about her.

Some of that irritation leaked out in a long, slow breath. He was as much to blame as the weather for what had happened to Carrie. He'd been so hell-bent on making it clear that neither was responsible for or accountable to, the other, that he might as well have sent her out in that blizzard himself.

The weight of his own culpability only added to his tension. "So what happened? You never did say."

She'd expected defensiveness, not interest. Not up to an argument, anyway, and not sure her headache was gone after all, she backed down herself. "He said he was sorry about my predicament, but he needs a reporter now." Her tone dropped. "He's hiring someone else."

"That's it? He just slammed the door?"

The sick feeling in Carrie's stomach had nothing to do with an aching head or exposure to the elements. The peculiar sensation she experienced now was all too familiar. She felt it every time something happened that yanked her security out from under her. The feeling was a little like being in a free fall with her stomach in her throat and her arms flailing as she tried to grab hold of something to slow the descent into a void of unknowns.

The only thing she'd ever had to grab onto was herself.

"He gave me one option," she conceded, hugging herself beneath the blankets. "He said that maybe we could talk in the future...*if* I come up with a blockbuster of an exclusive or a potential Pulitzer. The way I see it, my chances of doing that stuck in the middle of the Rockies with a bunch of bison and hibernating bears is somewhere between zip and nil."

She sunk a little lower into the blankets. "So now I have

no job in Seattle and not a single prospect for one anywhere else. I'm going to lose the lease on my apartment, and my deposit," she added when that distressing thought piled in with the rest, "and everything I own with the exception of one suitcase and a plant is buried under fifty feet of snow."

"It's only four feet," he murmured.

"This is my pity party, Jack. Don't ruin it."

He knew that look. He'd seen it before. She was trying hard to keep him from knowing that she was close to tears. He'd even be willing to bet that, under the blankets, her arms were crossed tightly enough to cut off her circulation.

"You're tired. Maybe this'll be easier to deal with after you get some more sleep."

"I'm not tired. What I am is scared. And you know something?" she asked, her eyes pooling as they met his. "I'm really tired of feeling that way."

The admission was out before she could even think to question it. Hearing it, hating it, she started to shove back her wildly tousled hair with her unbandaged hand, but the blanket slipped, baring her shoulders, so she jerked it back up to hold at the base of her throat. "I need some clothes."

He held up the gray sweatshirt.

Freeing her other arm from beneath the blanket, she reached for it.

Jack didn't let go. The haunting vulnerability in her eyes hit him like a physical blow, provoking responses he couldn't seem to fight.

"For what it's worth," he said, protectiveness shifting inside him, "you don't have to be scared right now. Just take it all in moments. Right now, this minute, you truly don't need to be afraid. Okay?"

"Is that how you do it?" Her voice faltered. "Live in moments?"

"For some of us, it's all we can do."

He'd learned how to live in those fleeting increments of

time, to take what peace he could from the hour or the minute at hand because there would always be the next moment, when that peace could be gone. He didn't mention that, though. He wanted to make her feel better. Not worse.

Her hair tumbled against her cheeks when she looked down at their hands, his clutching one arm of the folded sweatshirt, hers, the hem. Neither seemed to want to let go. Or, maybe, he thought, neither wanted to break that marginal hold on the other.

"I'm not even sure what it is I'm afraid of," she whispered.

He had the feeling he knew what she feared. But suspecting that they shared something so difficult to conquer wasn't a matter he wanted to consider just then. "You need sleep."

Hesitating, she shook her head. "That's not what I need." The sweatshirt bunched when she tightened her grip. "Would you do me one favor?"

"Only as long as I don't have to go outside."

The corners of her mouth tried to curve, but the smile never formed. "You don't," she returned, her voice soft and uncertain. "I just wondered if you'd hold me. Just for a minute."

Jack knew her defenses were shot. They had to be, because she'd never ask such a thing of him otherwise. She needed solace. The reassurance of a pair of arms. She needed for him to make her feel not so alone.

The fact that she needed anything at all from him should have had him bolting. Instead, drawn by that same, long-buried need of his own, he gathered her to him, blankets and all, and silenced the voice inside that told him he had nothing to give her. He could give her this. It had been so long since he'd offered anyone comfort that he wasn't sure he remembered how, but it felt good to know he could make her feel a little better. He knew he had, too, when he heard her sigh against his chest.

She curved her arms around his back, trapping blankets between them.

"I only need this for a minute," she said, as if she suspected he was acting under duress. "Just fifty-nine more seconds."

He smiled into her hair, then nudged her chin up. "No one's counting," he whispered, and touched his mouth to hers.

Jack's words shimmered at the edge of Carrie's consciousness. She hadn't expected his kiss, but it was as gentle as his touch, the sweetness of it almost more than she could bear. It was a kiss meant to console, to ease. And it did. The awful sensation in her stomach began to fade. So did the odd, bereft feeling that always came with it when he touched his lips to her temple, then pressed her head to his shoulder.

She would truly hate the moment when he would pull back from her. She'd only felt safe twice in her life since she was eight years old. When Jack had protected her from Felan, and when he'd lifted her out of the snow. What she felt in his arms now wasn't safety at all. The ache inside her was more like need. But she'd hate the moment he left her anyway. She didn't know when it had happened. Not precisely. But somewhere along the line, she'd fallen completely, unwisely and undeniably in love with him. He'd told her she knew nothing about him. But he was so wrong. She knew he was an inherently generous man who went out of his way to conceal that generosity. He was a man with a huge heart, yet he didn't want to let on that anything mattered to him. It was almost as if he couldn't allow anything to matter, and she found that so terribly sad. For both of them.

Through the blanket, she could feel the soothing motions

of his hand rubbing her back. The motions had slowed, though. Now, they stopped. Thinking he was about to let her go, she reluctantly lifted her head from where he'd held it at the side of his neck. As she did, their cheeks brushed and her lips grazed the side of his mouth.

He froze. So did she.

They were a scant, quarter-inch apart when she heard him pull a deep breath. He breathed out, warmth feathering over her skin.

"Carrie," he whispered, his voice a warning. "I'll hold you. But if I kiss you again, I won't want to stop."

"You said you didn't want to get involved."

"Yeah. Well, I'd say we already are."

"Jack?"

He hesitated, muscles tensed. "What?"

She truly had just wanted him to hold her. But that was before his grudging admissions gave birth to hope. It wasn't that he didn't want her. He didn't want to want her. The difference was huge.

"You don't have to stop."

For a moment, Jack did nothing. He just held her there with the blankets caught between their bodies and the temptation of that kiss hanging between them, until he slowly slid his hands to her shoulders and edged her back.

The awful knowledge that he'd pushed her away had her lowering her head. He tipped her chin right back up.

The chiseled lines of his face had gone taut. The intense blue of his eyes seemed to burn into her, through her, when their glances locked. Behind him, the fire flickered and danced. Outside the sturdy cabin walls, the glacial wind blew with the same ferocity it had for hours. She'd recognized those same elements in him before. The power. The ice. The fire.

Something feral washed over his expression. But he said nothing. His gaze never left her face as he eased her back down on the sofa's cushions. Her heart scrambling in her chest, she watched him lean toward her. Gathering the satin edge of the blanket from where she held it against her throat, he pulled it down to her waist as his mouth settled on hers.

The contrast of his hot mouth and the cool air on her body shocked her senses. The pressure of his lips increased, coaxing her to admit him more deeply. There was no gentleness in his kiss this time. No mistaking it for comfort or an experimental foray.

His work-roughened hand skimmed her ribs, moved gently, possessively over her breast. Slipping her arms around his neck, she cradled the back of his head to bring him closer. She wanted him next to her, to feel him holding her the way he had before. She told him that, too, and tugged his shirt over his shoulders as best she could with two fingers wrapped and stinging.

She'd forgotten all about that discomfort until that moment, and promptly forgot it the next. Jack stripped off his shirt, then sat as still as stone as she hesitantly touched the sculpted muscles of his chest, stroked her fingertips over his roped shoulders and arms. The heat in his eyes made her touch bolder and she pressed a kiss to the hard, steady pulse at the base of his throat.

"You're beautiful." She whispered the words, speaking of something far deeper than what she could see.

"And you're driving me crazy," he murmured in return.

He nudged her back down, drinking her soft gasp when he skimmed his hand over the back of her thigh. He had felt the scars before, knew what they were. Pushing the blankets aside, he angled her long, slender leg to expose the marks, and winced at the thought of how deep the wounds must have been. With more tenderness than he knew he possessed, he brushed his lips over the faintly puckered, white lines marring her silken skin, then traced a path of moist kisses over her hip to her belly. Hooking one finger under the narrow strip of pink satin and lace, he stripped her underpants down her legs and dropped them on his shirt.

The air whispered from Carrie's lungs at what Jack had done. But before she could reach for him, he covered her and reached for his zipper.

He peeled off denim and briefs, then the cushions gave beneath his weight and he was under the blankets with her. He gathered her to him, their bodies automatically twining as they had done before. She couldn't believe how natural it seemed to let him tuck her beneath him, or how uninhibited she felt meeting his hungry mouth. Her body craved his, sought it by straining closer. Loving Jack felt right, necessary in some way she couldn't yet define. With her senses swimming, she couldn't even begin to try.

What rationality she possessed had vaporized with his touch. His hands were everywhere, tracing, shaping, teasing. He taunted her with deep kisses, then soothed her with little nips as soft as the brush of a butterfly's wing. He carried those debilitating caresses down her throat while he traced the shape of her breast with his fingers, moving in circles toward the tightening bud so slowly she thought she'd die before he brushed his thumb over it. A heartbeat later, his mouth closed over her nipple and her senses nearly shattered.

Jack made a low, deep sound as she swelled against his tongue. The feel of her responses to him was nearly more than he could bear. She was so exquisitely sensitive to his touch, so artless in her desire to touch him as he did her. He could feel her trembling, taste her need. Soft shivers skimmed through her as she arched against him, inviting him closer, offering whatever he cared to take. He took what she offered, then demanded more. He would never get enough of her.

He knew he wouldn't last ten seconds once he was inside her. It had been too long and his need for her was too great. That was why he made himself wait while he wrung little moans from her with his mouth and his tongue, and tortured himself with the feel of her strong, supple body until he could wait no longer.

He eased back up, raising himself on his elbow. "Open your eyes," he whispered, his voice a rough rasp.

She looked up at him, touching his cheek, her eyes languid and her mouth damp and swollen from his kisses.

Slipping his hand beneath her, he settled himself in the cradle of her hips. He entered her slowly, watching her eyes darken as her body stretched to admit him. He gritted his teeth as her heat enveloped him, the storm outside echoing the one that had built within.

His name was a soft whimper on her lips when she sought his mouth; hers was a guttural groan that came from the depths of someplace long lost and nearly forgotten. Then, thoughts scattered, consciousness narrowed, and he drove her with him until she was gasping and he lay spent with her arms locked around his back.

Jack didn't know which one of them wakened first. Or even if they'd truly slept. Their breathing had quieted long ago, but he heard Carrie's quicken at the feel of his hand skimming her body. She reached for him as he reached for her, need growing so swiftly it should have frightened him. But he allowed himself no thought other than of her and scooped her into his arms.

He had no patience for the confines of the sofa, so he carried her to her bed, and there, in the dark, he took the time the frantic demands of his body had denied them before. This time, when they came together, it wasn't in frenzied desire. This time, long, easy caresses and tender explorations built to a slow burning heat that turned white-hot, seeming to fuse their souls, and left him tired, sated and oddly at peace.

In that peace, he lay holding her long after she'd fallen asleep in his arms, savoring what they'd shared. Tired as he was, he couldn't sleep. He knew what he had with her wouldn't last. It couldn't. So he wanted to relish it, forge the moments in his memory so he could remember the feel of that ephemeral calm after she was gone. That he might need her was something he couldn't let himself consider. So he just reminded himself that she would be gone soon; that she had a life away from there. Somewhere. This life was all he had. But right now, at this moment, he wanted nothing else.

Carrie wasn't sure what woke her. The thud against the wall. The pale light filtering through the window. Or the fact that Jack wasn't in her bed. She could hear him moving around in his room.

With her body aching in different places for different reasons, she stifled a groan and pulled on the old football jersey she'd won in an office pool. Her intention was to head straight for the bathroom, but when she stepped out into the hall, she saw Felan standing by his master's closed door.

The anxious feeling she'd wakened with had mostly to do with Jack and the possible consequences of what they'd done. She wasn't at all certain how he'd react to her this morning, either. The hesitation she experienced now, however, had to do with the dog watching her step toward him. She wasn't quite sure what Felan would do as she slowly held out her hand.

With a lazy wag of his bushy gray tail, the big dog promptly padded over and licked her fingers.

"Hey," she whispered, remembering the only other time she'd felt that warm, wet tongue. Relieved by the dog's reaction, pleased by her own, she gingerly touched one pointed gray ear. When he didn't move, she got a little bolder and stroked his head. His fur wasn't nearly as soft as it looked. "I think I owe you, big guy. Thanks." She stroked his coarse hair once more. "Ever thought of using cream rinse?"

The dog edged forward, shamelessly seeking more of a pet than she was giving him. But before he could get insistent about it, he heard his master's footfall. Ears cocked, he promptly wheeled around and returned to Jack's door.

Carrie was shoving her hair out of her eyes when she heard that door open. Jack, fully dressed, stepped out.

He hesitated the moment he saw her.

Feeling uncertainty snag in her chest, she offered a quiet, "Hi."

"Hi, yourself," he returned over the click of the closing door. "I'm just on my way out to shovel snow." Big and solid as an oak, he slowly walked toward her. As he did, his glance skimmed her face, his expression filled with a sort of tension she couldn't quite discern. "I don't think we got much new yesterday, but the wind sure rearranged what we had. The north windows are completely covered."

"Give me a few minutes and I'll help."

"No."

The flatness of his tone nearly stopped her heart. The touch of his fingers to her cheek, jerked it back to life again.

"You don't want to risk refreezing your fingers," he explained, skimming his knuckles along her jaw. "I'll be back in by the time you've showered."

He hesitated, suddenly looking uneasy. "There's something we didn't think about last night. Something we didn't talk about. I completely spaced it," he admitted, sounding almost as guilty as he did worried. His hand fell from her face. "I don't suppose you're on birth control, are you?"

She didn't know what it said for her priorities that she

should feel as relieved as she did just then. Her greatest fear had been that he would pull back from her again, but she felt none of the distance he was so good at creating. As long as he didn't regret what had happened between them, she could handle anything. Almost.

She'd suffered the same realization he had, about two seconds after she woke up. "It's been a long time since I've had a need for it. And this…" She shook her head, threading her fingers through her hair in subtle agitation. "I didn't think anything like this would ever happen. I'm not…I mean, I don't usually…ever—"

"Me, too," he agreed, looking very much as if he'd expected to hear her say pretty much what she just had. "I don't have anything for us to use, either, Carrie. Is this a bad time of the month for you?"

"Next week would have been worse."

There was no mistaking the relief in his expression. It washed over him like warm rain, easing the tightness in his features, relaxing the tension in his shoulders. He curved his hand over the back of her neck. "Then, we'll have to be very careful next week," he told her, and brushed his lips over hers.

The implication in his husky words jolted her with the same heat as his kiss when, seconds later, he pulled her into his arms. It seemed he had no intention of keeping his distance anymore. His hand swept down her back, drawing her to him, reminding her of just how very close they'd been, of how close he wanted to be.

"Hold that thought," he murmured, and left her leaning against the wall when he and Felan finally headed out.

Carrie felt dazed. She should have been sick with worry. She'd lost her job. She was still stuck. She didn't even know where she would go if she weren't. Yet, instead of the panic that should have had her pacing the walls, what she felt was a totally inexplicable combination of anticipation and...calm.

That oddly contented feeling stayed with her as the day faded into evening, and one day flowed into the next. She and Jack talked only of what immediately affected them, of what needed to be done, of the animals and the land, since both were affected by them, too. Because the wind had torn off a shutter, she helped him repair that, and she helped him clean up the mess at the lodge made by a tree branch the wind had tossed through a window, a task that took two days because of the amount of snow that had blown into the room. Sometimes she stayed at the cabin, tending it, mending the torn curtains Jack had taken down. Sometimes Jack stayed in all day with her, making love with her by the fire, carrying her off to her bed. Those were the moments she experienced the greatest contentment of all; whenever he held her, loved her. Living in moments, the way Jack did, she could have gone on forever. But forever only lasted a little over a week. That was when reality slithered through the calm.

The snowplow was coming through.

Carrie heard the steady drone of the plow's engine for hours before the dingy yellow vehicle appeared at the bend in the road. The moment she'd realized what it was, she'd felt dread freeze like a lump of ice in her stomach.

"I'll go talk to the driver" was all Jack had said before he'd taken off an hour ago. Now, hearing the muffled roar of his snowmobile returning from the highway, she stopped pacing, turned to the window by the long, pine table and made herself take deep breaths as he arced the big, silvery gray machine toward the garage.

Not a single cloud marked the crystalline blue sky. The snow sparkled a brilliant, almost blinding white. It had only been the past two days that the sun had come out and the views beyond the cabin seemed to shimmer in the cold, clear air. When she heard him cut the engine, she almost considered praying for a blizzard.

A full minute passed before she heard the porch door open and the stamp of his heavy boots on the planks. Seconds later, Jack stood in the kitchen doorway, his momentum stalled when he found her standing there.

His face was raw from the cold, his carved features molded into an unreadable mask.

"He's coming from the junction," he said, hanging his hat on the peg. "The road's been clear from there to Jackson off and on for the past few days. He's hoping to get to the milepost just beyond here before he finishes today. If it stays clear, he'll get to Moose Creek tomorrow."

"What about south of Jackson?"

"It's clear to the Interstate."

The lump in her stomach grew. Once the plow made it past her car, she was free to leave.

Jack knew that as well as she did.

"Do you know where you're going?"

He asked the question simply, his own desires completely veiled. She couldn't begin to guess what was going on behind those piercing blue eyes.

She knew she should have given some thought to her situation. At the very least, she should have considered how seriously unsettled it was. But she hadn't *felt* unsettled, and she'd needed the respite he'd offered too much to give any thought to her situation at all. She hadn't even been conscious of how desperately she'd needed that break until now. For over a week she hadn't struggled with worry. For over a week, she'd simply lost herself in the peace she'd found in Jack's world.

"No," she admitted, wishing he would touch her. The bond between them was too new, too fragile, to be tested this soon. "I haven't."

Jack watched uncertainty cloud her delicate features. He didn't think she had. She'd have mentioned it. And he hadn't brought up the matter of her finding another job himself because he didn't want to think about her leaving. As long as the road had been closed, he hadn't questioned the turn their relationship had taken. He'd made it clear from the beginning that he'd offer no promises, and she had accepted him on his terms. But what had seemed so cut-and-dried in his mind didn't feel that way in his heart and he was having a harder time every day divorcing the two. His physical desire for her had become all mixed up with a dangerous sense of need, and he didn't trust the combination at all.

"Do you have any ideas?" he asked.

She looked as guarded as he felt. "When I was looking before, I heard about a position opening after the first of the year in Portland. There are a couple of papers there I'll call."

"You want a big-city paper. Right?"

The sunlight pouring through the window caused her hair to shimmer when she gave a tense nod.

"What about Denver? That's only a day's drive south. Did you try there?"

He was trying to help. Carrie knew that. She would even have appreciated it, had it not been becoming apparent that her leaving wasn't going to make that much difference to him. "Not yet," she replied, crossing her arms over the sinking sensation in her stomach. "But I will."

The firm line of his mouth thinned. Taking a step closer, he lifted his hand and tucked her hair behind her ear.

"Make whatever calls you need and figure out what you're going to do."

He sifted his fingers through her hair, needing to memorize its texture, its shine. Having come to know her so well was only going to make it that much more difficult when she left. But he wouldn't ask her to stay. He couldn't. She really didn't know him. Even if she had, there was nothing for her here.

He let his hand fall and slipped it into his pocket. He wouldn't ask her to stay. But he knew she had no money to spare, and he could hardly turn her out with nothing. "You don't have to go anywhere until you've got something lined up."

Turning from the question in her eyes, he pulled his guard around him like a shroud, quietly damning himself for having let it down. "I'm going to the lodge to cut cornices."

"Jack?"

"Yeah?"

Carrie hesitated. She should have felt relief. And she did. It was somewhere beneath her confusion over the ambivalence in his eyes when he'd touched her. She wanted to thank him, to put her arms around him, to tell him she'd go with him and help if he wanted her to. Seeing his shuttered expression, all she said was, "Be careful."

He told her he would, then added that he'd be back by dark. She knew he had work to do, that he wasn't using the chore as an excuse to avoid her. What mattered was that he hadn't suggested that it was time for her to go. Still, despite his offer for her to stay, she couldn't help the uneasiness that swept through her. The ambivalence she'd sensed in Jack only fueled her own. Every call she would make to find a job held the potential for taking her away from him, but his suggestion that she make her calls told her that was what he wanted anyway. He hadn't asked her to wait.

That disquiet was still there when he returned that evening, cold, tired and hungry. While they ate, she told him of the calls she'd made to Portland, and of how little encouragement she'd received. He stroked the back of her

hand while she spoke, then told her he was sure she'd find
something and pulled back as if he hadn't meant to get that
close. She asked him what was wrong when he did that,
because his eyes had turned so bleak, but he said only that
he was tired, and headed for the sofa to pull off his boots.

She didn't doubt his fatigue. He looked exhausted from
the work he'd done that day. He didn't even stay awake
long enough for her to finish the dishes. They usually
stretched out on the sofa to watch the fire together, then,
eventually made their way to her bed. But he truly was
exhausted and, since she didn't want to disturb his hard-
earned sleep, she covered him up and went to bed alone.

Jack worked himself to near exhaustion the next day, too.
And the day after that. Carrie helped him when she could,
but after three days of watching him pull farther away, she
thought it would be easier on them both if she stayed at
the cabin and tended to her chores there. She had an errand
to run, anyway. Two agencies she'd called had asked for
her credentials, so Jack had helped her dig her car and
trailer out of the snowbank and she'd dug her résumé out
of her trunk. Now, she needed to get them to the post office
in Moose Creek, since the road was open and Moose Creek
was closest. Jack had said he'd be back for lunch, so she
would ask him to unhook her trailer for her when he returned. That way she wouldn't have to pull it all the way
to town and back.

Waiting for Jack, she finished the wash. His, hers and a
load of towels. When he'd handed her his laundry basket
after she'd asked for it, he'd told her to just leave his clean
clothes on his bed. So, with his shirts on hangers and everything else folded and back in the brown plastic laundry
basket, she opened his door and glanced from an oak armoire to the boxes stacked in the corners of the pale green
room. His bed was a mess.

It looked as if he'd done battle with the bedding and the

bedding had lost. Resisting the urge to straighten the blankets, wondering why his sleep was so restless when he hardly moved at all holding her, she set the basket on the tangled blue blankets. A paperback technothriller lay facedown on his nightstand, hanging half-off the edge as if he'd groped for the surface and barely made it. Next to it was a digital clock, a pine cone, a handful of assorted nuts and bolts.

She would have thought that here, in his most private space, he would surely have indulged some connection to a past. Wondering at the lack of pictures or mementos, wishing she understood what it was that kept him from her, she opened his closet to hang his shirts.

She'd thought it was a closet, anyway. As she stared at a computer sitting on a gray metal file cabinet, it looked more like storage—until she noticed charts of various stocks tacked to the wall behind them and an open box of files on the cabinet next to a printer. The files all bore the name Pineridge Lumber.

Pineridge, she thought, feeling the same tug of familiarity she experienced sometimes when she looked at Jack. But just as she started to wonder why that familiarity was there, she knew. And she knew who Jack was.

She'd seen pictures of him. In the newspaper. On television. His hair had been short then, the cut as conservative and trim as the mustache he'd worn. She remembered him mostly as being in a suit. In front of a courthouse.

Certainty suddenly vied with disbelief. Pineridge Lumber had been in the news when its two partners had been indicted for embezzling their employees' pension funds. The story had gone national when the mill went into bankruptcy during the trial and half the community had been left without work. It was inconceivable to her that the man she knew would steal from anyone. Yet, Jackson Holt Parker had been one of those partners.

She still clutched Jack's shirts in her hand when she started to close the closet door, only to hesitate once more. She remembered something else, too. Something that had kept the Pineridge story alive long after it should have ceased to be news. About a year ago, former employees of the mill began receiving cashier's checks in the exact amount of their pension contributions. No one had a clue where the money came from.

"I told you to leave my clothes on the bed."

Chapter Eleven

Jack's big frame filled the doorway. His chiseled face was ruddy from riding in the cold air, and he'd pulled the leather thong from his ponytail, leaving his dark hair flowing over the collar of his heavy denim shirt. As he stepped into the room, his cool blue gaze slid from the computer to Carrie and pinned her like a moth to a wall.

"What are you doing?"

The demand was almost too quiet, too controlled.

"I just wanted to hang these." She'd done nothing wrong. Still, feeling caught, she slipped the hangers over a knob on the armoire, shaking her head. "I thought that was your closet."

"It's not."

"I can see that now." Hesitant, concerned, she glanced behind her. "What is all…this?"

There was no mistaking his caution as he weighed what he wanted to tell her against what she might have already

surmised. It had only taken seconds for her to realize that
he played the stock market. That explained the charts on
the wall, and the sounds she heard so early in the mornings,
the opening and closing of the closet door to get to the
computer. It explained the books on his shelves. It did not
explain why he was so secretive about it.

Defensiveness sunk its claws deep. "I use the computer
to contact my broker. Okay? Now, when did you want to
leave for Moose Creek?"

"Not until you tell me what's going on," she said quietly. She wasn't going to let him change the subject. Not
now. She cared too much. Needed too badly to understand
what he'd done. What he was doing. "I've heard about
Pineridge, Jack. About what happened at the lumber mill
there." There was no accusation in her tone. No hint of
conclusion. "You were one of the partners."

For a moment, he said nothing. He just stood as silent
as the room itself, a vein in his temple throbbing with the
clench of his jaw. She'd wanted to know what lay at the
root of his bitterness. She had the feeling she was about to
find out. As the seconds ticked by, she could almost see
him pulling into that anger, cloaking himself in it. She
hated what the emotions did to him, and what it did to her
to see their effect. What bothered her more was that he
hadn't trusted her enough to share something so important.

The tension in his jaw made his voice tight. "Do you
think I took the money?"

"Does it matter?" she quietly returned.

Carrie immediately regretted the hurt-caused challenge.
With his past lying like a minefield between them, they had
enough to deal with at the moment. "I can't believe it of
the man I know," she stated, hating that he'd left room for
doubt. "Tell me what happened, Jack. Please?" She'd in-
stinctively trusted him from the beginning. Her instincts
needed to trust him now. "Where's your partner?"

He snorted, derision leaking from every pore. "I imagine Bill is with my accountant on a sunny beach somewhere sucking down the local suds."

"Your accountant?"

"Yeah," he muttered. "My accountant. They managed to disappear with everyone's nest egg just before the Feds came pounding on the door."

Confusion swept her features. "If they took the money, why were you indicted?"

"Because I authorized the withdrawals," Jack replied flatly, hating the feelings roiling in his gut. "My signature was on all the forms."

He truly didn't want to go into this. He didn't want to think about all those months of trying to get the authorities to listen to him while everything he'd worked for slowly fell apart. That much he'd managed to put behind him. "Let this go, will you? There's nothing here that concerns anyone but me and the people who got screwed out of their pensions."

"It concerns *me*," she insisted, grabbing his arm when he reached past her to close the closet door. For her own sake, she needed to know why he wasn't defending himself. He looked guilty. He sounded guilty. Refusing to talk to her, he even acted guilty. "Why did you authorize them to take the money?"

"I didn't know I was doing it," he snapped back, shaking off her hand. "Okay?"

"No. It's not okay. How could you not know something like that?"

The question did what the others had not. His tightly held control snapped, guilt surging forth, sharp and stinging.

"Because half the time I didn't read what my partner gave me to sign." He ground out the admission, his voice as hard as his expression. "Because I was always too busy out in the mill when he'd bring me something for signature

and I'd take his word for what was on the pages. It was
the same with the accountant. I believed the numbers she
showed me because my partner was sitting right there and
I never dreamed the two of them had worked up two sets
of books. I paid her good money to keep our records
straight and I thought I was getting what I paid for. What
I was getting was the royal shaft, but it was my own damn
fault.''

"It wasn't your fault. They set—''

"It *was*,'' he insisted, refusing to let her forgive what he
could not forgive himself. "I trusted the wrong people and
that caused me to fail the people who'd trusted me. Do you
know how many people I let down?'' he demanded, the
roots of his culpability suddenly exposed for her to see.
"Do you know how many people lost their jobs because
of me?

"Two hundred and twenty-seven,'' he spat out, neither
wanting nor expecting a response. "That's two hundred and
twenty-seven families that suddenly had to worry about
how to make their mortgage payments and how to feed
their kids. I was spending so much time with my lawyer
trying to figure out what other money was missing and
being hauled back and forth to Olympia for hearings that
business started dropping off. When that happened, I had
to put our house up for sale to pay the mill's suppliers, but
I couldn't get enough out of it to do any good and the
creditors put the mill into bankruptcy. The company that
bought it didn't keep it open. It sold the equipment off and
shut it down. Pineridge didn't have a lot of extra jobs, so
half my employees had to move. That meant leaving their
friends, their families.''

The town's losses were tremendous. An entire economy
had been demolished and the structure of people's lives
drastically altered. But Carrie had the awful suspicion that
the scope of Jack's losses was only beginning to form.

"What about your friends?" she asked, already knowing she would hate his answer. "And your wife?"

He turned from her, jamming his hands through his hair. When he let his hands fall, the look haunting his face was as bleak as winter rain.

"Once word got out that I'd authorized the withdrawals and things started falling apart for everybody, it didn't matter whether I'd signed on purpose or through carelessness. Since most of my friends lost their jobs, they found it a little hard to be sympathetic. As for Shelby," he muttered, speaking of his wife, "she couldn't handle the embarrassment or the pressure. She left long before the charges were dropped."

He'd said the demise of his marriage had been his own fault. Knowing now how ruthlessly he judged himself, Carrie wasn't inclined to accept the statement as totally true. She didn't doubt for a moment that the stresses had taken their toll on everyone, but he had suffered in ways she'd never suspected. He had been abandoned by his wife and his friends, and betrayed by his partner and his accountant. And he'd yet to do anything but blame himself.

"What about after the charges were dropped?"

"What about it? The damage had been done by then. The mill was closed. People were moving out. I was broke, and my life had been torn apart and spilled over the front pages of more newspapers than I care to consider."

There was nothing Carrie could say to defend her profession. Nothing she would say, just then. Over the course of the investigation, Jack had lost everything he'd ever worked for. His wife, his business, his home, his reputation. He was entitled to feel a little resentment toward those who'd undoubtedly escalated the process.

It was his harshness toward himself that concerned her.

"Don't you think all that was punishment enough?" she asked, wondering if he even realized how severely he'd sentenced himself for his mistake. He'd locked himself away in the wilderness as surely as if he'd been locked away in a prison. The only difference was that here, the walls weren't visible. "It's not as if you intended to do those people any harm. There's a huge difference between negligence and intent. Those other two deliberately set out to steal. You never took anything."

"But the result was the same," he shot back, his agitation refueled by frustration with her compassion. "And I'm not punishing myself. I'm protecting myself. It's like you and big dogs, Carrie. You don't trust any of them because one turned on you. But the difference between you and me is that you think you should be over the incident by now, and I think some lessons are meant to be remembered.

"I trusted the wrong people and I failed people who'd trusted me. I'm afraid to believe in anyone enough to let them affect any decision I make, or to put myself in a position where I can let somebody down. I won't let myself care. I don't think I even remember how."

He spoke with quiet vehemence, his words as much a warning as a statement. They found their mark, too, right in the middle of her heart.

Aching for him, hurting for herself, she curved her hand over his arm. "But you do care," she quietly insisted. "You wouldn't be making up what your employees lost if you didn't. Why don't you want anyone to know you're doing that?" It was such an honorable thing. Something few men would be noble enough, generous enough, to do.

"I'm not doing it because I care. I'm doing it to salve my conscience."

"Your conscience wouldn't be bothering you if you didn't—"

"You don't get it, do you?" He stepped back, holding his hands up as if he didn't know whether to fend her off or shake her. "The last thing I want is to have my life turned upside down by someone trying to figure out where the money is coming from. The embezzled funds still haven't been accounted for and I know of too many zealots in the D.A.'s office and in the press who'd be more than happy to believe I have part of them stashed away somewhere. I invest my salary because I don't need much to live on here, but I wouldn't put it past anyone to think I'm using those people's own money to pay them back. The digging would just start all over again if anyone found out.

"I couldn't stand that," he pronounced, edging back from her. "I'm sick of being investigated and questioned, and I sure as hell don't want to be the main topic of conversation ever again. I came here because I wanted to get away from people pointing fingers and speculating behind my back. When I go into Moose Creek, no one knows who I am."

At least, they hadn't known who he was. As Jack watched the furrows deepen in Carrie's brow, he could swear he could see the story forming in her mind. *I'm always looking for a story,* she'd said, and the sick feeling gnawing at him escalated.

So many people had turned their backs on him, that one more shouldn't make a difference. But it did. It mattered more than he would have believed—which was why his battered sense of self-protection had him lashing out before she could prove she was just as disloyal and self-serving as the rest of the people he'd once believed he could count on.

"I should have had you leave when the road opened," he said in a voice as cold as the air beyond the window. "The guy in Seattle said he'd give you a shot if you brought him an exclusive. You've got your story. Go get your job."

Carrie's sharp intake of breath was the only sound in the room before Jack turned and walked out the door. Stung beyond belief, she stood stunned as his angry footfall faded and she heard the jolting slam of the back door. Not for a fraction of an instant had it occurred to her to destroy the little bit of peace he had found here for himself. She'd confided in him, opened her heart to him, slept with him. Yet, he hadn't hesitated to believe that she would betray him just like everyone else.

Carrie didn't know how long she stood there in the deafening silence. She couldn't seem to move. Or to think. She was aware only of the free-fall sensation she knew only too well. Only this time, there was more to the feeling than just the bottom falling out of her world again. This time, she could also feel the ache of a breaking heart.

It was numb, that feeling. Almost protectively so. And when she realized that she'd been standing there long enough for the sun to shift the patterns of shadow in the room, she prayed the numbness would stay with her while she gathered the few things that were hers and carried them into the sunshine and out to her car. She had no idea where Jack had gone. She thought she'd heard him leave on the snowmobile, but she couldn't be absolutely sure. She wasn't sure of anything just then—except that he wanted her to leave. She didn't even know where she would go. Or what she would do when she got there.

Present

The cabin hadn't changed. The natural branch chairs Jack had made still sat in the deep snow that drifted over the porch. The bars that some previous winter-keeper had put up to keep out a marauding grizzly still braced the left window. And Carrie could still feel the same heavy sensation in her chest that had made it so hard to breathe when she'd been told to leave three months ago.

Since the snow had long since blocked the front door,

she headed for the other one. For the lost child's sake, she hoped Jack was home. For her own sake, she rather hoped she could just leave the note requesting his help and go.

That hope was dashed by a deep, ferocious bark as a flash of mottled gray darted from the garage.

Carrie wheeled around, her heart thudding as instinct shot past logic. But even before she could tell herself to not panic, the dog bearing down on her recognized her face and the threat instantly vanished.

She had her hands buried in Felan's coarse ruff and was trying to avoid having her face bathed when she felt the pull of enigmatic blue eyes. Jack was watching her. She could feel him. As if drawn by the sheer force of his presence, she straightened to see him standing just inside the garage.

His face was shadowed by the brim of his battered black Stetson and his coat hung open despite the frigid air. She had no idea what thoughts raced through his mind in the scattered seconds they stood there watching each other over the stretch of snow separating them. She wasn't even sure she formed a coherent thought of her own until she saw his glance cut toward the highway. Instead of her car parked at the end of the long, snowed-in driveway he saw the sheriff's white Jeep. The sheriff himself was out of the vehicle, pointing toward the cabin while he talked to the driver of a truck trailering two snowmobiles.

Jack's features turned as hard as the ice coating the eaves.

"You brought the sheriff?"

The accusation in his gruff voice sliced through her, reopening the wounds he'd inflicted with surgical precision. She remembered his being certain that he'd be investigated again if anyone knew he was the one sending checks to the old Pineridge employees. As she crossed her arms protectively around herself and the fragile little life inside her, it was abundantly clear he believed her interest in his story had led the authorities to serve him with another warrant. Given the fact that she was with the sheriff and that Jack so obviously expected betrayal, she could see where he might have leapt to that conclusion.

"A child is lost," she said, cutting to the heart of the matter before he could do any more damage to hers. "I told the sheriff about Felan. About how he led you to me in the blizzard. They're looking in the area down by the south ridge," she went on, desperately anxious to be out of there. "The little boy's been missing since this morning and it's only a couple of hours until dark. I understand he and his father have been camping for a couple of days and they've made so many tracks to and from the campsite that the dad can't tell which way his son went. Will you help?"

Her reason for being there caught him as off guard as her simple request. From the quick slash of his dark eyebrows, it was apparent that he now realized her presence was not as easily explained as he'd thought. But the urgency of the situation took precedence over that bit of guarded confusion. Beneath the shield of distrust, the caring nature he'd had so little luck killing worked its way past reluctance.

"If a kid's missing, yeah, sure I will." He allowed himself a step closer, his glance questioning as it moved from her white knit hat to where her arms were crossed at the waist of her long, white jacket. "They're searching the ridge?"

Carrie's hold tightened. "Apparently he and his father were camping below it. They're setting up a command post for volunteers just around the bend."

"I don't know how Felan will do with a lot of other people around. I'd better get a rope for a leash."

The lines fanning from the corners of his eyes were deeper, those at the sides of his mouth more prominently carved than she remembered them being. He looked tired and drawn and, as he started to turn away, the tension stretching between them drew so tight she thought it might snap.

"Where will you be?" he asked, glancing back over his shoulder.

"At the command post."

"I'll see you there."

The command post was nothing more than a place along the snow-packed road where a half-dozen volunteers had parked their vehicles. Little Dustin Raynes's father had already returned from his frantic drive for help and stood near the hood of a rusted, red truck surrounded by the small knot of parka-and-stocking-cap-clad volunteers. The worry etched in his young face identified him immediately as he pointed to a map held by a woman in a school-bus yellow snowsuit. Three snowmobiles were already on the snow-pack above the road, aimed like bullets toward the slope leading to the base of the ridge.

When Carrie joined the others gathered around Mr. Raynes, she could hear another of the powerful, efficient machines roaring toward them. Moments later, Jack pulled his slate gray snowmobile to a stop behind the Jeep. He deliberately stayed back, his attention on Felan as he spoke to the big gray-and-brown animal. Carrie didn't doubt for a moment that the dog hated being leashed, and he was clearly agitated by all the people. Snagging the sheriff's attention so she could introduce him to Jack, she felt a little agitated herself.

Jack had the growling animal by its collar and the free end of the thin, beige rope coiled in his other hand when she and the sheriff broke from the others. Behind her some of the conversation stopped, interest shifting to the big man with the wild-looking wolf-dog standing as rugged and still

as the craggy mountains. She wasn't sure who was giving
whom the more thorough once-over, but there was no denying the veiled assessments taking place between the
males as Jack and the rangy, rawboned sheriff closed ranks.

In the time it took Sheriff Evans to grip Jack's hand and
back away from his amber-eyed dog, he'd taken in his size,
his stance and the ponytail hanging over his sheepskin collar. Living in northwestern Wyoming, he'd no doubt seen
his share of self-styled individuals. He seemed to be one
himself. If his easy acceptance was any indication, he simply regarded Jack as one of the more reclusive ones when
he told him he was grateful for his willingness to help a
stranger, then relayed what he'd learned from the boy's
father so far. He then told him he planned to break everyone up into teams.

Because Felan didn't tend to work or play well with others, Jack wanted to search on his own, an approach the
sheriff wholeheartedly endorsed since the dog was still
practicing his guttural growls. Knowing Jack would need
something with the child's scent, Carrie told him she'd send
the boy's father over, then stayed with the others while an
anxious Mr. Raynes talked with him and the sheriff.

Six months ago, Carrie knew she would have been right
there with them, her tape recorder in their faces so she
wouldn't miss a word the distressed Mr. Raynes uttered.
She would have wanted to know what the sheriff's strategy
was, and how often something like this happened outside
a little town where not much seemed to happen at all. Now,
she knew she would write her story from what she heard
and observed and that would just have to be good enough.
With Jack part of the search, with a little boy out there all
alone, her professional edge turned as dull as a knife handle. Her only interests were in having someone find the
child, then in going home to the tiny room she "rented"
at Flo Leinhart's bed and breakfast and holing up for a

while. She'd just started to work past the hurt. Knowing Jack still believed her capable of betraying him had totally wiped out any progress she'd made in that direction.

Mr. Raynes left with Jack and Felan. Moments later, the sheriff was back with the map, breaking the search area into grids in case Felan couldn't pick up a scent and making sure everyone understood when they were to check back in. He had four radios. Muttering that he should have given one to Jack, he kept one for himself, gave one to a craggy-faced guy he called "Slim" who was about as wide as a toothpick and looked as if he'd spent most of his life sitting on a very wide horse, and handed one to Carrie. Since she'd volunteered to help, too, he wanted her to stay at the post to direct other volunteers who might show up and to relay messages to him from people checking in. Maxine Shaw, the lady in the neon yellow who owned the restaurant next to the paper, had apparently done this before. Since the sheriff's Jeep had been designated as headquarters, she lowered the tailgate on the dented black pickup in front of it and set up a large insulated container of hot coffee, one of cocoa, and a stack of foam cups.

"Just radio the Copper Bell if we get low and tell Ruby to have someone run more out here," she said to Carrie. "If this gets going too long and we haven't found the boy in a couple of hours, might have her run some food out, too."

Carrie gave the older woman a nod, liking her just a little bit more than she already did. One of the things she'd discovered about Moose Creek was that its people took care of one another when need be, but that they basically stayed out of each other's way. That was the antithesis of what she'd heard small town life was like, but that was how they did things in Moose Creek. She'd found that its citizens tended to be independent-minded people with a passion for wide-open spaces and a strong sense of individuality. She could understand perfectly why Jack chose to be near there.

Thinking about Jack was not what she wanted to do. Not now. Now, they all had a child to find. The good news was that it wasn't snowing and that the wind was little more than a breeze. The bad news was that they only had two hours until the sun set and that, even with more volunteers showing up, the odds of finding the child in the dark decreased dramatically. By the time Carrie sent a group of men on snowshoes into the last unassigned grid, those odds were already on the wane.

She figured they were at their worst as she sat alone on the bench seat of the Jeep, rubbing her gloves together to keep her hands warm because she didn't want to use up gas running the heater, and watching evening fade into a breathlessly clear night. Beyond the light thrown by the camp lantern on the tailgate in front of her, night settled dark and still. Had the moon been full, it would have been so bright its light would have faded the stars from the sky. Unfortunately only a crescent hung in that vast sky and its light was only strong enough to cast everything in shades of sapphire and indigo.

Twenty-nine people had gone out. Most of those on snowshoes or cross-country skis were back by dark. Three of the people on snowmobiles returned then, too. They gathered around the tailgate of the pickup, warming up with Maxine's coffee and talking about going back out when the moon was high enough to cast its pale light down through the trees. Two men took a truck and drove back to town for lanterns, high-beam flashlights and more help. Half a dozen men were still searching. Three brothers, the boy's father, the sheriff and Jack.

The brothers eventually returned to warm up and wait for lanterns. With a child missing, no one even mentioned calling off the search until morning. By seven o'clock, though, the only people out were the sheriff, Mr. Raynes and Jack. The sheriff had hooked up with Mr. Raynes when Jack and Felan left the man's campsite with one of Dustin's sweatshirts. Sheriff Evans had called in twenty minutes ago to say they were on their way in for lanterns. No one had seen or heard from Jack.

"I hear you know the guy with the dog," Maxine said, handing Carrie a cup of steaming cocoa as she propped a hip on the front fender of the Jeep.

From where Carrie leaned against the Jeep's door, she gave the pleasant woman her quick smile and accepted the offering.

"We were friends," she returned with a glance past the green stripe on Maxine's yellow shoulder. The men had knotted together around the front of the pickup, talking about whatever it is men talk about when there's something they need to do but can't.

"They're telling dirty jokes," Maxine muttered. She shook her head, but not even the breeze could budge the tight brown curls rimming the edge of her red knit cap. "Now, what's this 'were' business. He's a little too good-looking to let go, girl."

"It wasn't me that did the letting go."

Beneath the curls, Maxine's matronly features grew thoughtful. "I see," she murmured, squinting over the steam drifting from her own cup. She took a swallow of her cocoa, considering. "Well, for what it's worth," she finally concluded, "I don't think he's real happy with his decision."

The only person privy to Carrie's relationship with Jack, and its result, was Flo Leinhart. The retired, ex-ranch cook and owner of the B and B where Carrie stayed had brought her tea and toast every morning for a week before she'd finally insisted that Carrie tell her what was wrong. The only thing Maxine knew about her was that she'd been born in Moose Creek. Beyond that, they hadn't discussed anything more personal than the weather.

"I'm sure he's fine with it," she replied, though she couldn't help wondering what had prompted the observation. "But why do you say that?"

"Because he never took his eyes off of you any longer than he absolutely had to before he left. He was watching you like he wasn't sure he wanted to let you out of his sight." Raising her cup again, she gave a sage little nod. "Looked like a man full of regrets to me."

There was no arguing that last statement. But Carrie was certain the nature of Jack's regrets did not include her. She might have shared that conclusion, too, but the drone of a snowmobile cut through the deep rumble of nervous laughter coming from over by the pickup.

"That'll be the sheriff and the boy's dad," Maxine pronounced, moving on to more immediate concerns. "Heaven protect the rest of us from having to deal with what that poor man's going through."

The woman pushed herself off the Jeep to fill cups for the arriving men, ever so generously leaving Carrie with yet another worry for her unborn child. From the moment Carrie had realized her nausea was caused by more than the emotional turmoil of having her world fall apart, she'd vacillated between being terrified and overjoyed at the prospect of having a child of her own. "That's hormonal," Flo had knowingly informed her. "Mood swings are definitely part of pregnancy. I should know. I had five."

Since Carrie had been trying to choke down a piece of dry toast at the time, she'd only groaned. The emotional pendulum had become stuck firmly in the middle, though. Daunting as she found the responsibility, she wanted the precious secret she carried as much as she wanted her next breath. But, on top of having to worry about how she was going to provide for her child, give it the home it deserved and make sure she gave it all the love and attention and care she'd missed growing up, Maxine's comment now had her worrying about her little one getting lost in the snow someday.

Stress was obviously causing her to overreact. Telling herself that, she drew a calming breath and slowly blew it out. Stress wasn't good for the baby.

A dark snowmobile, its headlamp arcing wildly, slid down the incline from the snowpack and stopped in the road ahead. It wasn't the sheriff and Mr. Raynes, however. It was Jack. And with him was one very shy little seven-year-old boy no one could get near because Felan decided it was his duty to protect him from the people surging toward them.

"Hey, Carrie," the bow-legged Slim called back to her. "He wants you to take the boy."

The group separated, parting like the proverbial sea so she could get through. From where she'd stayed by the sheriff's Jeep, she saw Jack straddling the vibrating machine. Felan had leapt from the seat behind him and now stood straining at the rope his master held. Little Dustin sat between Jack's legs, holding onto the handles of the snowmobile his rescuer had let him "help" steer.

She knew why Jack wanted her to get the child. She was the only one Felan would trust to let past. So she headed for the snowsuited little boy, enormously relieved to discover that he'd been dressed for the weather. Being intimately familiar with what could happen in the cold, she hadn't wanted to even think about what the child might be going through. It was a good forty degrees warmer than when she'd been lost and Jack had found her, but it was still freezing out. As she drew close enough to see the freckles scattered over the brown-eyed child's little pug nose, she could see there wasn't much wrong with Dustin that food and a hug from his dad wouldn't cure.

She barely glanced at the caution marking Jack's expression. "How is he?"

"He's good."

She watched the little boy lean back into Jack's broad chest, shyness stealing over his fresh little face.

"I want my dad."

"I'm sure you do," Carrie returned, her smile soft. "And he should be here any minute. In the meantime, why don't we get you some hot cocoa and into a warm car? Would you like that?"

His head bobbed in a nod, just before he looked up at Jack. "Will you take me?"

"The lady can take care of you," he returned, his voice a gentle rumble. "I have to stay with Felan so he doesn't scare any of those people."

"Can't she stay with him?"

"I'll take Felan," Carrie said before Jack could respond. "It's okay," she added, reaching for the coiled rope in his gloved hand. "Dustin's day has been traumatic enough without being passed off to another stranger. He's comfortable with you, so you can take him to the Jeep. I'll bring Felan."

For a moment, Jack said nothing. He simply watched her as she gave the child her understanding smile and stepped back to stroke the agitated animal. Almost immediately the dog's pointed ears lifted from their flattened position and his growling quieted.

The little boy looked back up at the big man behind him. "She said it's okay."

"Then, I guess we'll do what she says," Jack agreed, good-naturedly rubbing the top of the boy's stocking cap.

Carrie stepped back, kneading Felan's favorite spots behind his ears, and watched Dustin peel himself away from Jack's chest. The child's quick attachment could have easily been rooted in gratitude to the big man who'd rescued him. It could have been, too, that his shyness truly didn't allow for much interaction with yet another stranger. But the way he'd leaned into Jack told Carrie something that the others watching the curious exchange wouldn't understand. Jack could sometimes make a person feel very safe. And that created a bond that was nearly impossible to resist.

The crowd ahead must have looked awfully daunting to Dustin. He wasn't a very big child and he was obviously tired. Jack apparently had that in mind when he swung himself off the seat, then scooped the boy up in one arm. With Dustin's head a head higher than his own, he strode toward the other volunteers as they surged back together.

Carrie was skirting the back of the group with Felan flanking her when she heard someone ask where he'd found the boy.

"By a thermal pool," she heard him reply and from the few words Dustin added, she knew the exact one they were talking about. The cornflower blue pool with the rime-coated trees. She also heard that Dustin had followed a herd of bison there, which was why no one had been able to find the light little pattern his snowshoes had made. They'd been overlooked in the churned-up tracks of the massive animals.

If anyone thought anything of the succinct way Jack dealt with their questions, they probably assumed that he was concerned only with getting the child out of the cold. Anxious to be on their way themselves, now that the crisis was over, people were already moving to their vehicles by the time Carrie led Felan to the Jeep and let him hop in back, then returned to where Maxine was filling a cup full of cocoa for Dustin.

"Seems like a good man," she said, handing the cup over. "Is he?"

Carrie glanced to where Jack had slid behind the wheel

of the Jeep to get its heater going. "Deep down, he's one of the best."

There was no mistaking the sympathy in the woman's eyes before Maxine turned back to collect her contributions from the back of the pickup and closed its tailgate. Like everyone else, she wanted to get home and out of the cold now that she was no longer needed there.

The shy little boy was sitting in the middle of the Jeep's bench seat with an old army blanket tucked around his legs and Felan hanging over his shoulder when Jack got out. Approaching the passenger door, he held it for Carrie while she handed Dustin the cocoa, then stopped her before she could get inside.

With his hand on her arm, he closed the door with barely a click. It must have sounded like the report of gunshot to Carrie. Beneath his glove, he felt her jolt.

She deliberately turned her back to the door, causing his hand to slide from her when she crossed her arms over her bulky jacket. So much wariness clouded her delicate features that he stepped back, but he put only enough distance between them to let her know he wouldn't reach for her again. She clearly didn't want his touch.

"The sheriff said you work at the paper." His words were quiet, as much in deference to the people still milling around as his own disbelief. "I thought you'd gone."

"I did. I went to Moose Creek."

That much he knew. What he didn't know was why she hadn't gone farther. When he'd seen her crouched over Felan by the cabin, he hadn't known what to think. He'd spent so many nights fighting memories of her and what he'd done and so many days trying to not think about the nights. Part of him almost believed his mind had conjured her up. Then, he'd seen the sheriff—and the lessons of the past had torn through what had almost felt like hope.

"Why there?" he asked, studying her in the illumination

of vehicle lights. She looked different to him somehow. Softer maybe, though he didn't know if that was it, either. He could see strain in her eyes, too, and a heavy dose of the same caution he felt. He couldn't believe how much he'd missed her. "I thought you'd be long gone by now."

Carrie glanced toward the child inside the Jeep, thinking how small he looked sitting there with his head bent and his mittens wrapped around his cup. He looked so alone. That was how she felt, too, how she'd felt ever since Jack had left her standing in his bedroom. He hadn't wanted her; didn't believe in her. He wanted nothing and no one. "I stayed because I had to stay somewhere while I figured out where to go."

Jack hesitated, seeming to weigh his words.

"I take it that what you learned about me didn't help you get the job in Seattle."

She closed her eyes, totally dispirited. For his own peace of mind, he needed to know where that information had gone. She supposed she couldn't blame him for that. But understanding didn't make her heart ache less.

"I never even thought about using it," she returned, still hurt that he thought she would. She looked up at him, valiantly trying to hide that hurt, failing miserably. "I loved you, Jack. If you would have given me half a chance, you'd have realized I would never do something like that to you. I'm not all the other people who turned on you."

There was more pain than defense in her words, but it was defense that kept her eyes locked on his before she reached for the handle beside her.

Jack caught the door the moment she opened it, trapping her hand beneath his. She could have used what she knew about him, but she hadn't. She hadn't even tried. Her admonishment stung. Her admission kept him silent. She said she'd loved him. Past tense. Love implied expectation, but she clearly expected nothing of him now.

Jack didn't want to consider why that stung, too. As someone shouted up ahead and Mr. Raynes came running toward the Jeep with the sheriff huffing behind him, he was conscious only of the pain in her eyes, and the realization that she hadn't deserved what he'd done to her. He'd hurt her to protect himself, and that made him no better than any of the people who'd once turned on him.

The thought that he'd caused her that kind of pain, had him backing away even before Mr. Raynes reached the door.

Chapter Twelve

The *Moose Creek Tribune*, circulation seven hundred, shared the last block on Lynx Street with the Copper Bell restaurant and a used-book store. Ben Harrison, the *Trib*'s owner and editor, did most of the reporting himself, but he hadn't been able to pass up the chance of having a "big-league" reporter on his staff of two, so he'd hired Carrie—which freed him up two days a week to go hunting or snowmobiling with his buddies. On Ben's days off, Carrie and Pete Calhoun, who'd been with the paper since the Tetons rose, took turns closing up.

It was Carrie's turn to close two days after the weekly edition of the *Trib* reported the story of Dustin Raynes's rescue. At four o'clock, since just about everything in Moose Creek except the restaurants and the bowling alley closed before dark, she pulled the peeling, glass-paned door closed and stepped out onto the shoveled sidewalk.

Her exhaled breath trailed off in a puff as she slipped on

her gloves and reached for the zipper of her long jacket. The storm that had been predicted that day had never materialized. It was cold and clear, the weather perfect for taking the long way home. She'd long ago traded daily jogs for walks, more due to lack of traction in the snow than because of her "condition," but today, she wasn't out just for exercise. She needed badly to work off the restlessness plaguing her. It had been three days since she'd seen Jack and she still felt unsettled by the encounter. Since she also felt tired because her body was using energy for the baby, the restlessness did little for her frame of mind.

The zipper pull slipped through her gloves, so she tried again, thinking as she did that she really had been doing okay until she'd seen him. She'd finally stopped struggling with the awful yearning he'd awakened in her, a yearning she would never have felt at all if he hadn't shown her a side of life she'd never experienced before. She'd just made the mistake of wanting more. She'd wanted the security she'd felt only with him, until he'd pulled it out from under her, and the home and the family she'd never allowed herself to think about. He'd been right about her. She hadn't been thriving. She'd merely been surviving. Getting by on her own. Like him. If she didn't love him so much, she could hate him for making her realize that.

She had a grip on the zipper pull, but now she couldn't get the metal end into the track. Telling herself she should have zipped up before she put her gloves on, wondering when her deductive abilities had taken a hike, she blew a foggy breath, dropped the zipper in frustration and whipped the sides of her long jacket over each other. Crossing her arms to keep in the warmth, she started past the high piles of snow and the snowmobiles and four-wheel-drive vehicles nosed into the curb.

She'd made it to the end of the block when she became

aware of heavy footfalls on the icy sidewalk behind her and saw the long, wide-shouldered shadow overtaking hers.

"Carrie. Wait."

The sound of Jack's voice froze her even before she looked up to see him duck to avoid the long icicles hanging from the bookstore's low eaves. He stepped in front of her, his black Stetson low over his piercing blue eyes and his granite hard features inscrutable.

"Do you have a few minutes?"

His coat hung open over a taupe fleece shirt. Far too susceptible where he was concerned, she found it easier to focus on his impossibly wide chest. "I have to go to work."

He frowned toward the newspaper office half a block away. "You're on your way to cover a story?"

"I only work part-time at the paper. I have another job where I'm staying."

The frown slipped into his voice. "What kind of a job?"

"I clean rooms and help with the baking. That's how I pay my rent." She tipped her chin up, showing a little of the pride she refused to swallow. "But I'm sure you didn't come to discuss how I'm making ends meet."

"No," he agreed, tension creeping through him. "I didn't."

Carrie felt herself back away. She still spent nights trying to imagine how she could have made him trust her; what she might have said or done to help him see that he couldn't judge everyone by the actions of others. By doing that, he hurt himself more deeply. He hurt *her* more deeply. She wanted so desperately to be in his arms, but that wasn't going to happen. He looked as unrelenting as he always did when his defenses were in place.

Being edgy and tired put her at a distinct disadvantage. She just couldn't face those formidable defenses now.

"I really have to go," she murmured.

Ducking her head, she started past him on the slick sidewalk.

"Come on, Carrie."

He immediately caught her arm, turning her to face him. As he did her arms fell to balance herself and her jacket swung open. She gathered it right back, in no danger of falling, but Jack's free hand had shot to her waist to catch her if she slipped.

He'd started to say something. Whatever it was, was forgotten. He suddenly went as still as the air around them. His eyes narrowed, uncomprehending, then jerked down to her recrossed arms.

Not quite believing the messages telegraphing to his brain, Jack ignored her attempt to pull back and curled his fingers over her forearms to pry them apart. The purple turtleneck and sweater she wore were nowhere near bulky enough to explain what he'd felt. He was intimately familiar with her body. He knew every surface and pore, every shape and curve. Her waist was small, small enough that he could nearly span it with his hands and, between her hipbones, her stomach was perfectly flat. It had been, anyway.

He couldn't begin to describe the feelings clamoring in his gut when he pulled back the sides of her jacket. The soft swell of her belly wasn't visible beneath the loose purple knit, but when he splayed his fingers at the side of her stomach, there was no mistaking what he felt beneath his hand. He *knew* what he could feel, and he knew that what he could feel was certainly possible. They hadn't been nearly as careful as he'd intended to be. It was just that his brain didn't want to process the information it was being fed. The possibility, the reality, caught him more unprepared than he'd ever felt in his life.

His eyes collided with hers. Breathing as if he'd been poleaxed, he whispered, "Why didn't you tell me?"

The look she gave him was one of abject disbelief. Her tone nearly echoed his own. "How can you ask such a thing? You practically threw me out, Jack. Even if we overlook that, you made it very clear from the beginning that you didn't want to be responsible for anyone other than yourself."

She took a step back, slowly folding the sides of her jacket together again. "You don't need to worry," she added, her expression one of complete assurance. "I've been taking care of myself for a long time. I don't expect anything from you for either me or the baby. I can take care of us just fine."

If anyone could make it on her own, she could. Jack didn't doubt that for a moment. But he couldn't stand the way she'd pulled from his touch. Now that his brain was functioning, he was also having a hard time with the thought of what she'd gone through alone, struggling to support herself while carrying his child.

"I don't blame you for not wanting to talk to me," he conceded, suddenly struggling himself. "But I'm not going anywhere until we do."

"If this is about the article in the paper, I'm sorry. There was no way to write it without mentioning you since you found the little boy."

He hesitated. "I haven't seen the article."

"Well, it identifies you as 'Jack Holt, a local.' That was the least I could get away with. Ben wanted a separate interview with you about your dog, but I told him I knew you weren't interested."

She'd protected him. Even now. "I appreciate that," he returned, not sure what it said about his state of mind that he'd totally forgotten she would write about that rescue. "But that's not why I'm here. I have two questions to ask you. I promise, it won't take long. We can either stand here with that lady watching us," he said flatly, nodding toward the owner of the bookstore peering shamelessly through the dirty window, "or we can find someplace less public to talk."

If the nervous smile she darted toward the woman was any indication, Carrie felt as edgy as he did. Looking as if she wanted only for that feeling—and him—to be gone, she tightened her grip on herself and stepped around the puddle of ice an icicle had dripped on the walk.

"We can go back to the newspaper," she said on her way past him. "There's no one there."

Jack didn't say another word while he followed her to the *Tribune* and stepped in behind her when she unlocked the door. The place smelled faintly of printer's ink and pipe tobacco and had outgrown itself years ago. Someone had made an attempt to organize the myriad stacks of paper filling the room, but the only uncluttered surfaces were the small service counter and a tiny desk wedged between a copier and a towering stack of old newspapers. The only color was in the travel posters on the wall beside him and the green folding customer chair.

What the place lacked in ambience it made up for in privacy. That was all Jack cared about as Carrie closed the door and flipped a switch. The lights flickered on with a faint buzz, picking out the highlights in her hair when she pulled off her gloves and hat and swiped at her bangs.

"What questions?" she asked, sounding as if she wasn't sure she really wanted to know but wasn't going to let herself stew about it.

"I think I already have the answer to the first one." He pulled off his hat. Contemplating its brim, he set it on the counter. "You said the other day that you came here because you needed to be somewhere while you decided where to go, but I couldn't figure out why you'd stuck around so long." His glance skimmed her stomach, the muscle in his jaw jumping as if he'd considered some other reason he'd already dismissed. "I can see now why that might not have been so easy."

She shrugged. "Employers don't like to hire pregnant women," she returned, her tone as philosophical as her gesture. "But I won't be pregnant forever. After I have more money saved, I'll move somewhere a little bigger to have the baby and find work from there. Don't worry," she quickly added, heading past a poster of Texas wildflowers to drop her hat and gloves into the chair. "I'm not going to ask anything of you."

That was twice now that she'd dismissed the idea of his help. One more and he had the feeling that he just might be out of the game completely. He couldn't let that happen.

"I know I've given you plenty of reason to expect nothing from me, Carrie. But all I'm worried about right now is you."

"Because I'm pregnant?"

"Yeah," he admitted, not sure what to make of the challenge. "Now that I know about it, I'd be crazy not to be concerned. I don't know much about pregnant women, but I don't imagine it's good for you to be upset."

The look she gave him would have melted Alaska. "This isn't upset, Jack. This is just protecting myself. Isn't that what you call it?"

He mentally winced. That was exactly what he'd called it, but she wasn't anywhere near as good as he'd been at building walls. As she stood with her back to a sea of bluebonnets, he could easily see the vulnerability she tried so hard to deny. She never had been able to hide it from him, though. He'd seen it the instant their eyes had first met.

He was also intimately familiar with her determination.

"Are you really intent on leaving?"

Carrie thought she heard hesitation in his voice. She

could even see it in the weary lines of his face. She just couldn't imagine why it was there.

"I don't see too many other options out there."

"You have options," he muttered. "I can think of a couple myself. Are you still interested in Seattle?"

Not at all sure what he was getting at, afraid to even consider the possibilities, she tipped her chin up. "Why?"

"Because maybe you could get that job back. If you think it would help, I'll tell you when the next check goes out and you can call the editor and tell him you're onto who's sending them. Or, I can call the guy and promise him an exclusive if he'll hire you."

Carrie didn't know what she'd expected, but that definitely wasn't it. For a moment, all she could do was stare. There wasn't anything Jack valued more than the privacy he'd finally managed. Yet, with his offer, his privacy would be invaded as surely as sunrise.

"Is that what you really want to do?"

"Hell no," he returned without hesitation. "It's about the last thing I want to do. What I really want is to leave the past where it is and start over. Here. With you. That's what I wanted to talk to you about. But if you feel you have to go, then we've got other things to discuss, because you're not the only one responsible for that child."

She needed to sit down.

"Carrie?"

"I'm fine," she murmured, reaching for the chair under a poster of Palm Springs. She sank onto the green plastic seat, pushing the fingers of both hands through her hair, and pulling a breath as she closed her eyes. When she opened them, Jack was crouched in front of her, one hand on the chair back, the other on her knee.

"What happened?" he demanded, worry slicing past guard.

Since she'd become pregnant, she tended to experience

light-headedness when she got up too fast or turned too quickly. Any sudden jolt to the equilibrium could bring it on. What Jack had just said definitely came under the "jolt" category. He wanted to start over? With her? "I know I didn't hear you right."

She must have looked okay to him. Concern faded to caution when his glance fell to where his hand rested on her corduroy covered knee. "Yes, you did." His voice dropped to a rough rasp. "I know you can get along without me, but maybe I can't get along without you."

As if he didn't trust himself to meet her eyes, he straightened, rising over her to clamp his hand over the back of his neck. "That isn't how I wanted to start."

He turned away, then hesitated, looking as if he were suddenly on unfamiliar ground and had no idea which way to step. "I wanted to apologize before I got into any of this, but I haven't handled much of anything well since we met, so I guess this is about par. I've spent three days trying to figure out how to say this and I still don't know how."

Exasperated with himself, his hand fell as he faced her again.

"I kept thinking about you and the animals," he said, diving in because he needed to start somewhere and the sooner he got started the sooner he'd get it over with. "About you and Felan and the bison and how it didn't make any sense to me that you'd be afraid of dogs but not of something so much bigger and meaner. But you'd pointed out that it wasn't a bison that attacked you, so you had no natural fear where they were concerned. Then with Felan," he went on, not sure she'd followed the leap that was as clear as crystal to him, "you had every reason to be afraid, but you were able to work past your fear once you realized he wasn't going to hurt you."

He shook his head, recrimination carved in the firm lines of his mouth. "You kept going even when you were scared, but not me. I was afraid, too, but instead of trying to work through it, I let my fear paralyze me."

His voice fell. "I'm saying this badly, Carrie. I know that. But if I'd accepted you for the person I know you are instead of lumping you in with everyone else to protect myself, I'd have known you wouldn't turn on me. I know you're not all those other people. And you didn't deserve the way I treated you."

Carrie watched him standing there, his hair combed back, the shirt under his coat looking suspiciously new and her heart lurched a little. He hadn't deserved what had happened to him, either. But life, she'd long ago learned, had a way of dumping all manner of obstacles along its rocky road.

"I think you said it just fine."

For a moment, Jack simply stood there, his eyes searching hers. Some of the tension seemed to be easing from his shoulders, but he didn't look relieved. He still seemed too guarded for that. Or maybe, she thought, he was just so far out of practice when it came to absolution, that he didn't recognize forgiveness when he heard it.

"So," he ventured, watching her carefully, "how do I make it up to you? Or do you even want me to try?"

He looked big and powerful standing there with his boots planted apart, his hands hanging loosely at his sides and his broad shoulders blocking her view of everything but him. But the fact that he hadn't moved toward her, told her he still wasn't sure just how close he should get.

"Is that the second question you'd wanted to ask?"

"No, but I'm getting there."

She rose from the chair, her heart bumping her ribs as she took the three steps that put her directly in front of him. "Did you mean what you said before? About wanting to start over?"

"Yeah, I did. If you're willing to give me a chance."

He lifted his hand, cautiously touching her cheek. "If you're willing to give yourself a chance," he quietly emphasized, relief finally washing over him when she didn't pull from his touch. His fingers drifted toward her temple, his eyes intent on hers. "When I was thinking about this before, I didn't know about the baby. But I can talk to my boss about adding onto the cabin. I still want to send those checks, but at the rate I'm going I'll be done with that in a few years. You've got your job on the paper here and I know how you feel about Moose Creek. If I plow the drive from the cabin to the road—" Seeming to realize he was getting ahead of himself, he cut himself off.

Carrie's heart felt a little too full for her chest. "You want us to live in the cabin?"

He must have thought she didn't like the idea. "It comes with the job, but we can work something else out if you don't want to live there. I know you might need time to think about this," he told her, looking more certain by the second, "but I know it would work with us. You once said you were tired of being scared, but you didn't know what you were afraid of. You and I are afraid of the same thing, Carrie. We're afraid of being alone. But we're more afraid of caring about someone and having them turn their back on us."

With the edge of his thumb, he brushed the corner of her mouth. "I won't turn my back on you. Ever. Or our child. I always wanted kids, Carrie. I want ours." The tantalizing motion of his thumb stopped. "I want you. I don't want to just survive anymore."

"Jack?"

"What?

She shook her head slowly. "Me, either."

His eyes went dark. "What does that mean?"

"It means that I want what you want. But what I really want is for you to put your arms around me."

She didn't know which one of them took the step that brought her up against him. It didn't matter. He closed his arms around her, burying his face at the side of her neck. She clung right back, breathing in the scents of fresh air and wood smoke in his clothes, drinking in the feelings she thought she'd never experience again. She felt so safe wrapped in his embrace. So secure. But those feelings had scarcely registered when he slipped his fingers into her hair and pulled back her head.

His mouth came down on hers, a little hard, a little hungry. He drew her closer, sweeping his hand under her jacket to her hips to bring her nearer still. Not until he'd completely altered their breathing and heart rates did he lift his head. Even then, it was only to touch his lips to her temple while he drew his hand possessively over her belly.

His eyes were filled with wonder and a touch of apprehension when he carried that touch to her face. "I can't believe this," he said, shaking his head. "How far along are we?"

"About four months. And 'we,'" she added, her mouth curving softly, "are all doing just fine."

She had always suspected that Jack would have a devastating smile. She'd just never suspected what seeing it could do to the stability of her knees. But that light slowly faded from his eyes as he smoothed her hair from her face.

"I need to ask that other question," he murmured, focusing on the motions of his hand. "I love you, Carrie. And I want us to get married. Not just because of the baby," he hurried to add. "I wanted that even before I knew about this. But the other day you said something that makes me wonder if what I've done has made it impossible for you to feel about me the way I do about you. You said how you'd felt, but it was sort of…past tense."

"You mean when I told you that I loved you?"

"Yeah."

"Oh, Jack," she whispered, her eyes shining as she touched his hard, chiseled jaw. "I've loved you from the minute I saw you. I've never stopped."

His glance swept over her delicate features, years seeming to vanish from his face as he let himself absorb the healing warmth in her eyes. As those shadows lifted, the smile she'd witnessed before slowly stole back to curve his mouth.

"You know," he said, as he lowered his head to hers. "I think that might have been about the time I started falling in love with you, too."

* * * * *

Take 4 bestselling love stories FREE

Plus get a FREE surprise gift!

Special Limited-time Offer

Mail to Silhouette Reader Service™

3010 Walden Avenue
P.O. Box 1867
Buffalo, N.Y. 14240-1867

YES! Please send me 4 free Silhouette Special Edition® novels and my free surprise gift. Then send me 6 brand-new novels every month, which I will receive months before they appear in bookstores. Bill me at the low price of $3.34 each plus 25¢ delivery and applicable sales tax, if any.* That's the complete price and a savings of over 10% off the cover prices—quite a bargain! I understand that accepting the books and gift places me under no obligation ever to buy any books. I can always return a shipment and cancel at any time. Even if I never buy another book from Silhouette, the 4 free books and the surprise gift are mine to keep forever.

235 BPA A3UV

Name	(PLEASE PRINT)	
Address	Apt. No.	
City	State	Zip

This offer is limited to one order per household and not valid to present Silhouette Special Edition® subscribers. *Terms and prices are subject to change without notice. Sales tax applicable in N.Y.

USPED-696   ©1990 Harlequin Enterprises Limited

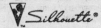

Coming this December 1997 from
Silhouette®SPECIAL EDITION®

AND BABY MAKES THREE: THE NEXT GENERATION:

The Adams women of Texas all find love—and motherhood—in the most unexpected ways!

The Adams family of Texas returns!
Bestselling author **Sherryl Woods** continues
the saga in these irresistible new books.
Don't miss the first three titles in the series:

In December 1997: **THE LITTLEST ANGEL** (SE #1142)
When Angela Adams told Clint Brady she was pregnant, she
was decidedly displeased with the rancher's reaction. Could
Clint convince Angela he wanted them to be a family?

In February 1998: **NATURAL BORN TROUBLE** (SE #1156)
Dani Adams resisted when single dad Duke Jenkins claimed
she'd be the perfect mother for his sons. But Dani was
captivated by the boys—and their sexy father!

In May 1998: **UNEXPECTED MOMMY** (SE #1171)
To claim his share of the White Pines ranch, Chance Adams
tried to seduce his uncle's lovely stepdaughter. But then he
fell in love with Jenny Adams for real....

Available at your favorite retail outlet.

SILHOUETTE WOMEN KNOW ROMANCE WHEN THEY SEE IT.

And they'll see it on **ROMANCE CLASSICS**, the new 24-hour TV channel devoted to romantic movies and original programs like the special **Romantically Speaking—Harlequin™ Goes Prime Time**.

Romantically Speaking—Harlequin™ Goes Prime Time introduces you to many of your favorite romance authors in a program developed exclusively for Harlequin® and Silhouette® readers.

Watch for **Romantically Speaking—Harlequin™ Goes Prime Time** beginning in the summer of 1997.

If you're not receiving ROMANCE CLASSICS,
call your local cable operator or satellite provider and
ask for it today!

ROMANCE CLASSICS

Escape to the network of your dreams.

See Ingrid Bergman and Gregory Peck in *Spellbound* on Romance Classics.

As seen on TV!
Free Gift Offer

With a Free Gift proof-of-purchase from any Silhouette® book,
you can receive a beautiful cubic zirconia pendant.

This gorgeous marquise-shaped stone is a genuine cubic
zirconia—accented by an 18" gold tone necklace.

(Approximate retail value $19.95)

Send for yours today...
compliments of *Silhouette*®

To receive your free gift, a cubic zirconia pendant, send us one original proof-of-purchase, photocopies not accepted, from the back of any Silhouette Romance™, Silhouette Desire®, Silhouette Special Edition®, Silhouette Intimate Moments® or Silhouette Yours Truly™ title available at your favorite retail outlet, together with the Free Gift Certificate, plus a check or money order for $1.65 U.S./$2.15 CAN. (do not send cash) to cover postage and handling, payable to Silhouette Free Gift Offer. We will send you the specified gift. Allow 6 to 8 weeks for delivery. Offer good until March 31, 1998, or while quantities last. Offer valid in the U.S. and Canada only.

Free Gift Certificate

Name: _____

Address: _____

City: _____ State/Province: _____ Zip/Postal Code: _____

Mail this certificate, one proof-of-purchase and a check or money order for postage and handling to: SILHOUETTE FREE GIFT OFFER 1998. In the U.S.: 3010 Walden Avenue, P.O. Box 9077, Buffalo, NY 14269-9077. In Canada: P.O. Box 613, Fort Erie, Ontario L2Z 5X3.

FREE GIFT OFFER   084-KFD
ONE PROOF-OF-PURCHASE
To collect your fabulous FREE GIFT, a cubic zirconia pendant, you must include this original proof-of-purchase for each gift with the properly completed Free Gift Certificate.

084-KFDR2

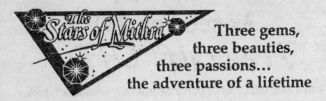